little black dress
· IT'S A GIRL THING ·

Dear Little Black Dress Reader,

Thanks for picking up this Little Black Dress book, one of the great new titles from our series of fun, page-turning romance novels. Lucky you — you're about to have a fantastic romantic read that we know you won't be able to put down!

Why don't you make your Little Black Dress experience even better by logging on to

www.littleblackdressbooks.com

where you can:

- ♥ Enter our **monthly competitions** to win **gorgeous** prizes
- ♥ Get **hot-off-the-press** news about our latest titles
- ♥ Read **exclusive** preview chapters both from your **favourite** authors and from brilliant new writing talent
- ♥ Buy **up-and-coming** books online
- ♥ Sign up for an essential slice of romance via our **fortnightly email** newsletter

We love nothing more than to curl up and indulge in an addictive romance, and so we're delighted to welcome you into the Little Black Dress club!

With love from,

The **little black dress** team

Five interesting things about Sally Anne Morris:

1. My bosom has been cupped by the actor Udo Kier who has also had his hands on Madonna.

2. I've always wanted to be a writer and as a girl, would write pony stories about foals born in the middle of storms and poor, hardworking girls who were given international show-jumpers by kindly strangers.

3. This year I shall start keeping bees.

4. The Young Me loved unsuitable boys, motorbikes, loud music and dressing in clothes from the fifties. Grown-Up Me lives with an ex-rock musician, has two fantastic children, loves vegetable gardening and still likes dressing in clothes from the fifties.

5. I know how to twirl tassles.

Trick or Treat

Sally Anne Morris

little
black
dress

First published in 2009 by
LITTLE BLACK DRESS
An imprint of HEADLINE PUBLISHING GROUP

A LITTLE BLACK DRESS paperback

1

Cataloguing in Publication Data is available from the British Library

ISBN 978 0 7553 5440 5

Typeset in Transit511BT by Avon DataSet Ltd,
Bidford-on-Avon, Warwickshire

Printed and bound in Great Britain by
Clays Ltd, St Ives plc

Headline's policy is to use papers that are natural, renewable and
recyclable products and made from wood grown in sustainable forests.
The logging and manufacturing processes are expected to conform to the
environmental regulations of the country of origin.

HEADLINE PUBLISHING GROUP
An Hachette UK Company
338 Euston Road
London NW1 3BH

www.littleblackdressbooks.com
www.headline.co.uk
www.hachette.co.uk

For Mom and Dad – for the best of beginnings.
For Paul – who believed I could all along.
For James and Lila – the reason for everything.
For Maggi – more love than you could
shake a stick at.
For Claire Baldwin – many, many thanks.

Lucy Diamond (Lucy Michelle Eleanor Jude Rita Diamond to be exact) does not, on the surface, have any of what the police might call 'distinguishing features'.

She has an ordinary job in Human Resources that involves endless meetings and tedious paperwork, and is not the sort of job that you dream of doing when you grow up. She has ordinary looks. No hook nose, no bat ears, no claw feet. On a good day, she might turn a few heads, and on a bad day you wouldn't exactly reel in horror, but you probably wouldn't even notice that she was there.

Lucy is pretty average and averagely pretty. Her good points are: nice grey eyes that with the right amount of kohl can look downright beautiful, and slim legs that can draw the eye in a miniskirt but would not be suited to hot pants on account of the little semicircle of cellulite puckering the top of each thigh. She has long straight hair – provided she has time to straighten it and it isn't in the slightest bit damp outside, which in Britain it usually is, so it can err on the side of frizzy – in a colour that the box from Boots describes as 'iced mocha'. She is not as small as Kylie nor as tall as Erin (who needs a surname for clarification – O'Connor – for although she is and has been the face of Marks & Spencer she does not have the superstar status of Ms Minogue). Lucy assumed she must also have very averagely sized feet – 5½ or 6 (depending on the style) – because she could never find a decent shoe in a sale, unlike her friends with childish size 3s or mannish size 8s.

Even her friends – Jojo, partner in crime since the first day at Our Lady and St Margaret of Cortona's Grammar School for Girls, and Nigel (GBF – Gay Best Friend and *the* essential accessory for the noughties, or so he claims) – would not seem unusual, out of step, wild or wacko. No, there was nothing to mark out Lucy Diamond in a crowd until this particular morning, although it wasn't until a good time later that she could trace the beginnings of it all to this very day and say, 'That was the day my life changed.'

It had started out with the all the hallmarks of a usual Monday. Lucy had risen with the hangover-recriminations that follow her Sunday night ritual with Jojo and a bottle of Oddbins' 'on offer'. She had break-fasted on her favourite cereal which still – to Lucy Diamond aged thirty and a half – tasted 'grrrrrrreaaaaat' and pretty soon, after some rudimentary personal grooming, she had found herself on the Victoria Line.

Lucy was flanked on the one hand by a man who may or may or not have urinated in his pants but certainly smelt as if he had and on the other by a power-suited woman who had power-napped between Seven Sisters and Finsbury Park and was now power-talking into her mobile phone.

Rocked by the shuttle of the tube, Lucy was being lulled into an almost dream-like state. Her horoscope in the free paper suggested new insights as Mercury entered the dark of the moon, but she was longing to be back in bed. Her favourite fantasy on wet days such as this was to imagine herself towel-robed and turbaned, sitting on a Mediterranean-style terrace with the lazy promises of a summer day stretching ahead of her. With the aid of the glaring overhead lights and the stuffiness of the overfull coach, she could almost imagine herself there.

The words of her fellow commuter drummed in Lucy's head. Maybe it was the nonsense of her office-speak forcing surreal images into Lucy's mind like 'someone's head's gonna roll for this' and 'you better get me a regional-size sticking plaster because this sore is getting out of control'. Maybe it was the constant, almost monastic drone of the woman's voice along with the cradle-like rocking of the tube. Maybe it was all those things and the heat and the fact that Lucy was not quite awake. Whatever the reason, Lucy's mind was wandering.

Her face had set into the glassy pan of the regular commuter – an almost corpse-like stare, entirely without expression. Thoughts of bed or sun terraces had dropped out of her conscious awareness. She was staring, unblinking, but not at anything. Certainly not at her reflection, just visible in the window opposite, because if she had been she would have started fiddling with her hair, because there is a part of Lucy Diamond that is really quite vain. Nor was she aware of the Jaeger-dressed middle-aged woman seated diagonally opposite who was scrutinising her from top to toe and thinking unkind thoughts about Lucy's already frizzing hair.

So she sat, eyes wide but not seeing, mind working

but not thinking. There was not a thought in her head until . . . *blaaam!*

A face appeared less than two inches from her nose and Lucy lurched in shock. The wild brown eyes of an ashen-faced young man bored into hers.

'At last! I need you to help me!'

'What?'

Not an intelligent response but appropriate, given that it was a little past seven forty-five in the morning and Lucy was more than a little surprised.

'You've got to help me. We haven't much time.' He had his hands on both of her armrests, corralling Lucy into her seat. She could feel the cold chill of his ungloved hands seeping through the sleeves of her pea-coat.

She shuddered involuntarily, acutely aware that Londoners travelling into the city from E17 were not renowned for their helpfulness to strangers in predicaments with crazy men, particularly if knives were involved. But years of commuting on the Underground had taught her to be polite to the mad, bad and potentially dangerous to know.

Not that this chap looked particularly dangerous. Agitated? Yes. Barking? Most certainly. But as he ran his hands through well-cut, thick sandy hair that Boots would probably label 'sun-kissed honey', a part of Lucy acknowledged that he was kind of cute in a rugby shirt/Labrador/sailing dinghy kind of way. Or at least he could be if he wasn't so pale and pasty looking. He reminded Lucy of a seedling that had been shut in the potting shed and not seen daylight for a very long time.

'I beg your pardon?' See how polite Lucy is? Even in extreme circumstances of shock and invasion of personal space her manners, drilled into her by the nuns at Our Lady and St Margaret of Cortona's, win out.

'Come with me.' The young man was insistent, desperate even. He was standing a little away from her now, alternately checking his watch and ramming his hands into the pockets of his putty-coloured trench. His distress was growing every minute and he was looking up and down the carriage as though watching for someone or waiting to be caught.

'I haven't got any money,' she began, still polite, but lying. The nuns had not taught the latter at Our Lady and St Margaret of Cortona's but seven years of observation of the Girl with Most Detentions in the History of the School – Jojo Gray – had. Lucy did, in fact, have ten pounds but that was for lunch and she'd held her breath at the cash point this morning waiting to see if there were sufficient funds in the overdraft to get it because pay day was still four days away.

'I don't want your money!' His Scottish accent was evident now but so soft that with her eyes closed he could probably have passed for Bond-era Sean Connery. Not that Lucy was planning to close her eyes. It is, after all, useful to be vigilant in such circumstances. 'I need you to talk to her. I need you to tell her it's all OK. She's over there. The girl in the yellow coat. Just there. Now come with me. She'll be getting off soon. I don't know how long I can do this for. Hurry!' He was moving off, head cocked in the direction he wanted, gesturing frantically for Lucy to follow him.

'Why don't you talk to her yourself?' Lucy asked softly in a manner she hoped implied 'helpfully concerned'. Why did she always attract the crazies, the religious zealots or the nutcases who believed that lizards ran the planet? Once she'd even literally been left holding the baby by a woman who jumped off the tube to avoid the ticket inspector.

She blamed her mother, of course. Bestowed by dear old hippy, dippy Beatles-mad mum, a name like Lucy Michelle Eleanor Jude Rita Diamond really was a curse. Laden with references to the acid trip that was the sixties and the most famous band on earth, she was tired of people breaking into spontaneous song whenever she had to fill in her name on a form. Lucy had no idea where all the 'lonely people' came from, but she sure as hell knew where they all ended up. Talking to her on public transport!

'I'm sure she'd rather talk to you,' Lucy offered again.

The young man was looking at her as though she was crazy. Lucy was about to elaborate and advise him that from a woman's point of view a direct approach in relationships worked best when a curt voice cut in.

'Do you mind? I'm trying to have a friggin' conversation here!' Power-Maid glared from behind her ironic but expensive heavy black glasses frames. She obviously had more 'fish to fry' or things to tell others to put on the 'back burner' or leave 'dead in the water'.

Lucy was stunned. This was so unjust! It was not yet eight o'clock and she was being assailed by nuts on all fronts. Was this some sort of elaborate piss-take with Jojo and Nigel behind it? Was Noel Edmonds about to appear in a dodgy disguise and give her some award for being a good sport? She was already formulating the slightly exaggerated 'forward to all recipients' e-mail to make the story funnier still. Not that people believed her stories at the best of times – certainly Jojo had never believed the one about the baby and the tube jumper.

'I'm sorry,' Lucy said in a voice that she hoped was assertive, yet still polite. (Thank goodness for Professional Development Day! Five hours shouting *No!* at potential assailants had seemed ludicrous at the time but a year ago she would not have replied at all.) 'But so are we.' She motioned behind her to Nut Job No. 1. 'This is *public* transport.' Feeling pretty pleased with herself, she turned back to her agitated travel companion and found he was gone.

She looked up and down the carriage now as frantically as he had and there was no sign of him anywhere. Where in hell had he got to? How could he have just disappeared in that split second? Lucy was furious that he'd ruined her peaceful journey and managed to make her look stupid at the same time. What a way to start the working week!

Power-Maid was rolling her eyes and doing the twirly index-finger thing to the temple to indicate to the rest of the carriage that Lucy was a lunatic, but Lucy was oblivious. She was locked in her own world of puzzlement.

Something caught her eye. The girl in the yellow coat was standing now, making ready to join the throng exiting at the next station.

Despite the remnants of a tan, she seemed as drained of colour and life as the man who had so desperately wanted Lucy to talk to her. And Lucy being Lucy, with the sort of generous soul that likes to do people good turns, felt she ought to tell the girl about him. It was probably a lovers' tiff, but on the other hand if he was a mad stalker at least she could warn her.

Lucy gathered up her bag and began to push

through the other commuters. Several 'Excuse me's' later, still polite, though anxious to keep sight of her quarry, she drew alongside the girl waiting to leave by the sliding doors.

Lucy could see by the swing of the glossy ponytail and the curve of the spot-free cheek that the Girl in the Yellow Coat was desperately pretty. Little wonder that she had driven a man deranged for contact. She had those universal wholesome good looks that win Miss World and in a split second of savage envy Lucy thought, *Yeah, and I bet you like children and animals too, dontcha?*

But as the girl turned her head towards Lucy and their eyes locked for a few brief seconds – summer-in-Provence blue with Lucy's British-skies grey – the heaviness behind her eyes, hollow and dead as they were, weighed instantly upon Lucy and she was filled with guilt for her mean thoughts.

'I'm sorry to bother you,' Lucy began, which, of course, was a far more civilised way to begin a conversation than *At last! I need you to help me* yelled in your face without warning, 'but this...um...guy came up to me and...' It really was very tricky to translate the latest episode of Crazy Man on the Tube to a stranger. The doors opened and Lucy was pushed on to the platform – a stop earlier than the one she wanted – and carried with the surge of nine-to-fivers towards the escalators. 'He really wanted to talk to you,' she blurted out.

'Thank you, but I'm not interested in going out with anyone.' The girl did not break her stride or look back.

'No, no.' Lucy struggled to keep up with the other woman's purposeful gait against the onslaught of commuters coming in the opposite direction. 'He didn't say anything about dating. He just wanted to say it was OK. That was the message. I thought he must already know you.'

The girl stopped, though they were both being buffeted by passers-by. She was in her late twenties, her face as yet unlined but the roundness of her teens replaced by sculpted cheekbones and an air of know-ingness that did not detract from her obvious beauty. She was so well groomed – smelling faintly of vanilla and Palmer's Cocoa Butter – and so well dressed in her startling yellow sixties-style coat that Lucy wanted to slink away to rot in a litter bin. The girl's mouth formed a smile though her sad eyes could not. She was being assertive now, Lucy observed; she was standing her ground. After all, it took one to know one.

'I'm really not interested in dating right now. Thank your friend for me. I'm sure he's very nice but it just wouldn't work for me to go out with anyone at the moment. Thank you again. Goodbye.'

Unlike Lucy, the Girl in the Yellow Coat was clearly used to requests for dates on her commute to work and had developed a strategy to deal with them. The crowd carried her forward and up and Lucy was left, being cursed by workers in a rush, standing rooted to the base of the escalator by the sheer weight of the departing girl's inexplicable sadness.

She'd done her best: she'd given the message. And overall she was pleased that, in a capital city where people will talk loudly into phones on station platforms about yeast infections or masturbate openly in a packed carriage, when one strange girl stops to talk to another the exchange can, at the very least, be civilised.

Her phone buzzed with the arrival of a text. She fumbled in her bag, moving out of the way of the Monday morning crush, and now she could not help smiling. The day was going to turn out fine after all. It was Nigel and he wanted to meet for lunch.

There's nothing like a meeting about forthcoming meetings to make you feel there's little point to living. Lucy had devised several strategies to ensure that meeting time wasn't wasted. At least it meant her pelvic floor got exercise, and today she had a free pen and promotional coaster to compensate for the two hours of flip-chart mind-maps and PowerPoint projections.

She was sucking one of the conference provider's complimentary mints with which she had filled her pockets as she hurried along the damp streets to the nearest coffee shop in response to Nigel's texted invitation to 'do lunch'. A reheated roasted vegetable panini or something similar beckoned. It would not be a grand affair.

She shook her umbrella into the street and entered the steamy heat of the coffee shop. Nigel had reserved a window seat sofa. Not that there was any point. The condensation clung to the windows and would obscure their view. So there would be no assessment of passers-by and their 'shagability' today.

A latte in a paper cup and some oozing, dripping, glorified cheese on toast were waiting. Nigel was trying desperately to look relaxed and casual but Lucy could tell his posture was staged and that he was desperately sucking his stomach in.

'Niiiice!' he hissed, his face forced into a smile as fixed as Eurovision voting whilst his eyes flicked past her shoulder.

Nigel was using his 'stranger voice'. He heteroed up and said 'larst' instead of his Midlands 'last' when they were in 'company'.

'Who's your friend?'

'What?'

'Don't be silly, just introduce us!'

'Who to?' Lucy folded her coat and stashed her umbrella under the table before kissing Nigel warmly.

'That guy you came in with. The one in the mac. Where's he gone? He had the look of Mickey Rourke in 9½ weeks. Before the surgery,' he stressed.

'I didn't come in with anyone. Is he at the counter?' Lucy was craning her neck this way and that.

'Don't!' Nigel hit her on the arm. 'You're making it obvious!'

'I can't see him. Must have gone to the loo or took it to go.'

Nigel groaned in disappointment but breathed out, letting his stomach relax and find its natural resting place over his waistband.

'You smell nice.' Already chomping a mouthful of mozzarella, she breathed in his scent. As ever, Nigel was groomed to male-model perfection. He was the only person she had ever known who made use of those travelling manicure sets. He knew the function of each and every surgical-looking tool, but then he was also familiar with the array of gadgets available in the Betterware catalogue. He actually owned a special three-pronged dusting device for cleaning his Venetian blinds. The macho male love of gadgetry and tools – mutated by his sexuality – seemed to have expressed itself in Nigel as something altogether different.

They had met on the first day of the first term in their first year of university. He had been playing Dolly Parton too loudly and when she went to ask him if he could just turn it down a little bit he had been so impressed by her knowledge of the lyrics to 'Coat of Many Colours' that he'd invited her to a stay for a small sherry. Nigel had not believed that her name was Lucy Michelle Eleanor Jude Rita Diamond so had lied and said that he was called Michael Jackson. At least when the truth came out he could commiserate with her. Seven years at an all-boys' comp had not been easy for a boy christened Nigel Leaks.

'Still, it could have been worse,' he had quipped at the time. 'Mum nearly called me Johnny.'

So they had bonded over several glasses of Tio Pepe and, thereafter, many people had assumed they were an item until Nigel came out a year later. It had been obvious to most of their friends that Nigel was, well . . . Nigel. After all, so many signs had been there. It had just taken Lucy a little longer than most to see them.

The stomach-churning, cheek-burning crush she had once felt for him had evolved into the fierce, accepting love of friendship, but looking at him now it was easy to see why her naïve little eighteen-year-old heart had beaten so quickly whenever he was near.

His long lean legs were encased in a Top Shop rip-off of Japanese denim and he had layered sky-blue cashmere over a grey marl tee. The labels might be

Florence & Fred, but he carried the look as though they were design pieces. Never mind that being over thirty was beginning to take its toll in the shape of a slightly less taut stomach – the whole look was still eminently touchable.

His dark hair fell over one eye in the Alex-James-of-Blur cut that he had favoured ever since an early beau had told him that it gave him the rakish air of a 1920s public school boy. Always fond of *Brideshead Revisted*, he kept the haircut and it became his signature. He used it to good effect – flicking it here and tossing it there – when he spouted his literary quotes and bitchy one-liners. She had fallen for his comedy timing and love of obscure eighties television as much as his big, denim eyes and angular jaw.

'I hear you had a freak-attack on the tube.' He had been texting back and forth with Jojo as he waited for Lucy to show.

'Nothing new there. So why aren't you in work? Day off?' Lucy enquired between mouthfuls.

'Duvet Day.' Nigel shrugged.

'Not man monthlies again!' Lucy almost choked. 'This is your third this month! Have you actually done a full week? They'll give you the sack!'

'They wouldn't dare!' Nigel bridled. 'I'd claim discrimination. I'd get the unions in and scream harassment. This is the civil service, you know, not the real world. Jeff in finance has been off sick for two years, claims that he was bullied because he was overweight. It still hasn't gone to court. Two years of "gardening leave" – imagine that! Think how long I could milk it for the Pink Cause! I might get a good pay-off to go quietly. I could spend two years just writing scripts.

I think I'll make it my next career move.'

Like Lucy, Nigel had drifted into the first decent graduate post he'd been offered and with rent, overdrafts and loans to pay found himself, nearly a decade later, stuck in a nightmare of being an extra in what felt like endless repeats of *The Office*, his dreams of being a playwright were not so much on the back burner as totally up in smoke. Lucy brought him back to earth.

'You're forgetting that you don't have any evidence, at all, whatsoever, of bullying. They all love you. Your boss sends you get-well cards if you're off sick more than two days, and don't you remember that little leg up the pay scale they gave you when they saw you with the *Guardian* and assumed you were looking for jobs even though you were actually just reading the TV listing? And just for the record, you used to call Jeff "Fatty Arbuckle" behind his back.'

Nigel smiled sheepishly. 'I'm just a bit peed off, that's all.'

'Aren't we all? I've actually had a complaint filed against me by Janet in accounts. *For real*. She said that I'm not adhering to the Equality of Opportunity Act.'

'My God! I'm sorry. This is serious stuff.' Nigel was all concern now, putting his arm round Lucy's shoulder protectively. Why did she always feel a little flutter as he did so? Even now, after all this time?

'That accusation will go on your file indefinitely. What did you do? You're not a racist! If anything, you're a world contender for Miss PC. And since you are officially the Gay Man's Friend, it can't be that. Is she a wheelchair user? Did you block her exit with your Primark bags?'

Ignoring the barbed comment about her shopping

habits, Lucy elaborated. 'She's a British, non-disabled heterosexual – although a glasses wearer – but when I gave out the stationery order I gave certain items to other people that I didn't give to her.' Nigel motioned for her to continue as he stuffed half a Skinny Muffin into his mouth. Sighing, Lucy added, 'I didn't give her a paperclip storage container in the shape of a house with the company logo on it. It has a magnetic roof for easy access to the clips.'

There was silence. Nigel looked at her blankly at first, and then contorted his face into an expression of disgust.

'You beast!' he spat, cake crumbs falling from his mouth, his voice getting louder. 'You foul, fucking beast. "Out of my sight! Thou dost infect my eyes."' People were staring now and he fell about laughing, flinging more Shakespearean quotes at Lucy to hold his audience.

The door burst open bringing in a gust of cold air and a pride of queens. They were talking animatedly, all androgynously skinny, all the under side of twenty-five with indie-band hair and skinny-leg jeans.

Nigel's mood shifted dramatically and he complained about first the coffee and then the food, ending his monologue with, 'And if I'd wanted to sit on a crap old sofa and look at a table coated in coffee rings I would have suggested we met at yours!'

When he saw how Lucy's face had fallen, he tried desperately to backtrack. Lunch hour was nearly over and in an attempt to make peace he walked her back to the concrete office block where she worked, holding her umbrella over her chivalrously. He demanded her keys and held her hands, pleading with her.

'I'll have dinner waiting for you, wine and

everything. Please forgive me. I love your flat. You know that. It just came out a bit wrong. I've had some of the best laughs of my life in Walthamstow Heights.' He used the pet name, coined long ago, for Lucy's move into home ownership. 'Come on. Give me your keys. We'll spend the evening planning our new lives as a detective duo.'

Lucy couldn't help but smile as she handed over her large bunch of keys, made larger by numerous souvenir key rings and dangly toys.

'I want Italian,' she ordered, before probing at Nigel's unhappiness. 'You should ask yourself why the young and thin make you feel so spiteful.'

Nigel denied it. 'They irritate me, those screaming little queens. They're all over the gay scene now. You can't go anywhere without tripping over one of them. They're like yappy little lap dogs and they look like girls.'

'But they don't spend all their time with girls.' Lucy was referring to Nigel's increasingly reclusive behaviour. Nigel had stopped clubbing, favouring DVDs and takeaways at Lucy's. His gay friends had stopped calling with invitations to dinner because he had refused so many and returned none. Although Lucy and Jojo joked that 'it' would fall off through lack of use, his lack of seeking a relationship – for a man whose bedpost had so many notches it looked woodwormed – was worrying.

He shook his head in irritation. 'We'll talk later. Now go – you'll be late.'

He was waving across the foyer from the revolving doors as she entered the lift. She pushed the button for floor seven and the doors were barely shut when a bibbly-bob sound heralded the arrival of a text. It was Nigel.

Mickey Rourke lookalikey from coffee shop is in lift wiv u now!!! Look over left shoulder. Give him my number.

She looked and started to text back as the doors opened at her floor. What on earth was wrong with him today? Why did he only ever see what he wanted to see? The lift doors closed shut behind her and the receptionist on her floor held out a wodge of papers for her attention. Lucy pressed send.

R u losing it?? Get new lenses. No one in lift but me.

It was dark when Lucy arrived back in Walthamstow Village. A misleading name, she felt, probably dreamt up by a slick estate agent eager to boost property values and consequently his commission. It suggested quaintness, community spirit and at the very least a rural location, none of which Walthamstow really had going in its favour. Although the drug dealer who operated from the squat at the end of the road did nod to her on a daily basis, which was a start.

Lucy had moved here long before the arty/foody couples and babies-in-slings brigade. A vintage shop selling second-hand furniture and home-made beaded jewellery had replaced the betting shop, but the kebab house still stood victorious amid the encroaching organic cafés.

Not that Lucy minded. It meant that when she was chatted up and said where she lived they said 'Oh!' in a 'You must have a good income and be interested in the arts and cooking with expensive vinegar' way. Previously the 'Oh!'s had implied pity mixed with admiration that she was somehow still alive.

So, back then, with first-time borrower's mortgage in tow, she'd been drawn to E17 by its low prices and a secret nostalgia for the boy-band of the same name. No one knew that about her. Not even Jojo and especially *not* Nigel.

She buzzed for Nigel to let her in and began the long climb to the top of the Victorian villa. Once the glorious residence of a doctor, it had now been chopped by property developers into five oddly shaped flats. Lucy loved running her hand up the smooth wood of the banister, imagining the black-booted, white-aproned children of the first owners of this house clattering their way down the stairs. Every day, the jarring sight of wonderful cornicing swallowed abruptly into hastily erected plasterboard troubled her. It wasn't just the ill-conceived architectural changes. For Lucy, it felt as if the house was groaning, choking with the distress of the 1980s 'champagne' bath suites and ugly fire doors. But then her grandma, Nan Peters, always did say that Lucy was at risk of an 'overactive' imagination.

'That daughter of yours needs a telly,' she would argue in broad Yorkshire tones to her daughter, Lucy's mum. 'She wouldn't need imaginary friends if there was something else to fill the space in 'er 'ead.' For extra emphasis Nan would point out that whenever Lucy was able to watch the horse-racing on the black and white portable (cheaper licence in those days) on one of their treks back 'home' to the north, there were no visits from the friend they couldn't see – Tobias Godough.

'But I kind of miss him when he's not around,' Jasmine would offer by way of passive defence.

Not that Lucy could remember anything about her invisible on-off companion from her pre-school years. This story, like others such as the day Grandad fell in the cesspit and the village whip-round to give Lucy's mum money for books at university, was a legend, part of the family folklore.

Her own flat was the least remodelled. High in the eaves, formerly servants' quarters, Lucy's flat was furnished with bottom-end and bargain-corner IKEA. She loved its simple white plastered walls – no elegant cornicing had been wasted on the serving classes. There was one original black grate surrounded by mismatched tiles as though remnants from other parts of the house had been bunged together with an air of 'That'll do for the likes of them!' Most of all she loved being at the top of one of the tallest buildings around, feeling safe and untouchable.

The door was ajar and Nigel was sprawled on the sofa watching a rerun of *Hart to Hart* on UK Gold. Kicking off her shoes, Lucy plonked herself into a throw-covered chair. As usual, the neat throw was sucked into the space beside her, exposing the shabby brown draylon of the arms beneath. Another of life's irritations.

'Drink!' she demanded, greeting Nigel with her best imitation of *Father Ted*'s Father Jack.

'Stopped raining then?' he said, taking in the only mild frizz of Lucy's hair and the dry shoulders of her coat. He began unscrewing a bottle.

'Oh, God, Nigel. Can't we even run to one with a cork? We're thir*ty*, not thir*teen*!'

'Look, are you flush at this point in the month, Ivana Trump? Because I'm not, and in two glasses' time you won't even care. Hush now – the Harts are closing in on the villains . . .'

He turned back to the TV and they watched in silence until the credits rolled. Nigel lit a cigarette and inhaled deeply before passing it to Lucy and lighting his own.

'God, it feels dirty, doesn't it? Since the ban all smokers are pariahs. We are the new demi-monde. And when a group of us meet to collectively puff away it feels more clandestine than a scoutmaster at a suburban swingers' meet. It's good to have a new vice,' he added with a hint of bitterness, 'now gay is so mainstream.'

Lucy was still sitting with her coat on, and as she started to peel off the layers she could sense where his little speech was leading. Nigel had Duvet Days for reasons which had nothing to do with idleness. For example: being dumped. This did not happen very often – such a good looking (though aware of it) man tended to be the dumper not the dumpee – so his brain could not compute when it did, which had been, actually, only three times in a decade of sexual activity. Another example might be the extreme good fortune of a friend, like a sudden inheritance from an unknown uncle. Half a million pounds had come in this way to Nigel's best work-pal Peter Carswell and Nigel had been rancid with envy for several weeks.

Lately, though, there had been a general creeping malaise for which no single event could be blamed. It was a depressed discontent with everything, all the more frightening because it seemed infectious.

Nigel and Lucy had an unspoken agreement that each would take it in turns to drag the other up the Ladder of Life. During moments of wobble when it seemed easiest to fling oneself off, whoever was firmer would grasp the other and through humour, theatre trips and good meals channel positive energy to the one who was losing their grip. But this time, today, when Nigel began quoting *Withnail and I* about their reduced state of being Lucy couldn't offer positives about their lot in life. She could only agree.

'What happened?' he demanded. 'We were young and full of spunk once.'

'Speak for yourself,' Lucy countered wryly, unable to resist a weak attempt to lift the conversation.

Nigel ignored her. Things were bad if he couldn't seize upon a double entendre. He continued, 'We thought we would be the new Bloomsbury set. Those halls at uni were full of talent in the raw – writers, musicians, activists and even those odd-ball scientists. Remember that night we all "did a turn"? Stand-up, improv, poetry . . .'

'We were pissed—' Lucy started but was cut short.

'We were fantastic! But where was the BBC then? Where was Channel 4's Talent Team? Fucking Oxford, that's where! Keep it in the old school, why don't you? Give the breaks to old pals Jinty Holden and Richard Farquhar-Smythe – talentless fuckers. Nothing's changed. We thought we could do anything! We believed that hype about "go to uni and live your wildest dreams". Of course you can – *if you've got a trust fund*. We thought we could change the world. All we got were fucking overdrafts larger than our likely inheritance and we're still paying off our student loans. And now where are we? Gone corporate! Suit wearers! Married with children—'

'If only,' Lucy sighed. Still Nigel ignored her. He was in full flow now.

'Slaves to the machine! On the payroll of the Man! Even we couldn't escape, Lucy, so there was no hope for the others. Working to pay off the debt we incur trying to cure the mind-numbing boredom of working. How did it come to this – our spirit, our youth, crushed and sucked from us by the evil twins of Xerox and Fax?'

He flung himself back down on the sofa, his speech complete. He had clearly been thinking of that finale for some time. Probably all afternoon. He was waiting for her reaction, for her denial that their lives were stuck on a one-way track to Deadendsville, but all she could manage in a quiet voice was a small 'I don't know' and an addition that unnerved and depressed him still further: 'I don't know what the point is at all.'

Suddenly, some might even say luckily, their spiral into mid-life crisis was halted by Lucy's horror-movie screams. Her cries were spontaneous and panic-driven, interspersed only by fishwife-type slandering and four-letter words. Lucy Diamond reserved the right *not* to be polite in her own home. She had stood up and was backing away towards the door.

'What are you doing here? Get out of my fucking flat! Get out! Get *oooout*! Nigel! Call the police! Call the police!'

Nigel's first response was to throw wine over himself and the mink ('I have to buy this or I will be a failure who has got to thirty without buying myself one non-reduced item of furniture never mind if it doesn't match the chair I'll use a throw') sofa.

'Lucy Diamond, by all that's holy . . .' In this testing moment, the repressed good Catholic boy was outed and Nigel resorted to his own mother's favourite exclamation.

Lucy continued screaming (and swearing). 'It's him! The one I told you about! The crazy guy from the tube! How the fuck did you get in here? Get out! Get *out*! Nigel – call the fucking police. Do it!'

The hairs on Nigel's neck and arms were standing up. He looked around the empty flat feeling suddenly sick and frightened. He moved towards his dearest friend to try to calm her down.

'Lucy-love, sit down. There's no one here.' His efforts were futile and his inner voice was paraphrasing a Thatcher quote – this lady was not for calming.

'No one there? Are you mad? He's standing right by the fireplace, as clear as fucking day in a trench coa— Oh my God! The guy in the trench! The Mickey Rourke-alike.'

Nigel looked even more confused.

'The crazy man on the tube is the same as the one in the coffee shop and the lift.' Nigel sat blank-faced, so Lucy yelled to enhance his understanding. 'THE ONE YOU FANCIED. REMEMBER?'

She turned her attention back to the man who might or might not be there. 'You've been stalking me all fucking day. You're a nutter. You need help.'

Lucy was pointing and shouting angrily at thin air. Nigel gripped her by her shoulders and forced her down into the chair. He held his eyes level with hers and spoke slowly and clearly.

'Lucy. There. Is. No one. There. You're a little stressed and you've been drinking on an empty stomach. Just close your eyes for a minute or two and when you open them again whatever you can see that I can't see won't be there. Trust me. Close your eyes.' Nigel enveloped her in his arms and because she trusted him and because she loved him, Lucy did as he asked.

'What's happening to me, Nigel? I swear to you it's real. I can see him. Why can't you? But you could earlier. Why can't you now? Am I going mad? Am I? Oh my God, what's happening to me?' As he held her and the adrenaline subsided, she began to cry. Nigel rubbed her back and she pressed her hands over her eyes, feeling safe in the circle of his arms.

'You're tired. You've been working very hard. That guy on the tube this morning obviously freaked you out more than you know. Sure, I saw a guy in a trench but there's nothing to say it was the same one. You've probably got some subconscious fear or something going on.' Nigel was grasping for some comforting phrase from pop-psychology.

He kept rubbing, Lucy kept crying and Nigel shushed her soothingly as he would a fretful toddler whilst simultaneously ringing Jojo on his mobile and talking about Lucy as though she wasn't there. Lucy sat passively listening to Nigel's half of the conversation, her eyes firmly clamped shut.

'Jojo. You've got to get here quickly. Lucy's had a freak-out. She's talking to things that aren't there . . . No, only half a bottle, but she hadn't eaten . . . Chianti . . . all right, it was a bloody screw top but it's not exactly LSD, is it?' There was a long pause followed by, 'Don't be ridiculous. None of us have smoked that stuff in years . . . Don't blame me! That was a decade ago! I wouldn't know how to roll it now . . . Oh, shit, that doesn't sound good. Say it again . . . Delayed Onset Psychosis.' Then, caustically, 'Let's look on the bright side, shall we? . . . Well, it might not be. She could just be tired . . . Oh, Jesus Christ . . . Shall I call an ambulance? . . . OK. I'll wait until you get here . . . No, I don't think she's a danger to herself . . .' and with a tremor running down his spine, 'or me . . . Of course I'll stay with her . . . Just bloody well hurry up, will you?'

Nigel threw the phone on to the wine-soaked sofa and crossed himself, adding quietly, 'Mary, Jesus and Joseph. If you make Lucy Michelle Eleanor Jude Rita Diamond well, I will *never* drink again.'

He wrapped Lucy up tight in his arms, kissing her hair as he did so, and was already reconsidering that maybe *never* drinking again was a little extreme when a small white vase that had sat quite happily on the mantelpiece for years – as the dust ring left behind would testify – shot across the room over their heads and smashed against the back wall.

Nigel screamed rather like a girl in a heated game of kiss-chase and scrabbled for cover behind the sofa, leaving Lucy to fend for herself. Now he was truly, utterly freaked out. He could tell that the vase had been thrown with force. It hadn't merely tumbled from the shelf and he was feeling thoroughly, totally out of his league.

'OK. Lucy.' He needed to speak calmly. He needed to reach some degree of understanding about this situation. 'How did that vase get over there? Can you tell me?' His voice was high and strangled as he wrestled to keep himself under control. Lucy did not answer. She was up and shouting obscenities again.

All the stories from his youth came flooding back to Nigel. Tales of ghosts, poltergeists, spectres and malicious fairies. These were the bedrock of a belief system derived from a doting Irish mother and four aunties who, despite living in a brand-new development in urban Coventry, still kept the superstitions of their country. Nigel was now thinking it was less an issue of overdoing the Chianti and more a case of demonic possession. Shit! He wished he'd had the guts to watch

The Exorcist. He hadn't got the script for this situation but that film just might have. Maybe he shouldn't have called Jojo after all; maybe he should have called a priest.

Lucy sought to get a handle on reality. But there was a man standing there that Nigel couldn't see. A man who could throw vases. She rambled a little incoherently, veering between talking to herself rationally and talking to the apparition.

'You're not really there. This isn't happening. I'm just tired, that's all. Why are you doing this? Why are you following me? Why am I talking to you at all? You're not there. You're just a figment of my imagination, that's all. Stop laughing!'

The desperate, pale face of the man she had encountered on the tube that morning contorted into a wide, wild grin. He was looking extremely pleased with himself as he took another ornament – a carved wooden cat – and flung it across the room where it splintered into shards against the door jamb to renewed squeals from Nigel.

Lucy ducked instinctively but realised, on the strength of Nigel's cries and the disapproving banging on the floor from Miss Crump the retired art teacher who lived below and was sure to be ramming her broom on the ceiling in anger (again), that some of what she was seeing was real.

Nigel's whimpering had taken on a fresh vigour. He was calling for God and Jojo in equal measure. Though he could not see the young man in the room, the flying ornaments had at least confirmed his presence.

Lucy's mind was whirling. She scanned the room for something to arm herself with. She gave the table lamp a couple of yanks but the plug was wedged into a socket that was itself wedged by an 'occasional' table. If ever there was an occasion this was it, but the lamp barely budged and though she tried to wave it threateningly she had only a few inches of spare flex to play with.

Judging by the young man's look of amusement, she had to admit it was a pretty useless idea. Then, in a moment of clarity, she leapt for a dusty grey figurine from the top shelf.

'Ahah!' Lucy was victorious as she waggled a candle of Buddha in the direction of her uninvited guest.

'What *are* you doing?' yelled Nigel from his position of cover. The evening was getting more surreal by the moment.

'Religious stuff is supposed to protect you from all things supernatural, isn't it?' Lucy said, still holding out the object as a barrier whilst side-stepping across the room towards Nigel.

'It's not exactly a crucifix, is it?' he said, ladling on the sarcasm.

'The sentiment is there.'

'Sentiment? Lucy, you're dealing with an apparition, not a wedding present.'

'Have you got a better idea?' Her savage response silenced Nigel. Then the 'thing' in the trench coat, whom Lucy could still see with remarkable clarity, spoke – without, thankfully, reaching for another missile.

'You're the only one who can help me, Lucy Michelle Eleanor Jude Rita Diamond. That is your name, isn't it? Your friend wasn't joking when he called you that?' He broke off and started singing a medley of Beatles hits. 'What were your parents thinking of?'

'Can you hear him, Nigel?' Lucy asked without addressing the rather rude and personal comment. The sort of comment that people feel they can make when you have an unusual name. 'He's talking to me now.'

'I can't hear him. What's he saying, Lucy-love? What's he saying?' Nigel had now adopted a tone akin to that of Denise the agony aunt from the golden days of Richard and Judy.

'He says I'm the only one who can help him.'

'Help him? *Help him?* Help him to do what?' Nigel's contribution to the conversation was unhelpful, still patronising in tone but tinged with a slightly hysterical fear. Nigel fervently hoped that the 'help' would not involve murder and the subsequent plea of 'the voices made me do it'.

'What do you want me to help you with?' she said in a slow monotone as though speaking to a foreign exchange student.

'I . . . want . . . you . . . to . . . talk . . . to . . . my girl-friend,' came the reply in the same stilted tone used by Lucy, then: 'You can hear me – I can hear you – talk normally! I may be Scottish but I'm not deaf or stupid. Or foreign, though you soft southerners may disagree,' he added as an afterthought.

Disregarding the insult, Lucy shouted to Nigel, 'He wants me to talk to his girlfriend.'

'Can't he just go to Relate?'

'Oh, for God's sake. Translate for him later, will you? This – *he* – is very irritating,' said the figure, gesturing towards Nigel, 'and I never know how much time I've got. It takes a lot of energy, this "appearing" thing, and I haven't quite figured out how to control it.'

'What *are* you talking about?'

Lucy was utterly confused. Her brain was in overdrive like a crashing computer scanning for files. Nothing made sense.

A man was in her flat and she hadn't a clue how he got there. He wanted her to do nothing more than talk to his girlfriend but apparently she was the only one who could do it. Oh – and Nigel couldn't see him, or at least he couldn't now but he could earlier.

It seemed that her grip on reality had loosened like her hold on the Buddha, who dropped to the floor from her limp fingers. She was frowning and her knees were buckling, every gesture an indication that the effort of trying to figure out what the hell was going on was just too overwhelming. She sank to her knees.

'What's he saying? What's he doing?' Nigel was frantic, frightened by Lucy's silence.

The figure spoke again, realising what needed to be done. He stooped to lock eyes with Lucy and lowered his voice. He seemed to be relishing what he was saying, studying her face, waiting for her reaction. He said each word slowly and deliberately, rolling his r's with extra Scottish flourish.

'You can see me, he can't? The Now I'm Here, Now I'm Not? Haven't you figured it out yet?'

Lucy shook her head dumbly and he stood back, spreading his arms wide and bending with a theatrical bow as though pleased to present himself.

'The name's Rayburn, Jonathan Rayburn, and let me clarify the situation for you. I'm dead, Lucy Diamond.'

Four hours later, all three of them – Jojo, Nigel and Lucy – were well on the road to Wales. One of them remained a gibbering wreck for most of the journey but the girls were doing what they could to make Nigel feel better. He was most fortified by the thought of another couple of days off work. What excuse could be better than a friend in need? A friend in need of sectioning!

Jojo had also been on the phone almost immediately begging urgent leave, telling her boss in no uncertain terms of the scene unfolding and her starring role. She was loving the drama of the situation and the sense of being grown up, being in command. She always seized opportunities like this because she so rarely felt mature, and certainly no one expected Jojo Gray to behave in ways other than immoral or illegal. After all, a girl who burnt her school tie to a four-inch stump – whilst she was wearing it – was never going to get awards for being sensible.

Jojo had arrived at Walthamstow Heights having road-raged her way across town in her Ka, and had quickly assessed the situation.

'There's nothing for it,' she had solemnly declared as though passing sentence, donning a black handkerchief and sending someone off to their death. 'We have to take her to Jasmine.'

A shocked silence filled the room. Jojo's belief in the mothering skills of Lucy's hippy maternal parent were markedly different from that of the others present. This category no longer included Jonathan Rayburn, who had made like Elvis and left the building, but Lucy lay curled in a foetal position on the damp wine stain on the sofa and was feeling too overcome to argue. Nigel rolled his eyes in horror at Jojo's suggestion.

Beautiful, leggy, naughty Jojo Gray, with her tumble of (non-frizzing) curls hanging down her back, her Queen's English accent, her well-heeled confidence and the ability to make even a high-necked blouse look slutty, was less a friend and more an honorary sister to Lucy, though each would have preferred the other's parents to be her own. Jojo could lean on Jasmine in ways that Lucy, her daughter, could not. Jojo loved being able to talk about everything that her bank manager father and teacher mother condemned, and loved that Jasmine was all for Letting It Hang Out and Being Free. So Jasmine and Jojo had talked pot smoking and sexual positions over the kitchen table with an honesty that made Lucy's toes curl. Lucy was glad that Jasmine was hardly ever around but happy that her mother at least liked her best friend. Nan Peters, whose back room had been Lucy's bedroom since she was eleven, did not. She had declared Jojo Gray a Bad Influence who was sure to come to a Bad End.

In turn, Jasmine admired Jojo's waywardness – in fact encouraged it, feeling, back then, a connection to the rebellious teen that she did not have with her own conventional, conservative daughter. Lucy never knew that the unshakeable bond had been forged over the secret of Jojo's teenage abortion and Jasmine's policy of non-judgemental support.

So in times of crisis Jojo turned to Jasmine, Lucy turned to Jojo and Jasmine always, always leaned on Lucy, forcing responsible and mature decisions and advice out of her only child. And so it had been since Lucy could remember. At an age when Lucy's only concern should have been Bagpuss, Jasmine would consult her toddling oracle on everything from How Are We Going to Find the Money for the Gas Bill? to Do You Think I Should Let Merlin Sleep with Other Women and Do His Own Thing? Jasmine called it Honesty. Nan Peters said it was Too Much Responsibility on a Young 'Un.

But then Jasmine had been young herself, having had Lucy in her second year of university whilst studying anthropology. Lucy's was not a conventional upbringing. Her first steps were taken in the university quadrangle cheered on by dope-smoking, didgeridoo-playing animal activists. Her first memories were of running along corridors of books in the university library and the flashing lights as she whirled around, the only child in a throbbing sea of psychedelically dressed adults, at a Roc Soc disco.

Jasmine had been briefly and unsuccessfully married to Lucy's biological father. A hasty visit to a registry office joined Dave Diamond and Jasmine Peters in matrimony and saved face for her parents back in the village. The marriage was over so quickly that Lucy had no recollection of a home with Dave or indeed a dad of any description. But there had been a colourful changing parade of long-haired, flare-wearing, slim-as-a-string-bean prog rock fans.

Dave – he was never Daddy – was just one of them and one day he had 'Gone to Morocco' and did not come back into their lives again for several years. There were no tears, no bitter divorce and no court dates for back maintenance. And when Dave Diamond did return to meet his progeny there was awkwardness and embarrassment all round.

Gone was the concave chest, Gillan-haired wearer of T-shirts with catchy titles such as Keep on Truckin' and I'm With This Idiot that Lucy was familiar with from photographs. Suddenly, he was a shorn, suit-wearing sold out, regional sales rep and the conversation had been stilted to say the least. But Lucy never felt the lack of him in her life, never resented the new men in Jasmine's, and was never the victim of any cruel step-parenting about which she could now write a bestseller.

She should have been screwed up, a therapist's dream, but she wasn't. Nor was she In Denial. Between the bohemian life of houseboats and artists' communes with Jasmine and the steadiness of life in Ploxbury with Nan and Pop Peters, Lucy had never felt the lack of a Marillion-loving man who now won awards for selling the most panty-pads in the South East. No lurid chat show confessionals to be had here. Lucy had endured her unconventional childhood to emerge nice, polite, friendly and, well, ordinary. Ordinary up to the day that Jonathan Rayburn appeared, anyhow.

And because he had appeared and Lucy was in meltdown, Jojo needed Jasmine's Buddhist/pagan/self-help manual pick-and-mix wisdom. Hence they were on the road to Wales.

Nigel really did not want to go. Though he was now

crammed into the back seat along with old newspapers and decaying food (Jojo had famously never cleaned the inside of any car she possessed) he had put up as many excuses and employed as many delaying tactics as he could muster, without success. The truth was he was so spooked that he doubted he would ever sleep alone again. Not that he had ever needed an excuse to bring home strangers – good-looking strangers – but although he was never going to sink to grab-a-grandad level, the way he was feeling, a hasty pick-up seemed less trouble than a trip to Jasmine's.

'It's not as if we are taking her "home", is it?' was his first try and he had even done the annoying rabbit-ear thing to denote inverted commas. 'Lucy's never lived there.'

'But Jasmine is her mother and Lucy needs round the clock TLC,' Jojo had countered.

'Well, let's take her to Nan Peters.'

'Yeah, right. Let's unleash poltergeist activity and a granddaughter with a nervous breakdown on a pensioner.'

Nigel had made a not-very-attractive-grumpy face at Jojo.

'It's a bit remote, though, isn't it? A bit in the back of beyond, don't you think? I mean you can't even get a mobile signal, can you?'

'Perfect!' declared Jojo, not to be swayed from her decided responsible course of action. 'Peace and quiet. A bit of R&R.'

'Rock and roll?' queried Nigel. 'That isn't what she needs.'

'Rest and recuperation,' corrected Jojo, already throwing things into a dusty weekend bag dragged off the top of Lucy's wardrobe.

'I have no clean pants,' had been Nigel's final excuse, and to emphasise the point he had added, 'and you know I can't bear to wear underwear for more than eight hours at a stretch.'

'Why? What in hell do you do in it?' Jojo's patience was thinned.

Then, speaking for the first time in what had seemed an age, a quiet voice from the sofa said, 'I have a pair of your boxers in my top drawer. You left them here when you stayed over that time, remember? The blue check ones. One hundred per cent cotton. I've washed them for you and they're ironed. I know how you always iron your boxers. I just kept them because I thought you might need them one day. Like today.'

So it was decided. No more excuses, though Jojo and Nigel had thought it a little weird that the pants had been idling in a drawer for several months unmentioned, both washed and ironed. Neither had sought eye contact over this point; in fact each studiously ignored the other, but the fact was filed under For Later Discussion and Jojo was already mentally rehearsing the It's Not Healthy speech to give to Lucy.

Then, armed with a carrier bag of travel-size toiletries scooped from the sticky depths of the bath-room cabinet, a large bag of Doritos and four blackening bananas, they hit the road. They were heading for Jasmine's eco-commune of sustainable housing deep in the heart of Pembrokeshire. It was collection of tipis and shanty-town shacks made from reclaimed materials surrounded by allotments and wind turbines where a mixed bag of aromatherapists and professional benefits claimants lived off the land. Straggle-haired children who seemed to belong to nobody yet everybody galloped bareback between the dwellings on semi-wild ponies. Jasmine and her battered leather cowboy hat had at last found a place they could call home.

The nearer they got the twitchier Nigel became. He could almost hear the twanging of country banjos. It wasn't just the lack of twenty-four-hour garages or that at Jasmine's he had to share a solar-powered shower that was always, only ever, *just about* lukewarm. No, he could cope with that if he could be sure it would all be over within a weekend. Nigel's Big Fear was that he would have some sort of terrible accident and that rather than call out the paramedics, who would pollute the atmosphere of dung heap and joss-stick with ambulance diesel, Jasmine would bind him in a nettle wrap and stitch him together with birch fibres. And he hadn't felt too good lately. His body just didn't feel as it had done when he was younger. He shouldn't take chances. Anything could happen. Nigel fought hard to quell the rising panic.

The journey was almost over. It had gone smoothly and the conversation had switched from banalities like 'Would you rather shag Ant or Dec?' to probing Lucy. Had she seen this imaginary/ghost fella before? Could she see him now? What did he look like? What did he sound like? What did he say? Tell us again. And so it went on until Lucy had grown tired and irritated, like a parent of a six year old asking 'Are we there yet?'

The car bumped and lurched down narrow dark country lanes. These city slickers who could pass hoodies on the Underground without breaking a sweat screamed in fear as a cow's head leaned over a gatepost. The lanes gave way to a single off-road track that required the opening and shutting of several farm gates. The task fell to Lucy. Nigel simply refused to help on account of his new trainers and the risk of sheep poo. He claimed to be still traumatised from their last visit when he had actually slipped over on ovine afterbirth.

'That bloody Farmer Llewellyn-Jones or whatever his name is was bloody lucky I didn't go to bloody Claims Direct. I've seen the adverts,' Nigel ranted.

'Yes, they always show them in the daytime,' was Jojo's spiky reference to his Duvet Days.

Several tracks later, their conversation had dried up completely. They resorted to stating the obvious to each other.

'Brr! It's cold out.'

'It's so dark, isn't it?'

Eventually, lights gleamed in the distance and a log cabin reminiscent of Laura Ingalls Wilder's Little House on the Prairie mushroomed from the darkness. Night-time and the dim light thrown by the headlights of Jojo's Ka lent Jasmine's home a pioneer romance that daylight would bluntly strip away, revealing it for what it was: a cabin constructed of old doors, tarpaulin, reclaimed floorboards and wonky windows. But now it was a welcome sight for the weary travellers peeling themselves from the fuggy interior of the car.

Jasmine was framed in the doorway, short and squat, her long hair forming a capital A across her shoulders. She was hand in hand with the taller silhouette of her younger Swedish live-in lover Ert. She was running to them now, flip-flops slapping, reaching out to the girls and pulling them into a warm, woolly-shawled embrace.

'Blessed be! Blessed be!' Jasmine offered her pagan greetings and babbled away like a stream as she stroked the girls' faces and hair and beamed benevolently. 'I'm so happy to see you. They came up from the farm with the message that you were coming and I couldn't even settle to meditation, could I, Ert? I had to have a foot rub instead. Ert is learning reflexology – he's really very good.' She rattled on.

Nigel was holding back from the embrace, pretending to check for a mobile signal though he knew there wouldn't be one. He loved women. He loved Jasmine, but he preferred to be around more artificial glamour: Veet hairlessness, Bambi-mascaraed eyelashes and alcohol-based perfumes. Ever since Jasmine had 'embraced the crone', as she called her menopause, he had found her earthy, natural approach to grooming a little off-putting.

Her armpit hair flourished like sheltering anemones, grey streaks ran slug trails of silver through her mousy hair (untamed by Frizz-ease) and whiskers curled on her upper lip, adding an extra, uncomfortable tickle to any kiss she might give. Nigel harboured scary desires to attack her with strip-wax during the night. Lucy also had reservations about Jasmine *au naturel*, knowing that unchecked, undepilated and without hair product she might very likely look exactly the same.

One lentil curry and a few glasses of home-made damson wine later – the wine having burned a path through the oesophagus – they were finally warmed through by the wood-burning stove. In the light of a few candles the reason for their visit was made clear. Only Jasmine could respond to a daughter's 'I can see a man who says he's dead' with clasped hands and a face of wonderment.

'At last! At last!' Jasmine murmured, eyes raised to the heavens.

'What do you mean "At last", Mother?' The last word was spoken with exasperated irritation. Lucy was tired, worn out by the journey and the hair-raising spectacle of Jonathan Rayburn, but she might have known that this had something to do with Jasmine. The ridiculous and irregular things in her life always did – like the hand-whittled clogs Jasmine once sent her for Christmas and the trip to a Green Festival two years ago where everyone had shed their clothes and danced around naked, even the ones who should really have covered up in the spirit of consideration for others. Lucy recalled with a shudder how she had eventually had to peel off too as she was the only one left wearing clothes but she had never, ever forgiven Jasmine for that one.

'Remember Sioux? Your spiritual mother?' Lucy nodded, recalling a woman very similar to her own mother but with flaming red hennaed hair whose real name was dull Susannah Brown until she became a self-appointed Native American shaman. 'Well, when you were born we decided to do a little moon magic. An all-female ritual to sanctify your start in life—'

Lucy harrumphed and Nigel squirmed uncomfort-ably as Jasmine described the burial of the placenta under a tree by the light of the moon. He inwardly thanked God that Jasmine hadn't described eating it. She continued, 'Sioux compiled your astro-chart and we checked how suitable your name was with numerology. I mean, we all know the true powers of the Beatles, right? I mean, why do you think the government arranged the shooting of John Lennon?'

Nobody questioned her. Lucy knew better than to start her mum 'off on one', Nigel had always thought Jasmine had used far too many drugs in her past, and

Jojo sat in rapture, absorbing every word that was said, which contrasted so sharply with her father's conservative party political broadcast-type speeches.

'And then we wanted to give you a gift. A Life Gift like in the traditional folk tales. Like in *The Sleeping Beauty*.'

'Trust you to end up with a little prick on your finger,' whispered Nigel. Lucy hit him by means of reply. She was curled on a bean bag resting against Nigel's legs. At least his mood was much improved by the passive smoking of Ert's home-grown dope. If Jasmine had heard, she didn't respond. She was deep into her tale-telling now.

'I'm so happy, Lucy – I never thought we had the true power to do it. I mean, we followed the ritual to the letter. Sioux had found it in some antiquated book shop, bound in leather along with charms to eliminate warts.'

'Why are you all looking at me?' Nigel bridled, paranoid about a past intimate infection. 'Like you're all Snow White!'

Jasmine pressed on. 'I kind of doubted we could really do it. But hey, we did! We really did it! When you were little, there was Tobias. Tobias Godough – your invisible friend. I never called him imaginary. Never. Just because I couldn't see him didn't mean he wasn't real and I always believed he was a spirit child. As for energy fields! You could sense whether a building or even a street was good or bad within seconds. It was as if you could *read* the atmosphere, sense its whole past and the souls that had rested there. Don't you remember? You couldn't even go inside the stone circle at Avebury!'

Lucy seemed to recall it was because of a dispute

over an ice cream that Jasmine had refused to buy because mass-produced lactose products represented bovine exploitation. Lucy had merely gone off in a nine year old's sulk, but there was no point arguing with Jasmine's version of events. And there *had* been Tobias Godough . . .

'Then, as you grew older, you kind of . . . stopped believing. Closed your mind to that part of yourself. Tobias stopped visiting. But remember, Lucy – this is a gift. A Gift,' Jasmine repeated for additional mystical emphasis.

'Ask her if she's got the receipt,' hissed Nigel and received a dig from Lucy's elbows.

'I've gotta tell Sioux – this'll blow her mind!' and Jasmine was up and off to an area screened by a batik wall-hanging. They all sat looking into the flames behind the little glass door of the woodburner. Ert skinned up. Again.

'I didn't think Jasmine had a phone,' Nigel finally said.

'She doesn't,' Lucy answered. 'She's gone to tell her telepathically and no, I'm not joking.'

Jojo's eyes were dancing and her mind racing with all she'd heard. The fug of Ert's spliffs and the potent damson wine were helping to move her mood along.

'Lucy – this is your Gift! Your spiritual birthright! This is what you were born to do!' Jojo invariably got caught up in the theatrics of any situation and always threw herself into Jasmine's world – the polar opposite of her parents' sphere of golf sweaters, choir practice and the WI.

'Oh, for God's sake! You don't believe all that mumbo-jumbo, do you?' Lucy was scathing. 'Thank God you're here, Nigel, as the representative of common sense or they'd have me drinking deadly nightshade and riding a broomstick. I think you'll find I'm just tired. It was all just the product of an overactive mind, that's all. I'm just overworked and in need of a detox. Nothing more and nothing magic!'

Though Lucy's tone was matter-of-fact, dismissing Jasmine's claims of spiritual gift-giving, she did not feel it at all. In fact she knew there were things around Jasmine that sometimes defied explanation. Herbs that healed faster than chemist's medicine. Tarot readings that came true. Wild animals that turned up at the door.

They lapsed back into a tired silence, mesmerised by the hissing and popping of the woodstove's flames, each absorbed in their own thoughts. Then Ert spoke and they all jumped with the shock of it and sat gaping, open-mouthed.

Ert rarely spoke. As a consequence it was very easy to forget he was even there. It wasn't anything to do with a language barrier – he spoke perfect English – but actually due to the fact that he was perpetually totally stoned. He had the effortless good looks, clear skin and white-blond hair of a Nordic-themed Benetton advert. Quite how he had migrated to Pembrokeshire was a mystery, as was his evident adoration of Jasmine who was old enough to be his mother and looked it. He was always touching her – massaging a shoulder, stroking an arm, running his long fingers over her calloused feet – or gazing in wonderment as she offered some enlightened wisdom or another.

Despite Nigel's cruel nick-naming – he called him In-Ert because of his slothful manner – he was always skittish and coy whenever Ert looked in his direction. Nigel frequently claimed he'd swap his Camden flat for a one-room shack if he could share it with him, although he could never quite get past the fact that Jasmine and Ert ran very successful and well-attended practical tantric sex workshops. He said his imagination was too vivid to cope with the concept. Technically, Ert was a common-law step-parent to Lucy, but he did supermodel much better and it was a revelation to find that he did conversation at all.

'Lucy, you don't like your life much at the moment. Yes?' Lucy nodded, struck mute because in the five years Ert had been part of her mother's life she had never heard him say so much. 'You don't like your job and you say you need a new direction. Maybe this is eet. This is your chance. You do this as your job. Yes? This will be your new life. People will want to pay you for your gift. You can take enough money for living and you help The Dead. It is perfect. No?' And he nodded at his own sage words and lit another joint.

'I don't think I want this Gift,' whispered Lucy to Jojo and Nigel as they made up beds in another screened-off corner of the cabin. There was a double futon and a single hammock strung between two beams. She was beginning to think that maybe Jasmine had a point after all and it was certainly easier to think that she could connect with the so-called spirit world than to consider herself psychotic. 'I mean, it's creepy, isn't it? It's weird. It's Not What People Do. It's not real and it's not scientific. I can't prove Jonathan Rayburn exists – or should I say existed. What if it was all in my mind? Although Jasmine's got a point about my imaginary friends – perhaps they were ghosts. They did all wear what we would call period costume.'

'You had multiple imaginary friends?' carped Nigel. 'I couldn't even get one. Even the invisible kids wouldn't pick me for the team.' Somehow Nigel always made it about him. Lucy threw him a pillowcase to stuff and continued.

'The Dead is quite a broad term, isn't it? There must be legions of them. Will this mean that I can only see The Dead who want to speak with me or can I dial a connection to any old spirit on the other side? Can I speak to Shakespeare or only people who have died in my lifetime? Will I speak in tongues? Will I be possessed? Will I be able to hold a séance? And if so, should I ask Jasmine for an ethnic headscarf and gypsy earrings?' Lucy's tone was verging on hysterical.

Jojo was the Chilled Out Voice of Reason as she tucked a sheet around a futon reeking of incense.

'There's too much to take on board at once. You'll have to take it in stages. Read books. Surf the Web. See if you can find other people like you. You'll have to learn how to do it. I guess you'll have to train.'

'Well, I can't exactly take a GCSE in it, can I?' Lucy was in no mood for her friend's chilled vibe.

'What do *you* think happened? What do you *want* to happen, Lucy? How do you want to explain it all?' Jojo lay back on the scatter cushions of the futon. Nigel was still making a ham-fisted attempt on the pillows – a typical ploy. Make a bad job of it and the others will do the work.

'Right now, I want it to just all go away. I want it to be a one-off. A flashback caused by all those dodgy E's and acid we had at Creamfields. I just want to be normal again.'

She moved instinctively towards Nigel for comfort and he snaked his arms round her neck, making little cooing noises and reassuring her that it would be all right and he'd get her the best straitjacket and padded cell that his income could afford. She leaned into the embrace, enjoying his strong arms round her and his good, clean smell, chuckling at his usual wicked humour, and then she saw Jasmine with an armful of bedlinen watching with her bright bird's eyes.

Lucy jerked herself away and knew that Jasmine would want to have another of those Why Are You Doing This to Yourself? conversations. The one they had had so many times before. The one that began with Jasmine being all concerned, drifted into Jasmine's self-pitying guilt-laden Is It Because I Didn't Stick It Out With Dave? Was I Wrong to be a Nomadic Mother? and ended with Lucy consoling Jasmine that Everything was Fine and that it had Nothing to Do With Any of That and that she was Completely Over her Crush on Nigel. Then tomorrow – because even hippy mothers can't help matchmaking – Lucy would be introduced to some hapless, anaemic-looking bearded vegan at the log pile who couldn't possibly match Nigel in terms of either good looks or wit.

He was being witty now, or at least something that rhymed with it, as he leapt into the double futon with Jojo and hissed in the darkness, 'I'm not moving. You lot dragged me here against my will and I refuse to sleep in that hammock. You can't make me. Can you hear me, Lucy Diamond? I absolutely refuse to sleep in that fucking hammock.'

It was going to be to hard to slip back into the mundane of routine nine-to-five after all the high drama of the previous week. Lucy had stayed on in Pembrokeshire until Friday, returning via a convoluted route involving tractor, bus and late, overpriced and overstuffed train in time for the weekend. The whole time, Jasmine had waited desperately for Lucy to commune with The Dead and it didn't happen, despite Jasmine's candle circles, pentagrams and oil burning.

Perhaps it had been a figment of her imagination after all – like her 'friends' from childhood – and Jasmine's memory of the gift ritual just a coincidence. Lucy felt pretty stupid about the whole affair but she had been glad of the rest – and Jasmine's macrobiotic cooking. It had made her feel good and righteous even if she was now craving a slab of Cadbury's. She had a carrier bag of the commune's communal books as emergency guidance if any of The Dead should happen to reappear. Titles such as *Spiritualism for Dummies*, *Knock Once for Yes*, *The Small Book for Mediums* and the ominous-sounding *When Séances Go Bad*. She had also been given the phone number of a white witch in Cheam. After all, you never know when you will need one.

She was glad to be heading back to London. To grimy air thick enough to chew on, nose-to-tail traffic and locals who ask 'Wha' you looking at?' As soon as Lucy's phone had a signal, it blip-blopped the arrival of text after text. The other passengers scowled in annoyance and Lucy's thumbs worked like a masseuse's as she replied to first Jojo, then Nigel, then workmates. Then the name Tony R popped into the inbox.

Tony R – Tony Russell to be exact – had joined the accounts department about six months ago. He had talked to her a few times on work-related matters and then chatted TV and music in the kind of chummy way she evoked in men. There had been joke e-mails exchanged, nothing out of the ordinary in an office environment, but Lucy did think there had been a bit of lingering eye contact and unnecessary journeys to retrieve unimportant paperwork on his part. He was nice looking in a Jack-the-lad sort of way – all mussed-up hair and a cocky grin – and he caused quite a stir in the girls who were once called office juniors but now had preposterously long titles like Administrative, Communications and Clerical Support Professional.

Lucy pushed View and the message *R u free Sat 4 dinner?* appeared.

Her stomach churned. This was not expected. She ignored the old-style texting – obviously he hadn't mastered predictive text – and checked the date. It had been languishing somewhere in mobile phone land since Monday. Without a reply! And the first thought she had before even considering what to reply was *That'll seem very rude*, because it is after all (as you have learned) in her nature to be polite.

When was the last time Lucy Diamond had a date?

A while ago.

Let's be honest.

A long while ago.

Come on . . .

OK. Nine months. Nine, long, arid, dry, dateless months.

So what's the problem? Is it her or is it them?

It's the men. So Lucy says. There is always something wrong with them so that she doesn't ever get beyond the 'mild interest' phase even if they like her. For example, a perfectly nice fella might have poor posture or ears without lobes or a name like Kevin or George that she could not imagine screaming in the throes of passion.

And then there's Nigel with his intelligence and charm and overall edible appearance stuck up there on a pedestal, flying the Rainbow Flag and totally unattainable. Somehow – rightly or wrongly – inside the head of Lucy Diamond, Nigel has become the Golden Standard of Manhood. So how could any heterosexual man compete? Most of them couldn't even pass the Basic Hygiene test.

Don't feel too sorry for her. Everyone has had their fair share of bad dates, haven't they? Lucy has had her share of good ones too. There have been ones she was interested in who ticked most of the boxes on the eligibility list and have been interested in her. There have been repeat dates. Some of them repeated for weeks, months and even a year at a time. But some have ended badly, and though Lucy says it's the men – fifty per cent of it is also her.

One of the problems, one of her faults, is that Lucy Diamond is one of the last of the True Romantics. She shouldn't be – not growing up as she did without the psychologist-recommended father figure and a list of very colourful 'uncles'. But Lucy wants to believe in love at first sight (she had often confused it with lust), Happy Ever After and even poisoned apples. She wants a Brief Encounter with Mr Darcy in Casablanca.

She did realise years ago that in the Rules of Modern Dating romance rarely enters into it and her standards – including the Nigel factor – are incredibly high, so she constantly feels short-changed and disappointed. Her true wishes are not compatible with today's world. What hope for romance when magazines for 'ladies' give advice on First Night Sex Tips That'll Blow More Than His Mind and the lads' mags have Blue Peter presenters presenting themselves half-dressed? Lucy can't bear the current expectations that she should know how to pole dance *and* every position in the Kama Sutra.

Lucy yearns for times of mystery when women kept the bits only a gynaecologist should see covered. All the sex in adverts, on TV and in magazines makes her want to rebel – to wear pastel pinks, aprons and a (no longer appropriate for her by fifteen years) virginity pin. She wants to be pursued, desired, respected. Jasmine's generation may have thrown away the rule book but Lucy Diamond wants to reclaim it.

Just because she wears cheap clothes it doesn't mean she has to be a cheap date though she has certainly behaved like one at times. It is not the stuff of Great Romances to sleep with someone because you feel sorry for them or because it seems – and we know this is an issue for Lucy – *polite*.

She read the message again and thought carefully. OK – so Tony Russell was no Rhett Butler, but he was no Shrek either. He must be intelligent or he wouldn't be an accountant and the 'round robin' e-mails of funny YouTube clips and 100 Best Blonde Jokes indicated there might be humour of some sort. Plus, the invitation had come out of the blue and could therefore be loosely considered 'romantic'. Perhaps he was harbouring a secret longing for her?

Lucy stared out of the train window, her face furrowed in thought. The fields and farms flew past, the countryside less wild now they were out of Wales. It was neat, patchworked and would soon give way to the suburbs of Birmingham and then its packed centre, and she would have to change trains for London.

Her thumbs moved quickly. She pressed send and now there was no stopping her reply. Never mind visitations from the Other Side, Lucy Diamond had a date!

She had just over twenty-four hours to prepare.

First, there is the harvesting of unwanted hair from leg, pit and what the advertisers discreetly refer to as the 'bikini area'. Not that Lucy was planning for the latter to be on view, but it was best to be prepared and would add to her sense of being 'groomed' in a way that stray spider legs sneaking around the edges of a tanga brief never could. Luckily, an early grounding in yoga and a strategically placed mirror enabled Lucy to strip-wax from places she could never ask a beautician to go.

Then there is buffing. A battered old body-brush, bought during the first wave of celebrity detox diets – probably on Carol Vorderman's say-so – was used to scrape away at her epidermis on bumpy thigh, pimply upper arm and scaly calf. Lucy sloughed away at the offending dead cells, built up into a rhinoceros-hard layer from months of hiding under winter-wear man-made fibres and heavy duty opaque tights.

It was only when she came to cover herself in some of last Christmas's gift box body lotion which had lost its perfume that she discovered that the brush had etched deep welts into her limbs. Deep, red, *raw* welts that did not react well to body lotion. Her eyes smarted and she leapt back into the bath to ease the pain.

Lucy topped up the hot water, swished up the foam and lay back. Her face pack drying in the steam, she sighed contentedly. The bathroom resembled a war zone but she was temporarily dyed, conditioned and set into rollers for bounce. Her pores were being sucked clean and the hard skin of her feet shaved and pummelled with a lotion containing ground-up apricot kernel. She was on schedule and Tony Russell was in target. He was coming to fetch her at eight which gave ample time for nail painting, cuticle removing and the filing of ridged toenails. Never mind that she was wearing boots and not open-toed sandals – it was the *knowing* that her big toenails were smooth that counted.

It was only later that Lucy realised that she had created the right conditions for it to happen again. She was relaxed, warm. The gentle swaying motion of the water in the bath was like the cradling, rocking motion of the tube. Her mind was emptying of thoughts as she slipped from anticipating her date to a blank canvas, an empty space, and—

BlaaaaMMM!

'Lucy Diamond – you've got to help me!'

Lucy screamed, splashing water this way and that as she came to, opened her eyes and found Jonathan

Rayburn standing in the centre of her bathroom floor. Her face pack splintered into a thousand cracks. Naturally, she panicked – as any girl would if they were naked in the bath with an unknown man in a trench coat staring down at them.

Her first reaction was to cover her eyes. A foolish move as she quickly realised it left her breasts fully exposed. Jerking around like a fish on a line, water sloshing on to the floor and probably leaking (again) into the ceiling of Miss Crump below, Lucy covered herself and slipped under the bubbles, nearly drowning herself in the effort to drown out the image of Jonathan Rayburn.

And what happened next? Well, there was a lot of what had gone on before. A lot of You're All in My Head – No I'm Not, You Don't Exist – Yes I Do, This Isn't Happening to Me – Yes It Is type stuff. Jonathan was beginning to find it boring.

'Why won't you accept it, Lucy Diamond?' Jonathan had made it clear he was going nowhere until she did. 'It's who you are. This is what you can do and I need your help.'

Lucy sat there grumpily, refusing to look at him. She was trapped in the bath with her hands covering her breasts and her face pack flaking off into the water. Her mind was churning everything over. Jasmine's ritual. Ert's wise (and rare) words. How easily she had accepted and played with her childhood imaginary/ invisible/ghostly friends. Maybe it was because he had the persuasive approach of a good manager – his clothes, his bearing, his confident manner all indicated he was used to getting people to do what he wanted. Maybe it was his smooth Scottish brogue that convinced her – after all, it's the voice the advertisers prefer when they want you to trust them, whether they're selling ISAs or toothpaste.

Finally, she spoke in a tone of resignation. 'For Pete's sake. Why me? Why now? Why here?'

'You've been shutting me out.' Jonathan settled himself on the toilet lid as if speaking to a mud-faced naked girl in the bath was the most natural thing in the world.

'I haven't been doing any such thing.'

'Well, I couldn't get through until now, and believe me I've been trying. I can't control this thing any better than you can. I just trust to luck and keep hoping. It's your fault if the only place that you've let your guard down is in the bath.'

'And in view of that fact do you think you could just turn away or something? Or at least hand me a bloody bath towel?'

'Oh, don't worry,' Jonathan said simply. 'I'm dead. It's different. Your nakedness has no effect on me at all. I suppose it's one of the "earthly pleasures" that doesn't really concern me any more.'

'Well, it concerns me, so will you pass me a towel.' Jonathan didn't move. 'OK. Pass me a towel – *please*.'

To illustrate a point, Jonathan reached for the towel. His hand passed straight through it. He shrugged his shoulders and grinned. Lucy shuddered.

'Can't you move it with your mind or something? You were able to throw my vase pretty accurately.'

'It's not as simple as that. I was very, very focused that day on getting your attention.'

'And I would appreciate not having yours. If you don't mind?' Lucy made a little spinny gesture with her index finger and Jonathan swivelled on the toilet seat until he had his back to her and she could reach for a towel.

'OK, you can look now. How come you don't fall through the lid?' It was a reasonable question to ask in the circumstances.

'The physics of this are not my area, Lucy Diamond.'

Lucy was now full of questions. 'Why am I the only person who can help you? Why not . . .' Lucy groped around for an appropriate name, 'why not Mystic Meg? Or – or Sally whatshername, Psychic to the Stars?'

'It's something to do with vibrations. Apparently, we are on the same wavelength and you are what we – The Dead, the passed-over – call a Perceptive.'

Lucy rolled her eyes. It was like listening to Jasmine all over again.

'So I have no choice that it's me you can talk to?'

''Fraid not. But remember that I have no choice who I can connect to. By the way, your eyes – the mascara – you look a little . . . Alice Cooper.' Lucy wiped the smudges away and Jonathan continued.

'I had been up and down that tube, in and out of bars and buses, back and forth, time and time again. Not even my own family responded to me. There was nothing until I met you that morning. I'm sure this isn't the way you wanted things, Lucy, but trust me, this isn't exactly what I wanted either. I didn't ask to be run over by a white van at the start of September.'

As Jonathan talked Lucy settled herself back into the water under the bubbles and allowed herself to really study him. He had the looks, the confidence and the good teeth that come from a comfortable income and an independent education. Her mind wandered, flooded with images and sensations, and she could clearly picture his life – it had not been perfect but as near to it as a life could get.

His loving parents, their strong marriage, his closeness to a younger brother. It was a life of music exams and swimming certificates, excellence on the sports field and prefect badges. A solid red-brick university education, a few wild parties and then, in his second year, Laura – that was the name – the girl he knew instantly he wanted to marry. The beautiful girl in the yellow coat! Of course!

Lucy was suddenly, icily aware that the cold tap was pouring into her bath. She struggled to turn it off whilst shielding any grey, lumpy or fleshy bits that might have accidentally slipped on show. Jonathan was grinning.

'A new trick to add to my act.' Then, more seriously, 'You weren't listening to a word I was saying, were you?'

'I was too.' Lucy felt chastised. It took her right back to school and being made to stand in shame throughout assembly because she was talking. Many times she had been brought to justice for Jojo's wrongdoings because Jojo, whilst clearly the naughtier of the two, had the face of an angel, whereas Lucy at that point with her lank greasy ponytail, spots and large outdated spectacle frames looked like a budding serial killer.

'So what did I just say?' The classic line used by parents and teachers alike.

'I don't know . . . but' – Lucy pulled her knees to cover her chest – 'I could picture things about you,' and she told him, even naming the girl he loved.

A little blush registered on the pale cheeks of Jonathan Rayburn. Lucy laughed and found herself feeling surprisingly relaxed in the presence of a genuine ghost. There *was* a connection – a vibration or whatever Jasmine would call it – between them, and having peeped (metaphorically speaking) beneath the stereotypical clothing of a man who works 'in the City' she had found someone she rather liked. A nice person. A good soul. A boy scout in banker's clothing.

'You were telling me about how it happened – something about a white van.' Lucy didn't want to say death, dying or anything like it. After all, it might offend. She topped up the hot water, pouring more bubble bath under the flow.

'The morning it happened we'd had a bit of a row. The usual thing. I hadn't put my socks in the wash basket and the cleaner was coming round and Laura was saying it wasn't her job to pick up my things . . .'

Jonathan carried on documenting his domestic fracas whilst Lucy silently marvelled at how easily some people talk about cleaners as though having 'staff' when you are young, fit and childless is the most natural thing in the world. In her university days, Lucy had *been* a cleaner and could never imagine a life where she would be rich enough or busy enough to have one . . .

'Lucy!'

Maybe, I have self-limiting expectations, she thought. *Maybe if I assume I should have a cleaner then I will have a cleaner.*

'Lucy! Will you listen? You're drifting off again. Anyway, I left the house in a wee bit of a mood, I suppose—'

Lucy arched an eyebrow as if to say 'A *bit* of a mood?'

'OK. OK. But I was under a lot of pressure at work! That morning I should have given a presentation to one of the big chiefs that would have secured my future – and Laura's – in lots of ways. You have no idea how cut-throat, how pressurised, the world of finance is, especially at the moment. Anyway, I gave the door a bloody good slam as I left, but before that I said a whole bunch of mean stuff that I can't take back. About how hard I work and how her job is hardly as demanding, and if she didn't want to support me in my job then maybe we shouldn't even be together.'

'So there was no *bit* of a mood about it, was there?' It was Lucy's turn to chastise. 'You were in a full-on mood. So what was Laura's job that can be nowhere near as demanding as anything a big man does in the City?' Lucy felt strong female solidarity. It should always be the job of any self-respecting woman to tell a man who has argued with his girlfriend that he is wrong, particularly – especially – in matters concerning housework.

'Don't talk about her in the past tense. It gives me the creeps. She's still alive. I'm the dead one. Anyway she's a primary school teacher. It's what she always wanted to do. She just loves it and yes, she works damn hard. She's always marking or doing lesson plans. I know full well that I was being – that I was behaving like a . . . well, I was being an arse.

'The worst part is I was already trying to text to say that I was sorry when it happened. I was so engrossed in trying to type a message as I crossed the corner of our road that I didn't see the van coming and the next thing I know she's leaning over my body on a hospital bed and I'm floating off up in a corner trying not to go into the light and my parents are making arrangements to shut off the life support machines.'

Jonathan ran his hands through his sandy hair and his eyes filled, heavy with misery. He stared into space and sighed. 'It all happened very quickly. One morning,

I'm alive. That afternoon – I'm dead. I try not to think of what I had ahead of me, the life I could have had. I look back and think of all the time I wasted – but it's over for me now and I guess I've just got to get used to it.'

'Why didn't you want to go into the light, Jonathan?' Lucy's voice was soft and tentative. 'I thought everyone headed to the light.'

'Because of Laura. I couldn't go and leave things the way they were between us. I couldn't leave when she was standing there sobbing. Crying because I'm dead and crying because she thinks I walked out of the door and didn't want her any more. She even asked my parents if they thought I might have walked in front of the van on purpose because I couldn't bear my life with her any more. Truly, Lucy, that's something I would never do. I loved Laura. I loved life. I loved *my* life, and given the choice between life and death I'd choose life every time. Isn't that what Irvine Welsh – the greatest modern Scottish writer – wrote about in *Trainspotting*? And I would, Lucy Diamond, I would. I'd choose life. Every time.'

Trust a Scot to be loyally patriotic even in his darkest hour. Jonathan put his head in his hands, that universal symbol of despair, and Lucy instinctively reached out to comfort him. Her hand shot through the solid-looking shoulder into thin air.

Her action made Jonathan lurch as though punch-drunk and he became visibly paler and more nauseous-looking. He was fading in front of her, like a TV with the brightness turning up too high.

'Jonathan! What's happening? Oh, God – I'm sorry. Jonathan!'

Lucy was holding helplessly to the edge of the bath

as a chill cold breeze flicked around the room and Jonathan faded from view, looking as though he was fighting with every ounce of his energy to stay.

Suddenly, he was back. His image was grainy and untuned and his voice crackled like an old-school mobile phone connection.

'Lucy – will you help me? Will you speak to Laura? Let her know it was just a silly argument?'

'Just tell me how! Where?'

But he was gone, and, like her only meeting with Laura, Eleanor was left with the heart-dragging weight of his sorrow.

She would help him. She'd take a message to the beautiful girl in the yellow coat and ease her pain and then maybe Jonathan could cross over and find some peace too. It would be easy, and if The Dead were all as civil and wholesome and decent as Jonathan Rayburn, then this medium-thing wouldn't be too bad at all. The good thing was that Jonathan didn't look like a ghost. There was no head under the arm, pale cataract-eyes, pointy skeletal fingers or drifting shroud. He just looked like a sepia print of a Boden catalogue. He also had that lovely accent – there was no wailing or echoing portent of doom.

But The Dead aren't all nice and Lucy Diamond will find that out. Being a medium isn't all meeting new people (living or otherwise) and 'now head towards the light'. In fact, what people were in life they are in death and there're many, many folk on this side and the other that you wouldn't want to meet on a dark night – or in broad daylight, come to think of that.

Lucy Diamond isn't worried. She's feeling hopeful, optimistic. She has the typical Glass Half Full approach to life. She likes helping people and she's beginning to get quite fond of Jonathan Rayburn, in the way you might become fond of a cat or a needy pigeon that adopts you as its own. But right now, Lucy Diamond has a date to get ready for and she's way behind schedule. She has hair to dry and make-up to apply. All in half an hour before her date turns up? And she's not yet decided what to wear. It simply can't be done. Can it?

The evening was going well. Tony Russell had arrived on time bearing a non-garage-bought, tasteful bouquet of flowers. Not entirely self-selected – they were wrapped in chain-store cellophane – but it was a hopeful start.

Lucy had insisted that Tony come to the flat to escort her to the restaurant instead of her usual See You There approach. It was just as well. Jonathan's visit had ruined her schedule and there had been no time to put on primer before foundation or to experiment with eyeshadows.

She had to try hard to push Jonathan from her mind. Their meeting had left her feeling adrenalised, sick and faint, but the drilling buzz of the intercom that announced the arrival of her date helped to sharpen her focus. Unfortunately, the first words Tony uttered as he crossed the threshold were, 'Are you OK? You're very pale. You look as though you've seen a ghost.'

Lucy was pleased with herself for demanding old-fashioned courtesy and dating principles. It was the first time. Over a decade of bad dating had caused her to resort to her Nan Peters's advice. After all, it was no use using Jasmine's because that could well involve a pot of magic mushroom tea and a spot of naked moon-bathing.

She had tried Jojo's approach, which was to wow

them with a liberated woman's demand for sexual satisfaction. But that was Jojo's style, not hers. Let's face it, Jojo often dispensed with the date altogether, greeting them at the door naked with a rose between her teeth. Often, she didn't even bother learning their names. Jojo had an appetite for the carnal that was shocking. Not long after the school-underground award for most detentions she was winning her hall of residence award for most nocturnal visitors in one week. Maybe it was true what the legends said about Catholic girls' schools; maybe it was because Jojo had grown up with Madonna during her *Erotica* phase as the primary media female role model. Maybe it was just as Jojo said – she got itches that she just had to scratch. To which Nigel had quipped, 'If they itch that bad, honey, you better get to a GU clinic and fast.'

When it came to sex and dating, Nigel had always given advice. He'd recommended *Behind Every Great Woman is a Fabulous Gay Man: Dating Advice From a Guy Who Gives it to You Straight*. Anyone would think he had written it (secretly he wished he had written it) but it was easy for him to give out pearls of wisdom. His only trouble was *refusing* dates. Everywhere he went he was drooled over. Tables were moved in restaurants, spotty youths at cash registers dropped loose change with shaking hands. Once a bus had even mounted the pavement, causing pedestrians to leap for safety, just because he bent to tie a shoelace. When Lucy Diamond was out with Nigel it was as if the whole world had gone gay and the whole world loved Nigel.

So Jojo and Nigel were happy with sex the naughty-noughties way, but romantic, idealistic Lucy Diamond wasn't. She knew what it was to be stood up. She knew the disappointment of a date who drove you home in the rain on the back of a motorbike when you were wearing a miniskirt. She knew the prickle of fear that came when dinner conversation with a seemingly ordinary insurance broker turned to his love of Nazi memorabilia. She knew it was a jungle out there and that she kept dating the monkeys.

She wanted to get it right this time. Knowing that looks could be deceiving, she had sent urgent texts to the right people in the office and had gleaned some information about Tony Russell. There didn't seem to be any obvious glaring faults. Tony Russell was from Kent. He was thirty-one and he liked water sports.

Nigel had reddened, spluttered and sniggered away to himself when Lucy had told him this fact. Sometimes, his constant double-entendres wore a little thin. As usual, Jojo and Nigel had treated the potential date of Lucy Diamond as a huge joke. They couldn't wait to dissect the evening with her and hear the exaggerated retelling of things said and done. But this time Lucy had had enough of bad-dating for her friends' amusement. This time she wouldn't focus on the negative. This time she would get it right.

Starters had been eaten, the main course was on its way and the evening was going well. They had laughed at each other's jokes. They had talked childhood and education – she embellishing hers and employing a bit of careful editing. After all, a full explanation of Jasmine and early home-schooling would test the resolve of any man, but they found that they shared a single-sex senior education and northern grandmas, although his 'Nana' was rarely visited and had, for a long while, been packed off into a home.

Lucy tried not to focus on this, especially when he rolled his eyes and complained about his inheritance being wasted on her twenty-four-hour care. This jarred against Lucy's principles, but she told herself that he must have been joking. It was easier to focus on the Potentially Eligible facts that his father was a lawyer and that Tony already owned his own home. She also pretended not to notice when he checked his reflection in the dessert spoon.

It was warm in the restaurant and she had stripped off her little cardie to reveal her cleavage-enhancing top, but that was not where Tony's eyes were lingering. Either he was staring with a frown at Lucy's arms or his gaze was wandering all over a particularly pert and petite blonde waitress whenever she passed the table.

After the table next to them also began to stare (at Lucy's arms not the puke-makingly pretty waitress) Lucy followed their gaze. Her arms were covered from shoulder to wrist with what looked like the healed slashes of serious self-harm. Far from being mortified, the relaxing glass or two of wine meant that Lucy giggled. She had to say something. Tony was sure to see the funny side. He didn't.

'. . . so you see, it's that old exfoliating brush – it's a bit raggedy and I was a bit too enthusiastic—'

'Whatever.' Tony brusquely shoved her comment aside. 'Would you mind putting your cardigan back on? It's a bit off-putting for the other diners.'

Lucy slunk her cardigan around her shoulders, feeling humiliated. She had never been told that she was putting people off their meals before. However, it strengthened her resolve to challenge his wandering eyes. That assertiveness training course really was worth every penny of the company's money.

'Do you know her?' she asked innocently as Blondie Pretty Thing sashayed past the table with Tony's eyes following like a hungry dog.

'Erm – no. No, I don't,' and thereafter he studiously looked the other way or directly at Lucy whenever the blonde neared their table.

After that minor blip, the evening seemed to be running smoothly again. Sweets were ordered, although Lucy's waistband was feeling a little tight, but then so was she. They were nearing the end of the second bottle of house red. The wine that Lucy had knocked back nervously meant that she had to try really, really hard to concentrate on everything Tony was telling her – the list of his marvellous achievements, how wonderful he was at his job and how hilariously funny he and all his mates were. It was especially difficult since the script to the adverts advising women with tight waistbands to eat yogurt to stop them feeling like a football kept going round in her head.

Plus, she was feeling very, very warm wearing her cardigan in the steamy heat of the restaurant, and added to the warmth that comes with imbibing the grape – that sultry body-heat that begins in the chest and spreads to the groin – Lucy was feeling very relaxed indeed.

She was aware that she was flirting, and he with her. There had been casual 'accidental' touchings of each other: fingers resting too long on a hand here, a foot nudging another foot there. Lucy was twirling her hair round her index finger, her other hand resting at her throat, trying to imagine what he would look like old and making all those judgements that women are programmed to make when considering whether it's worth investing a few eggs in a man. Were they going to have children with wild hair like hers or one eye slightly bigger than the other like his?

Tony was in the middle of another of his 'hilariously funny' stories about yachting off the Greek coast, involving his sleeping best friend, a pair of baggy shorts and a cruelly placed sea urchin. Lucy was nodding and smiling along but secretly obsessed with the size of his eyes. Was one eye really bigger than the other? Was it because he was tired? Was it because he worked on computers all day? Was it the wine? Was it because *she* had drunk too much wine?

Her mind was free to leap from thought to thought because Tony hadn't asked her a single question since the starter and didn't look like he was going to draw breath.

'Boo!' Jonathan Rayburn's face appeared between her and Tony. Lucy gave a yell of surprise and the glass of red wine that she had been swirling slowly – she had hoped seductively – in her hand shot from her grasp into the lap of a shocked Tony Russell. The darkening stain not only had the look of a urinary accident but looked – on his dry-clean-only trousers – like it was going to be permanent. Jonathan had vanished.

'Oh my God! I'm so sorry. I'm so, *so* sorry.' Lucy was up and trying to dab at his lap with a white linen napkin, at the same time craning her head this way and that looking for that gate-crashing ghost of a Jonathan Rayburn.

'No – it's all right. Really, it's fine. It's just an accident. I can sort it.' Tony was being polite, but then with a trace of irritation he batted Lucy's hand away. 'It's nothing. Really.' He tried to cover his groin with another napkin.

'I know!' Lucy brightened with the arrival of a Great Idea. 'A glass of white wine will do the trick. One counteracts the other. Waiter! Waiter!'

It wasn't just the waiting staff's attention they had now. It was the whole restaurant. Lucy was oblivious, so focused was she on fixing the problem, but Tony was not comfortable at all with being in the spotlight.

'Lucy – leave it! It's fine. I don't want to go adding anything else to the fabric. They're Paul Smith—'

'Here's the wine.' Lucy took it from the tray of Blondie-waitress and rather too loudly advised, 'Now take it into the Gents and dab away until it all comes out.'

Tony was backing away with his arms raised in protestation, but as Lucy moved insistently to hand it over the wine glass was lifted out of her hand by some supernatural force and a second spillage was heaped directly on to Tony's crotch. A shocked gasp rippled around the watching diners.

'Jonathan! What the hell are you doing?' Lucy was looking from side to side up and down but there was not a trace of him anywhere.

'Tony – my name's Tony.' Tony had a rictus of a smile on his face and was trying very hard to maintain his manners.

'Oh, I'm not talking to you,' Lucy answered honestly, but did not get any further in her explanation as waiters vied to fuss over the slapstick pair and Tony was hurried along to the Gents.

Gradually, the other diners returned to their meals and Lucy slunk down into her seat, one shaking hand pouring another drink into the water glass, the other over her mouth suppressing either a scream or a sob, she couldn't decide which. She tried to make herself very, very small, winding one leg around the other and hunching herself together. She downed the drink in one.

She was angry (with Jonathan), embarrassed (for herself and Tony), humiliated (self again) and quite, quite certain that Tony Russell would not be asking her out on another date.

She willed Jonathan Rayburn to appear with every cell in her body. If Jonathan had known Lucy Diamond better, he would have kept a low profile at this point because inside Lucy there is a temper. It seldom appears – there has to be gross injustice or outright lying – and it is always over with very quickly. But right now, Lucy boiled with rage as she closed her eyes tight shut and juddered with determination to make Jonathan return.

Of course, this gave Lucy a slightly mad appearance and people on adjacent tables shifted uncomfortably in their seats. *He wants me to sort out his love life whilst he does his best to wreck mine!* Lucy was seething, muttering under her breath. It was not a good look.

'You!' She pointed accusingly. 'You've ruined my evening!' People were turning to the maître d' with begging looks that said Get the Mad Woman Out of Here. Jonathan was sitting in Tony's chair now with the surprised look of someone who has been dragged unexpectedly through a rift in the space/time continuum in a blue police box. *Everyone* has seen at least one episode of *Doctor Who* so you will know exactly how Jonathan looked. Jaw open, eyes boggling. He had not expected to arrive back in the restaurant by Lucy's will alone.

'The first glass was my doing.' Jonathan raised his hands surrender-style. He could tell she was angry and he didn't like it one bit. He tried the Coming Clean approach. 'And the second one – all right, I helped it along a little bit.'

Lucy snappily folded her arms and her nostrils flared in anger. Now Jonathan changed tack. Coming Clean wasn't working. He now tried Justification.

'But you know he deserved it.'

Lucy cut in. 'His Paul Smith trousers are ruined! And he will probably ask me to pay for them!' Suddenly, realising that she was still providing entertainment for the restaurant, she lowered her voice to a whisper and loosened her body language to a minimum. She was hissing between gritted teeth.

'You have made us look like fools! So it's all gone wrong for you, Jonathan, and I'm sorry for you, I really am!' Lucy laid her hand on her chest because angry though she was she still felt for Jonathan's predicament. 'You're dead and you don't want to be and you really, really hurt for and miss the woman of your dreams. I get it, I really do. And you're used to people jumping to your orders and life being how you want it, but for the rest of us *mortals*' – she emphasised the last word with more than a little spite; Lucy Diamond was a loyal friend but a bitter enemy – 'we still have lives to get on with. Still got soulmates to meet. And some of us have to search a little bit longer than people who have it all falling so perfectly into place with such perfect bloody timing.'

Jonathan hung his head and his hands fumbled in the pockets of his mac for want of something to do. He did look sorry, although he didn't say so. 'Well, I heard him say some very disrespectful things into his phone while you were in the Ladies. Words to the effect that he might be "on a promise" here – *and* he took a call off another woman.'

'It could have been his sister for all you know.' Lucy's anger with Jonathan was subsiding and she was always fair – she would always listen to another point of view.

'Has he mentioned a sister?' Jonathan asked more than a little sulkily. Both of them knew he hadn't. Lucy tried to ignore the possibility that Jonathan might have a point. She might be open to listening to another's point of view – didn't mean she had to accept it.

'That's not the point!' she exclaimed. 'Why are you here? You knew I was going on a date. You knew this was important to me and there's nothing I can do for you right now, is there?'

'But our last conversation ended a little abruptly, don't you think? And when you are all relaxed and dreamy – or should I say *drunk* – it's much easier to get through.'

Lucy stared at him like an angry wasp and Jonathan started some serious back-pedalling.

'But look how easy it was for you to get me when you were determined enough.' His tone was light and jolly, as if he was cajoling a child, and then it lowered. 'I just wanted to talk to you, that's all, Lucy. It's pretty bloody lonely where I am right now. I'm not on one side or the other. There are others, but they pass by me with dead eyes. We're like fish passing each other in a bowl, but that's not as bad as The Living – they literally pass right through me. I can be on either side or a place in between but I belong nowhere. Nowhere at all. I'm sorry if I ruined your evening, Lucy Diamond.'

Lucy felt her anger evaporating and she found herself agreeing to talk to him again as soon as they could on the proviso that Jonathan would pick his moments carefully – very carefully. That meant no bathroom visits and no interfering on 'date-time'. Even if he could get through he had to hang back if the moment wasn't right.

Then Tony's mobile started ringing with some naff R&B ringtone better suited to a fifteen year old and the name Chloe flashed on the screen.

'Answer it,' Jonathan teased. 'It could be his sister.'

The attention-seeking ringtone stopped as it went to answerphone and Jonathan added, 'And if you were my sister I'd say you could do a lot better than him. Have you got a brother?'

Jonathan started asking Lucy questions about her life. She had so easily seen into his own and now he wanted to know about her. Lucy noticed, but tried to push away the thought that they were questions Tony had not asked. As a dried Tony emerged from the Gents carrying his trousers in a paper doggy-bag and wearing a spare pair of the chef's checks his first view of Lucy Diamond was of her waving her hands around as she always did when deep in conversation. She didn't look up – she was too busy nodding and smiling to Tony's empty chair.

The maître d' appeared at Tony's elbow, having also taken in the spectacle, and made a swift response to Tony's expression.

'Allow me to get the bill, sir.'

7

No one was more surprised than Lucy Diamond when Tony Russell asked her out for a second date. After all, there had been more than a few negative aspects to their first evening and she was sure that she had heard the other diners cheer as they shut the restaurant door behind them.

Tony had approached her coyly whilst she was getting the latest gossip from the receptionist – the sort of girl you would tell 'in the strictest confidence' if you wanted everyone to know some nugget of information. Lucy had just assumed after Saturday evening that she wouldn't hear from him again, and by the time Wednesday rolled around and she'd not even seen him at the water-cooler she suspected that he was trying his best to avoid her altogether. So when he finally appeared lurking behind the fake dragon ferns in the reception area it seemed feasible that he didn't want to be seen. Lucy deliberately ignored him to make it easier for both of them.

Tony eventually stopped loitering behind the potted palms and interrupted Lucy's conversation with the receptionist, whose eyes immediately bulged on stalks. He said it had been a fun evening and would Lucy mind coming out again? Just like that! He even made a little joke about wearing wipe-clean trousers next time. So a weekend date was agreed, he promised to call nearer Saturday and Lucy knew that everyone, absolutely everyone, in the building would know about it within the hour.

Lucy walked away feeling lighter than air. He'd asked her out again! He'd seen the funny side of it after all and it was very funny when you thought about it. He must have liked her enough to get past having his best trousers ruined, and he probably only talked about himself so much out of nerves. Plus, he *was* nice looking, and what could be more ego-boosting and self-esteem-raising than being asked out by someone universally known as an office hottie, even if he wasn't exactly Prince Charming. And he'd asked her! Lucy Diamond! In front of reception! That was like shouting it out from a megaphone. She spent the rest of the day giving loose change to buskers and smiling at snot-faced babies. What wonders a date can do for the soul!

But what she didn't see was Tony high-fiving another member of the accounts department who had observed the entire exchange through the rippled glass of the double doors, a skinny brown-suited man known for humping and dumping any temp he could lay his slimy hands on who was unfortunately Tony's new best friend. Would Lucy Diamond have smilingly tipped the *Big Issue* seller at lunchtime if she'd seen the ten-pound note exchanged as part of a bet settled? How kindly disposed towards Tony and forgiving of his self-obsession would she feel if she knew his Boys' Club challenge was to sleep with her before the end of the month and finish with her before Christmas? What? You can't believe that anyone would be so callous, so disregarding of another person's feelings? Have you never dated a member of this species before? Never had a little bet of your own or seen what people put up on the Internet about each other?

Lucy wasn't to know that Tony was a wolf in designer clothing, but Jonathan Rayburn did. He was now in the habit of popping in to visit since the two of them had embarked on 'training'. This involved Lucy's testing out various positions (lying, sitting, lotus), places (bed, chair, floor), accessories (candles, whale music, Buddhist prayer bells) and times for communing with not so much The Dead as A Dead because, after all, so far it had been only Jonathan who had materialised. Unfortunately, despite Lucy's protests, it seemed that a bath containing a drop or two of Liz Earle's Bliss bath oil produced the best results, for no sooner was her bum in the water than Jonathan was winkled out from the other side. He swore he had no control over the matter and did cover his eyes with polite apologies. Lucy, always believing the best of people, believed him.

Today it wasn't only Tony who had been lingering around the fake office plants and Jonathan had seen everything. He tried telling Lucy at lunchtime, but she wouldn't listen. He tried telling her on the journey home and she told him very patiently that a date with Tony would not be a threat to their working relationship and that he should 'butt out'. Those were her exact words. And once again, having spoken aloud to what appeared to be thin air, Lucy suffered the indignity of being the tube carriage's Honorary Crazy Person for the ride home.

Jonathan was determined to find a way to make her

see sense. He liked her. She was a good person. That was startlingly evident, as though she wore her goodness like a lapel pin. She was too good to waste her time on a man with a Vegas cabaret singer's name. He would help her. Protect her. After all, she didn't have a big brother who could do it. He was going to look out for Lucy Diamond.

Lucy was quite enjoying being under the spotlight. Not only was she basking in the attention of Tony Russell but she was 'largin'' it as a medium too. It made a change from being in Nigel's shadow or being the straight man in her and Jojo's double-act. As a bonus, it all seemed to distract Nigel from his Oh Crap! My Twenties Are Over and I Still Don't Feel Like a Grown-Up blues. Lucy had even been able to exploit a recent visitation from Jonathan by getting Nigel – yes, *Nigel*! – to bring her a coffee as she lay 'exhausted' on the sofa. It was odd having a feeling of power over Nigel. He was usually so superior, so sure of being right about everything, that to see him defer to her, to actually ask her opinion, to actually say, 'What do you want on your pizza?' instead of making assumptions – 'I've ordered you the large vegetarian, OK?' (a comment that was always followed by 'So your mother will be here any minute') – well, it was all a bit unsettling.

The intercom buzzed and Nigel came up the stairs, the lights flickering on and off all the way.

'Ha-ha. Very funny, Jonathan.' Nigel spoke sarcastically. 'I swear he's torturing me on purpose. Honestly, my nerves are shot to bits. How can I give up smoking under these circumstances?'

'I didn't know you were.' Lucy was staggered. How

much weirder was life going to get? Nigel saying bye-bye to B&H? 'Since when?'

'Since I decided. I'm going to look after myself more. Healthly living and all that. You could join me or you could wait until the cellulite reaches your knees before acting. I'm doing vitamins too!'

'Nigel, you don't *do* vitamins – you take them.'

'Whatever. I'm doing it.' There was more to it than this. Lucy didn't need to be a psychic when it came to reading someone she loved so much and knew so well. For a start, he had averted his gaze, looking down instead of over her head as usual. Add that to the cutting back on social engagements, the non-existent sex-life and his sudden meek and mild What Can I Do for You? manner . . . and now he was in the kitchen pouring a glass of . . . water!

'Are you thinking of joining a monastery?'

He stuck two fingers up at her, perched on her bar stool and carried on reading the free paper as Lucy started cooking dinner around him. Nigel was always scouring the small ads. Secretly he was searching for eighties He-man toys to add to his collection. The irony of the gayest boy at school being the biggest fan of He-man wasn't lost on Nigel, although for a long time he had thought She-ra (Princess of Power) shared the same surname as Alan Shearer, ex-footballer turned TV sports pundit. He was forever asking 'But what's her first name?' and when no one could answer he decided that it was Tina.

'I'd like to know the story behind this ad.' Nigel read aloud, ' "Wedding dress – never worn." It's so tragic. A tale of heartbreak would unfold from that one.' Then, after a pause: 'Do you still want the whole trad white wedding thing?' He took another slug of water.

'Sometimes.' Lucy went a bit dreamy at the thought.

'But you'd wear Vera Wang and not a meringue – right?' Nigel did a quick style check.

'Definitely – and no sugared almonds in the netting either. Nan Peters's teeth couldn't cope with that.' Lucy leaned on her elbows on the kitchen counter. 'I don't see the day itself as the pinnacle of my achievement. Not like all the fairy stories and old-style Mills & Boon. It's not the end of the story, is it? I think it would just be the beginning, you know? But I want kids and I would like it in that set-up. A proper family. Mum *and* Dad.'

'Only cos you've never had it. Trust me – it's over-rated.'

'Don't! You had a lovely childhood. You sound like Jasmine. She's always banging on about alternative ways of raising children and kicking off the patriarchal traces of the enslavement of marriage, but I would like someone – a life partner, a friend. Someone to go through it all with. Someone who's batting on my side. What about you?'

'I'm batting for the other team, I'm afraid.' But despite his attempt at a joke, a look flickered over his face that Lucy couldn't quite place. 'But if Daniel Craig has a free afternoon – who knows? How's whatsisface?'

Nigel turned his attention back to the newspaper, feigning disinterest, yet using a tone that managed to convey a low opinion of Tony Russell (whom he'd never met), a slight disgust at the thought of their heterosexual coupling and a sort of jealous hurt, all at the same time. He was like a Jewish and a Catholic mother rolled into one.

'I've got a second date!' There. She'd said it. Clearly, Nigel had not expected to hear that, not after hearing the blow-by-blow – or spill-by-spill – account of the first evening. He looked up in astonishment, his mouth forming a surprised perfect O.

'He's a glutton for punishment then, isn't he?' That tone again.

Every time Lucy Diamond had a boyfriend there were these mixed messages that made her feel he didn't want her to have another man in her life, and yet it wasn't as if he would ever be capable of having the relationship with her that she had once so wanted. Lucy wanted to shake him and scream in his face, *What do you want from me? What do you waaaaant?* But instead she said nothing and Nigel turned his attention to the What's On section of the paper. Obviously, discussion of her forthcoming date was considered o.v.e.r.

'There's line-dancing at the day centre on Saturday morning.'

'I think I'm busy,' Lucy lied.

'Don't knock it till you try it.' In more youthful, social times, Nigel was always dragging them off to new 'entertainment experiences'. Jojo had won a tin of fruit salad at lunchtime bingo at the local Gala, and at a Knitting Night in Shoreditch Nigel had proved a natural at pearl stitch and made a good start on a woollen mohican wig.

'We've . . . *you've* got to go to this!' Nigel was suddenly more enthusiastic than Lucy had seen him in weeks.

She groaned. 'What is it now?'

'A Psychic Fair – well, actually they spell it f.a.y.r.e. to add to its spooky otherworldliness. Is that a word –

otherworldliness? Anyway, it's on Saturday, twelve till four at the Unity Hall. You've gotta go! There will be tarot reading, crystal healing, aura analysis and who knows? There might be someone there just like you . . . one of your own people,' he added in a dramatic Brian Blessed Does Shakespeare voice. 'Well, what are you waiting for? Call Jojo and tell her to drop whatever . . . *who*ever she's doing on Saturday, polish her crystal ball and get herself over here for midday. I'll get here a bit earlier, say ten thirty, and we can do brunch. That's all right with you, isn't it? I mean, you were joking when you said you were busy?'

Lucy didn't know what to say. She just nodded dumbly. It was good to see Nigel taking an interest in something outside himself *and* he'd asked her if it was okay instead of railroading her along.

Suddenly, the metal utensils on the wall rack started rattling and a tea canister next to the kettle slowly rose about six inches off the work surface. Jonathan was honing his supernatural skills again. He had started playing little jokes like this. First it was moving pens and hiding the toothpaste. Yesterday, he had managed to conceal a sizzling pan of stir fry.

'Tell him to stop, Lucy, or I'm going to find out all about exorcism at that fuckin' fayre and there'll be holy water and priests all over this flat faster than you can say "deceased". I mean it!'

The canister dropped abruptly and there was no other sign that Jonathan was there. Nigel was back to poring over the free adverts again.

'My God! They're selling body parts in the small ads now! Listen! "Kidney . . ." Oh! False alarm. "Kidney-shaped dressing table."'

They both laughed. The pasta was boiling and the bottled sauce was simmering nicely. Lucy reached for her cigarettes and lit up. Nigel immediately began flapping his arms around and coughing. Then Lucy pulled a bottle of wine from the rack, but Nigel shook his head and produced a packet of herbal tea from his mansatchel.

By the time dinner was over and the plates stacked for Nigel to do the washing up that he never would, they were both sitting nursing a glass of red and were nearly through Lucy's 'social-smoking' pack of twenty.

'I did go all day without a fag, you know!' Nigel was defensive about his weak resolve. 'There's no point trying to do it all at once. I'll start the healthy thing tomorrow. Cheers.' They chinked glasses and Nigel downed his in one.

'Don't you have clocks over there?' Lucy had just woken up with that nagging feeling you get when you think you are being watched. And she was, by Jonathan Rayburn. 'I thought we had an agreement about appropriate times?'

'We do, but this was an emergency.' He reeled back in mock horror as Lucy sat up and snapped on the bedside light. 'Geez! You look like the love child of Brian May and Anita Dobson!'

Lucy had made the mistake of going to bed with her hair damp from the shower. It was the sort of comment she had come to expect from Nigel but from polite, well-mannered Jonathan Rayburn delivered at three in the morning when your defences about such things are not fully in place – well, it was more than a little unnerving.

'And I suppose the love of your life wakes at this hour

with the breath of angels and a blow-dried 'do, does she?' Her retort was as chilly as the room and Lucy pulled the duvet around herself.

'Now listen, Lucy. Be serious for a moment here. Things are not as simple as we thought. You can't just go calling me up and me popping over every time we feel like it. Apparently, there are rules. Regulations. Risks.'

Lucy started to protest that it was he who had started it all in the first place, but Jonathan talked over her.

'There's someone I want you to meet. It was just a chance meeting and he had to come now because it was the only time he was free. He's an expert on this Crossing Over business. Lucy, may I introduce Keith Richards?'

It was the early hours of the morning and Lucy was being formally introduced to someone who was yet to materialise in her bedroom. As she struggled to comprehend what was going on, she braced herself for a Rolling Stone to appear. Maybe it wasn't only the Beatles who had special gifts (according to Jasmine) but when did he die? Granted, he had always looked close to death's door, but how did she miss that one? Weren't they touring again soon anyway?

'Keith Richards isn't dead,' she exclaimed, just as she realised that Jonathan clearly hadn't meant *that* Keith Richards judging by the balding, pot-bellied man in a Fair Isle V-neck who was waving cheerily in greeting.

Jonathan and Keith looked pretty pleased with themselves, as if they had rambled an ancient footpath and raised money for Cancer Research at the same time. They shook hands and Keith beamed like a head teacher on Prize Day.

'Well done, you two! Well done! I didn't know whether the Channel would open enough for me to slip through with Jonathan this time but we thought we'd give it a go. I must say you two have been working hard, though it's obvious you're naturals. Naturals! Now are you clairvoyant, clairaudient or clairsentient?'

'I'm not called Claire – my name's Lucy Diamond.'

Keith Richards chuckled. He had a slight Brummie twang and a National Trust volunteer name-tag. He wore the sort of trousers that have earned the name *slacks* in that nondescript beige favoured by men of a certain vintage.

'No, no, no! Do you mostly see, hear or sense spirits?'

'Well, all three really, but I only ever see – I've only ever seen Jonathan.'

'Are you sure about that? Not even as a child?' He had an owl-like wisdom about him and Lucy found herself telling this chubby Brummie all about her imaginary friends and her ability to pick up over-powering smells of cigars or perfume that no one else could detect and her strong, instinctive fears or liking of houses, rooms or streets. Clearly, Keith found this all very exciting and kept blurting, 'Natural! A natural!' He clasped and unclasped his hands as he talked and looked totally absorbed and fascinated by the whole subject. 'I just wish there were more like you and then there'd be fewer lost.' Suddenly, he looked very serious.

'Lost?'

'Yes, lost, Lucy.' Keith did not elaborate. 'Now, I need to talk to you kids about protection.' He clasped his hands together over his little protruding tummy and looked, for all the world, as if he was about to deliver a lecture on using condoms. 'You and Jonathan have a special bond but the work you're doing should not be taken lightly. This isn't satellite channel entertainment, you know. This work is valuable and it can be very, very dangerous indeed.'

He was walking up and down now, hands clutched in front, looking up to the ceiling. He was in his element. He was in the 'Zone'.

'It may reassure you to know that I've passed my Level 5 certificate in Orientation to the Light and have been granted unrestricted access to Limbow – Life In the Middle of and Between Other Worlds, which is its correct title. You may know of it with no W and the meaning of the acronym forgotten. Sorry for getting bogged down in the technicalities. Anyway, all this and I've only been dead three years.'

Keith stood still and his chest puffed out a little. Lucy felt congratulations were in order although she had absolutely no idea what he was talking about.

'Erm . . . well done,' she offered.

'There's not many rise through the ranks as I have, but I love study and new challenges. Eternity is a very long time, Lucy. You've got to find things to fill it. But, rest assured, you're in safe hands, Lucy Diamond. Very safe hands,' and he waggled them at her to illustrate his point.

For the next hour and a half, Keith Richards talked Jonathan and Lucy through some of the mechanics of mediumship. He told them how to have a formal 'opening' and 'closing down' and told them a string of nonsensical words which he declared 'classified, ancient and more powerful than a ten-ton truck' that should accompany the start and finish of every session as a safeguard against unwanted spirit contact. Not that Lucy could remember any of them.

'You will have to guard yourselves and Jonathan's lady friend when the time comes to make the connection, and remember, it's always better in a group of like-minded individuals than alone. The more the merrier, as it were. And never' – Keith lowered his voice and spoke so seriously that it caused the hairs to rise on Lucy's arms – 'never, ever do it when you feel negative, ill or tired. There must be not a trace of negativity. That's like an invitation to the wraiths. They can smell it, they can. Like sharks can smell blood, and they'll channel themselves through and attach themselves to any weak or willing soul. Living or dead.'

'Wraiths?' Lucy pulled her knees up and clasped them protectively. She didn't like the sound of it one bit. This medium thing didn't seem like a laugh any more.

'Horrid things they are. Lost souls. Sticky, foul-smelling things. Always moaning. You should hear 'em. Moan, moan, moan. Oh, it's terrible.' Keith wrinkled up his face in disgust. 'Took a wrong turn from the light, they did, and they can't get in. But they can get back here all right and in the meantime they wander Limbow looking for lost souls that they can claim as their own. Vampires to the energy they are. Vampires.'

'But how will I know if I've let one in? How do I know that I haven't let one in already?' Lucy was looking fearfully around the room, and judging by Jonathan's face he wasn't feeling too confident about the whole thing either.

'Oh, you'd know all right. You'd know.' Keith chuckled to himself in the vein of One Who Knows. 'And up to now you've been very lucky. Very lucky indeed, but it's not you who's my main worry at the moment. It's this fella here,' and he gestured towards Jonathan. 'He keeps passing from this side to the other and each time he's got to cross Limbow. Well, that's fine if you know how to keep your strength up and you don't lose your way. That's fine if you know how to cross over and close the rift so those wraith-buggers don't get in. But I can't teach him all I know in five minutes. I mean, it's not as if he's got much time, is it?'

'Isn't it?' Lucy and Jonathan chorused together.

'Oh, no! He can't keep wandering between worlds indefinitely. There're regulations about that sort of thing and the Powers That Be don't like unauthorised souls going back and forth willy-nilly as they please. Causes all sorts of problems it does.'

'When does his time run out?' Lucy was horrified. It was like a death sentence hanging over Jonathan all over again, and Jonathan certainly looked like the time limit was news to him.

'It's not earth time, Lucy. It's Life Time, and every time Jonathan crosses over unnecessarily he'll use a little bit more of it up. You can't time it in minutes or seconds – it's down to energy. The last little bits of life force that're in him. And to tell you all that – well, that's a whole Level 5 certificate in itself.'

Jonathan was pacing up and down now doing his familiar stress response of running his hands through his hair.

'So, all these jokes I've been playing, all the practising of coming here pinching Lucy's cutlery and messing with the electrics, I've actually been wasting Life Time?'

'I'm afraid so, Jonathan. Haven't you noticed that

you've become less and less – how can I put it? Substantial?'

Jonathan looked down at himself, turning his hands this way and that and holding them up to the bedroom light.

'You do look a bit paler,' Lucy agreed with a pained look on her face.

'That's not very comforting, Lucy,' Jonathan complained, still checking himself all over. She murmured her apologies and Keith continued.

'The thing is – you made the choice to turn from the light for a reason. If you don't deal with that before the time runs out you can't cross over – the light won't come again. But if you spend too much Life Time trying to solve your problem you'll become weak. Vulnerable. And there's every chance a wraith will get to you before the light does. Then you'll be one of them. A ghost stuck in Limbow. For good.'

They all fell silent and Keith let the enormity of it all sink in before clapping his hands together and clasping them (again) in his head-teacher-about-to-start-assembly mode.

'No one said it was going to be easy. It's a lot of responsibility for you, young woman, to assist Jonathan in his hour of need, but everything about you tells me you're up to the job. Now I'm a bit tied up at the moment finishing my Advanced Psychic Energy Creation, but I wonder – would you mind teaming up with me, Lucy, when I do my Connecting With the Earthly Plain, Spirit Guide certificate? It would be an honour!'

Lucy, always trying to please, found herself agreeing and Keith's cheery last words before he faded from view were, 'Just follow my advice and everything'll be hunky-dory.'

Jonathan and Lucy were no longer so sure. He made a hasty retreat, not wishing to waste more Life Time, and Lucy fell into a fitful, exhausted sleep full of troubled dreams about wraiths trying to eat her whole. But before she entirely succumbed to unconsciousness, she marvelled at how typical it was that mediums you heard about in books or on TV get glamorous Native American shamans or Mesopotamian priests as their spirit guides while she, Lucy Diamond, got an ex-National Trust volunteer from Birmingham wearing a pullover of dubious acrylic mix.

'Well, there's not much point you going at all, is there?' Nigel had the hump. He was not pleased to hear about the enlightening visit from Keith Richards the night before. He wanted Lucy to learn all about her craft from the Psychic Fayre that *he* had read about. In short, *he* wanted the glory, the gratitude, the story to tell beginning with '. . . and I found the advert for the fair in the free paper and said, "Why don't we go?" . . .'

Lucy was busy placating Nigel with warm chocolate croissants when a text arrived. As her face fell, he grabbed the phone off her.

Can we rearrange to Sun night? Don't feel too well xx

Between the lines the message was loud and clear. Tony Russell had a better offer for Saturday night. In a rare moment of tact and sensitivity, Nigel said nothing, and the arrival of Jojo still in the clothes that she had gone out in the night before was a welcome distraction.

'Who was it this time?' Nigel asked in a wearied voice.

'Someone in publishing – no one special.' Jojo was vague about the personal particulars but precise in the physical details to the point where Nigel eventually put his fingers in his ears and sang 'La-la-la – I can't hear you!' until she stopped.

Jojo always batted away questions directly related to her job. She did 'something' in publishing, went to functions with 'people' from publishing and sometimes ran into famous authors. Nigel said – a little unkindly but with more than an element of truth – that it was a job Daddy had arranged through friends and that Jojo was killing time until she could marry someone in her father's income bracket. Either way, Jojo had a more exciting job than Nigel or Lucy and an enviable debt-free lifestyle. Not that she crowed about it – she didn't – but the needy (Nigel and Lucy) couldn't help but notice the It Bag dropped to the floor, the casual way she could pick up the tab for all of them more than once in a while, and the clothes that came from the sort of shop that stocked only half a dozen items at a time in sparse 'industrial' units.

Now they would be setting off much later than they had planned because Jojo was struggling to find something of Lucy's to borrow – size was not the issue but 'statement' was. Thank God she had her Dior aviator shades in her handbag and that there were a couple of her cast-offs in the back of Lucy's wardrobe. After all, you never knew who you might run into. Jojo could never admit to her best friend her real thoughts about Lucy's sale-rail wardrobe collection so dressed up her fears as a veto on wearing anything that might have been produced by child labour. Nigel and Lucy tried to act suitably impressed by this new and entirely unbeliev-able sentiment. It was past one o'clock by the time they set off.

*

There was a lot of ethnic print and sandals in the queue at the entrance of the Unity Hall. Nigel nudged Lucy and smirked.

'Home from home for you, isn't it?'

They paid their entrance fees, but when it came to Nigel's turn the man said, 'Student?'

Nigel answered 'Yes' like a breathy Marilyn Monroe. The girls said nothing until they were in the hall.

'He didn't think you were a student because you look young but because you look scruffy. You know – unemployed.' Jojo knew how to needle, and couldn't ignore the fact that she was more often addressed as Madame than Mademoiselle in French restaurants these days. Funny how you make the assumption that you will always be young.

'Just remember, Nigel, they're all psychics here. They'll know that you've been lying.' Even Lucy enjoyed watching the paranoia creeping over him.

Rows of stalls were set up in the hall and the room buzzed with chatter and pan pipes as ancient speakers played the sort of ambient music that ought to calm you down but actually raises the blood pressure to levels requiring beta-blockers.

Scattered amongst the Jasmine generation were young dreadlocked teenagers and the occasional pensioner seeking herbal remedies for arthritis. Jojo – in her opinion – was the most stylish person there. Lucy was skimming all the stalls but could see nothing that directly related to her and Nigel had his eye on a free Indian massage but only because he was quite attracted to the stallholder – a tattooed, shaven-headed, pierced New-Ager in a wife-beater vest and leather trousers.

There were stalls offering Hopi ear candle

treatments, cupping (which made Nigel snigger) and iridology. There were palm readers, tarot cards and ball-gazing. Nigel actually didn't comment on this. There was no lewd joke, no play on words, not even 'They're welcome to look at mine if they want.'

Nothing.

Lucy and Jojo both looked at him expectantly, waiting for the risqué remark, and he walked by without comment.

As is the case when you attend an event – any event, be it a Scouts' Bring and Buy, for example, or a French Farmers' Market – where things are sold, there is a need to buy something. Anything. However unlikely it is that you will wear the silver and turquoise copies of Native American jewellery (Jojo) or drink the obnoxious-smelling concoction of detoxifying herbs (Nigel) or need a crystal angel-shaped talisman to hang from a window (Lucy). These things will be purchased. In this way, the three of them whiled away a couple of hours going from stall to stall and between them frittered away well over fifty pounds.

They were invited to attend a workshop in automatic writing in a side room off the hall. Lucy practically skipped into the room she was so excited. She even introduced herself as a 'budding medium' in the warm-up task. Nigel kicked her under the chair for 'being an arse' as he later put it. Jojo raised an eyebrow but nobody else batted an eye. After all there was a woman there who spoke with confidence about her life on another planet, so who could compete with that?

A little wizened man with a ponytail, long past the age when it was respectable to have one, talked the group through a meditation with shoes and lights off.

The smell of feet was more than a little off-putting. Even the essential oils in the burner couldn't mask the odour. Someone had serious sole-sweat-gland issues. Then they began.

Nigel doodled cruel caricatures of everyone in the room and tried to pass it off as the work of some malevolent spirit. Jojo had her eyes shut and was biting her lip in concentration but was rewarded by only random squiggles. Lady from Another Planet claimed her sheet filled with runic script was her home planet trying to connect with her and Lucy's sheet had 'Lucy Diamond is a Poo Face' written in big letters.

'That's not my writing,' she tried to explain to Ponytail Man who made some snide comment about people who don't take connecting with the other side seriously and ruin it for others. She tried again and in a neat cursive script the words 'Lucy is a fatty bum-bum' appeared.

'This really is not my writing!' Lucy protested and screwed up the paper in frustration when the words 'Lucy loves Nigel' appeared in a heart crossed with an arrow. 'You're wasting your Life Time, Jonathan,' she snapped, then: 'Did I say that aloud?'

She was asked to leave the workshop.

Jojo 'modelled' in a photograph for the local paper as a volunteer for the reflexology demonstration. Her pretty pedicured feet looked perfect in the picture published the following week though she was livid that her face was not included. She had enjoyed the crowd gathering round to watch until Nigel had called out in a voice ladelled with innuendo, 'Not the sort of modelling you're used to, is it?'

Nigel had also been the centre of attention and

unusually was most uncomfortable with it. They had been hanging around the stall devoted to angels – Lucy was taking a long time to choose which lucky crystal charm would go best in her sitting room. Angels seemed to be a popular theme throughout the fayre – there were tapes, prayers, poems, CDs. There were books with advice on *Finding the Angel Within*, *Listening to the Angel on Your Shoulder* and *Connecting with Your Angel Above*. So far all this was the closest thing Lucy could find to mediumship but it just wasn't her. Having taken up so much of the stallholder's time with questions, she felt duty bound to buy something.

The stall was adjacent to a three-sided display board covered in coloured posters explaining auras. There was an invitation to have your own aura photographed for a small fee and though a number of people were taking an interest, the mumsy-looking middle-aged woman running the stall kept looking across at Nigel. He and the girls wrote it off as further evidence of his Incredible Powers of Attraction but as they moved away towards another stall the woman caught Nigel by the sleeve.

'I'm sorry, but I've got to speak to you,' she began. This sort of thing had happened so often that Nigel and Lucy had developed a routine for such times. Immediately, Lucy linked arms with him and he leaned in to her as though they were an item. Nigel adopted a pitying look that was meant to say 'I'm so sorry about my Incredible Powers of Attraction but I'm already attached.'

'You need to see a doctor.' The mumsy woman stood there wringing her hands and looking anxious. As a chat-up line it was somewhat lacking.

'I beg your pardon?' Nigel – like Lucy – was a great

believer in manners, especially when all around people were shocked into stunned, traffic accident-type voyeurism. It's always best to be seen as well mannered when there is a witnesses. Silence reigned except for the deep tones of the didgeridoo which had replaced the pan pipes.

'I don't normally do this but your aura is so strong, the message is so clear, I feel it's my duty – in fact, it *is* my duty . . .' The woman kept rubbing and squeezing her hands together. More fayre-goers gathered to hear the worst. 'I signed an oath with the International Federation of Divination Masters and Healers. I *have* to tell you. I'm no doctor but I do have a diploma from the IFDMH and your colours are so . . . so muddy. It's your health, you see, it's not as it should be and it's obviously something that's on your mind because your aura's got Worry stamped all over it.'

'I think you must be mistaken.' Nigel tried in vain to move off but the woman caught him by the sleeve again.

'Whatever the problem is it won't go away. I could say more about it but you may not want me to because of the region we're talking about . . .'

'I think everyone can hazard a guess, with the clues you've just given them. Now if you don't mind . . .' Nigel had reddened at first but now the colour had drained from his face and he was pale and thin-lipped. He was desperately trying to get away, dragging Lucy with him. The crowd that had gathered seemed to close ranks around him. Usually Nigel would have verbally torn the woman to shreds, but this time he was visibly embarrassed and, cornered, he started to push roughly past people. Someone shouted, 'See a doctor, man,' and another voice added, 'Let the lady speak.'

Someone shoved a glossy flyer into Lucy's hand as they made off towards the exit and the last thing they saw was an orderly queue forming for aura photography.

'Of all the nerve!' Nigel's chest was heaving with the speed of their getaway as they stood on the pavement outside Unity Hall. 'Talk about drumming up business! I ought to charge her for using me as her unpaid assistant like that! The bloody cheek of it! And what a bunch of mugs for believing all that rubbish. I'm glad you don't have to use such ridiculous Barnum statements to get our attention. What a cheap bloody trick!'

'What do you mean "Barnum statements"?'

'Leading questions, open statements. The sort of thing that could apply to most of the population. That's how a lot of these people operate. It comes from P. T. Barnum, the circus fella from the States. Oh, come on, Lucy! For fuck's sake! We saw the bloody musical together!' Nigel got very irritated in response to Lucy's blank face. 'He demonstrated how general statements can sound personal. It's all part of the trickery.' Nigel put on a wheedling voice. ' "You're inwardly very shy except around people you love." "You need to see a doctor about something you're worried about." For God's sake, pick anyone over thirty and we've all got something that doesn't work like it used to, right? What's this?'

He took the flyer from Lucy's hands in an act that the girls did not realise was designed to deflect attention away from himself. Under the scroll lettering declaring 'Valerie Andreas – Psychic to the Celebs' was a photograph inspired by Lady Singers of Country 1984. A bleached blonde and bouffanted woman posed in a vivid cobalt-blue tasselled jacket with shoulder pads that could easily take out the eye of a passer-by. The blurb stated that as part of the Walthamstow Psychic Festival, Valerie Andreas would be appearing 'by special invitation' and 'for one night only'. A list of her credentials stated that she had 'done readings' for Jeremy Beadle and Les Dennis and the flyer invited you to 'Take a Walk with Valerie to the Other Side'.

'Oh, we are going!' asserted Nigel, back to his usual form, without consulting either Lucy or Jojo. 'Never mind broken dates, Lucy Diamond!' Jojo looked at Lucy, who ignored her on purpose. 'It's Saturday night and you *shall* go to the ball! And better than that it's only ten pounds a ticket. Somebody give me a phone – I've run out of talk time – and I'll book the tickets now.'

Whilst Jojo handed over her phone, complaining that he was always running out of talk time and saying that no she didn't have anything planned for tonight but he could have asked, Lucy, unnoticed because she wanted to be, since the others would only tell her she was being a mug, sent a text. It was good to hear Nigel back to his bossy self. She hoped it would last. She searched her phone book for Tony R and pressed send.

Yes – Sun will be fine, hope u feel ok soon.

It is always better to think the best of people. Give the benefit of the doubt. Trust. It's just a shame that not everyone deserves it, Lucy Diamond. Haven't you learned that by now?

The crowd at the theatre was mostly post-menopausal ladies and people of a certain social standing.

'Now, I'm not a snob . . .' began Nigel.

'Yes you are!' chorused Lucy and Jojo together before he could add anything further. Both could think of clear examples of Nigel's snobbery. Evidence that in a trial of snobbery would have him convicted. For life. Jojo was thinking of her old car, an almost-chic retro Ford Escort painted a semi-luminous orange. Nigel had declared it a Car of the Masses and would only sit in it if he could hold the *Guardian* aloft as if to prove his status as a sun-dried-tomato-eating holiday-in-Tuscany member of the middle classes. Lucy was mentally listing his dislike of winners of TV talent competitions and people who say 'parnd' instead of 'pounds'.

Nigel shuddered as some ladies in pastel jumpers sauntered by clutching their rum and Cokes.

'Someone should tell them that they are at risk of yeast infections if they spend much longer in those all-polyester trousers.'

'Oh, just stop it, Nigel!' Jojo flashed.

'I was only joking!'

The trouble was it was very difficult to tell when he

was. Lucy knew that even if they were at an opera in Covent Garden, he'd find some way to sneer at the crowd. It was his policy to criticise everything and everyone. It was part of his defence about where he came from, where he felt he ought to be and where he felt he didn't belong. Not everyone understood that about him. Lucy did. She had supported him through his turbulent 'coming out' phase, despite the hurt it caused her and her aching love for him. She had seen what it was to be the boy from Coventry at a university where nobody had a regional accent. She knew what he'd gone through as a gay teenager on an estate where Page 3 and football players are cultural icons. Still, it could be very tiring at times.

Jojo was reading aloud from the programme.

' "You will have seen Valerie Andreas in *Have a Chat!* and *Perk Up* magazines." '

'Top end of the market then,' snorted Nigel derisively, but before Jojo and Lucy could remind him that it was *he* who had booked the tickets an announcement was made that people should take their seats. They moved with the shuffling crowd through the fire doors and into the auditorium, where they pushed past the knees of old ladies nursing bags of Werther's Originals and took their places in the Grand Circle.

'Oh, God, why did we come?' Nigel rolled his eyes about some overweight women who were squeezing along the row and cackling with raucous laughter. His endless snide remarks were beginning to irritate Lucy. She was already adrenalised by hopes of seeing a professional in action and Nigel's moaning was jangling her nerves. She'd been disappointed at the Psychic Fair and now she was looking forward to meeting people like herself who could share advice and tips. People who would make her feel less crazy and less alone. Less freakish. Less like the only person on the planet who could contact the spirit world. Less . . . well, you get the picture. But here was Nigel's negative side creeping back like the acrid smoke of a snuffed candle and throwing a big wet blanket over what might just turn out to be an illuminating and enjoyable evening.

Jojo instinctively stepped in with the tone of a brisk matron dealing with a difficult OAP. 'We are here, Nigel, because you read the flyer and booked the tickets. Lucy wants to be here and we are here to support her and none of us had anywhere else to go anyway. So stop complaining.' And she shoved a packet of Toffee Poppets at him so that at least his mouth would be stuck shut by chewing on them for a while, even if he ran a serious risk of losing a filling.

The lights dimmed and the chattering of the crowd sank to a murmur. Slowly the fire screen rose and then the red velvet curtains opened. A hush fell over the theatre and the hairs on Lucy's arms prickled. Jojo reached over Nigel – who was as ever at the centre of things – and patted Lucy's hand in a show of solidarity and excitement. None of the three of them knew what to expect beyond the acts seen on television where clever editing can make anything credible. All of them wanted to believe.

Stage lights were swirling; there was a drum roll from somewhere though the tiny orchestra pit was empty. A spotlight searched stage left, then stage right, and a disembodied voice boomed out from the speakers. The voice was as slick as any advert for a half-price spring sale on sofas where Everything Must Go. It spoke with precise pronunciation. Every word had gravitas, giving the message that 'what I am saying is very, very important.'

'With extraordinary powers passed on from her Romany Gypsy heritage, discovered in a funeral parlour in the back streets of Rochdale and now a regular in the front parlours of the rich and famous – signed copies of her life story can be purchased for the special price of five ninety-nine in the foyer during the interval – Walthamstow Psychic Festival is proud to present' – there was another drum roll – 'Val-aaa-reeeee Aaaannnndrrrreas!'

The crowd went wild and were on their feet, stamping, cheering and whistling, and Jojo, Nigel and Eleanor stood and clapped along with the rest. With the sort of build-up reserved for American wrestlers, clearly this woman must have something special about her.

Suddenly, there was a theatrical flash and a previously empty stool standing centre stage with only a small bar table to accompany it was filled. The audience gasped a little and fell silent. Lucy's expectations were raised, but once the smoke had cleared there was a swift anticlimax as she took in the round-shouldered pensioner, two stone heavier than her flyer picture, whose perch on top of the bar stool looked far more stable than that of the incongruous Dolly Parton blond wig balancing precariously on her head.

Lucy pushed away the desire to snigger and even without looking she could picture Nigel's scornful face. She braced herself for his next comment, but then she caught her breath.

Figures were emerging from the shadows as if they had been part of the backdrop and beginning to walk towards the seated woman in her loud floral dress and odd wig. There were old men leaning on sticks, a young man in a motorcycle jacket, an old lady in overcoat and church hat with a heavy-duty handbag over her forearm. There were children, too. Babies in arms and a little girl of around five looking uncertain and holding the hand of a grandmotherly looking woman and fidgeting as though she needed the toilet. One by one, they seemed to materialise out of the curtains until the stage was filled and Valerie Andreas, whose out-of-date promotional picture was so doctored as to make a mockery of the Trades Descriptions Act, was surrounded by a semicircle of supporting spirits.

'Can you see them?' Lucy was sitting forward and gripping Nigel's arm.

But one look at his bored, sceptical face told her he couldn't.

Lucy was almost out of her seat now. She hadn't felt this excited since Nan Peters had taken her on the Mouse Trap, a rickety wooden roller coaster, in Blackpool.

'Jojo, can you see them? Can you see all the people on the stage?'

People in the row behind were hissing 'Sssshhh!' Jojo and Nigel were looking from the solitary figure on the stage to Lucy and back again.

'There're so many! They're all trying to get through and I can see them!' Lucy was delighted with her new skill. First Jonathan, then Keith, now a whole chorus line of ghosts had taken the stage and she could see them! Valerie Andreas was fiddling with her microphone stand and the little crowd of spirits were moving as though being jostled. Someone was elbowing their way through them to get to the front and there, dressed in his trench, grinning and waving straight at Lucy Diamond in a very 'Can you see me, Mother?' kind of way, was the late Mr Rayburn himself.

Lucy gave a little squeal and waved back. 'There's Jonathan! He's there at the front just to the left! He's waving again!' She clutched her hands together in pride.

'Is she going to sing "Jolene" for us?' Nigel whispered sarcastically. He really couldn't help himself. There was audible tutting from the row behind, who shushed at them yet again.

Valerie Andreas was enjoying her moment of glory as if she knew it couldn't last the night. She slipped stiffly down from the too-high stool and in an accent thick with her Lancashire roots addressed the audience. 'Good evening, Walthamstow!' She held her arms out up to the balcony and the crowd went crazy again. She turned to the boxes, then bowed low to the stalls, remaining regal even though there was obvious wig slippage. She made quietening motions with her hands and the cheering died until there was silence again within the theatre. There was not a rustle of a sweet wrapper nor a cough of a bronchial lung.

The spirits surged forward around Valerie, trying to get her attention. Hands were raised as if by eager students with the right answers in class. Valerie had her eyes shut and the fingertips of each hand at her temples. She was obviously trying to get into her 'flow'. Lucy could barely breathe with anticipation, and then Valerie spoke.

'I've got a Doris.'

No one in the theatre responded. Valerie tried again. Clearly there was interference on the direct line from the spirit world.

'An Iris?' Valerie had her eyes open now, darting across the rows, looking for a response. Still nothing. Then, a little impatiently, face wrinkled in concentration, 'A Vera?' and the audience gave a collective sigh of relief when a tentative hand was raised in the stalls. The spirit crowd seemed to shrink back, and no one looking like a Vera moved to Valerie's side.

A woman in her late fifties was ushered by waistcoated theatre staff to the front of the stage where she stood blinking nervously in the fringes of the spotlight, alternately wringing a handkerchief in her hands and dabbing at her nose with it. She was already close to tears.

'I'm getting that she was a mother figure . . .' Valerie Andreas was wafting her hands around as though immersing herself in the ether of the other world.

'Not really . . .' The woman was a little hesitant.

'*Like* a mother figure,' Valerie quickly corrected. It sounded as if she was correcting the audience member rather than herself.

'Well . . .' The relative still didn't sound too sure. 'She was my sister.'

'That's right,' Valerie soothed. 'And she took a motherly role . . .'

'Umm . . . she was younger than me.'

Before any other disagreement could take place Valerie changed tack entirely. 'I'm sensing a pain here or here.' The medium's hand waved from groin to chest and back again, covering all bases.

'Yes, it was heart failure.' Vera's sister was more confident now and Valerie nodded smugly.

'I know, love. I know.' Then Valerie clamped her forehead with her hand as though in pain. 'Vera was quiet in front of people she didn't know but she could let herself go with those she loved. Am I right?'

'That's a Barnum statement if ever I heard one,' Nigel exclaimed too loudly and someone in the row behind muttered, 'Quiet, you!'

Vera's sister was sobbing and nodding, all of her raw grief and restrained emotion unleashed. The spirits were looking from one to the other as if searching for the lucky ghost who got heard and it was clear that Vera wasn't on this stage. Jonathan Rayburn was aghast. His mouth flopped further open with every trick Valerie Andreas pulled until catching Lucy's eye he shook his head in disgust, made an 'I'm washing my hands of it' gesture and was gone. This event was not worth wasting his Life Time on. Other souls on the stage were popping away like burst bubbles as the fraud that was 'Valerie Andreas – Psychic to the Celebs' became apparent.

Lucy slumped back in her seat as one after another, members of the audience were duped with banalities and ambiguities. Valerie had a complete repertoire. She fired her comments out at the audience like a machine gun: 'I've got a Dave, a David, Daniel, Duncan . . .' and kept going until something hit home, following up with non-specific statements that anyone could apply to their lives.

'I sense an older male figure who says despite your disagreements he still loves you.'

'There's a feminine presence who says you've been

through a bad time recently but it's all over now. Does it apply to anyone?'

And there were the openly mercenary: 'Who here has been seeing a lot of psychics and phoning those telephone lines in the paper?' A hand shot up. 'Well, love, I've got a grandfatherly/uncle spirit here who says you mustn't waste your money. See me after the show to arrange a one-on-one. Very reasonable rates.'

Valerie Andreas also had her 'Quick Fire Contacts': one or two lines designed to confirm that she could reach many members of the audience. Comments that on the surface were personal but were so general that they could apply to one in ten of the population at any given time. 'Who's had the living room redecorated or is thinking about it?', 'I'm getting something about a car accident . . .' or 'A girl who loves horses or a woman who used to love horses . . .' would be followed by a comment like 'Your loved one just wants you to know that they're thinking of you,' or 'They still visit from time to time – if you feel a sudden draught, that's them.'

Then there were the stooges, obvious 'plants' where the accuracy was so precise and the responses so perfectly timed that they had to be rehearsed. Plus they all had accents like the cast of *Coronation Street* in a theatre where the majority of punters sounded like extras in *EastEnders*.

With each disappointment of a voice not heard and a presence unfelt, the remaining visitors from the other side turned back into the dark recesses of the stage wings and were gone. Finally, Valerie Andreas stood alone on the deserted stage claiming direct contact with The Dead.

Lucy's illusions weren't just shattered, they were

smashed, stamped on and ground into a fine powder. She felt more alone and freakish than ever before. But something was keeping her there. She didn't walk out. They didn't even leave at the interval. Lucy was in shock. Jojo was plain bored and had spent the last fifteen minutes deleting messages from her mobile inbox and texting an unnamed 'someone from work', and any minute now Lucy was expecting a scathing attack from Nigel. Instead he laughed. He was finding it funny. He reframed the act as kitsch, camp, music hall; glugging back the vinegary house red before the performance had helped.

'Lucy Diamond, we've been on some shit nights out together and this is certainly one of them, but I'm getting my full tenner's worth before we go home.' He pressed the girls back towards their seats.

The second half of 'An audience with Valerie Andreas' was no better and Nigel, fuelled with more vino during the interval, started sniggering at anything that could be interpreted as having a double meaning.

'I can see a pearl necklace . . . wait a minute . . . something's coming . . .'

Nigel's shoulders began to shake.

'I've got the feeling of something big in my hand . . .'

Nigel snorted and covered his mouth.

'She's showing me fur now . . .' and Nigel guffawed so loudly that Valerie and half the stalls turned to look at him.

Lucy just winced at her lack of finesse – 'I've got a lad 'ere what hung himself' – and stared opened-eyed as Valerie Andreas argued aggressively with anyone who questioned what she had to say.

'He wore a hat.'

'He didn't.'

'Well, he used to have a friend who wore a hat.'

'He didn't.'

'Listen, love, check the facts, OK? I think you'll find I'm right.'

Looking round, Lucy realised that there were empty seats where previously there hadn't been. Clearly, some people had walked out in disgust, but the remainder sat on, hopeful that it just might be their turn next, desperate for any contact with a departed loved one, however lacking in anything concrete. All around, people had tissues at the ready and wore their grief openly, etched as it was in the lines on their faces. Clinging to any word, accepting the sham that was Valerie Andreas because they needed to hear that there was an afterlife, a place where they might just get to meet a beloved again. Where hands might be held, cheeks kissed and harsh words or bad deeds forgotten. A place where there might be resolution to the difficult questions left unanswered by death – the who, the where, the why that torture the sleep of those left behind.

These people deserved better than this. So they were old, perhaps uneducated or misinformed. Few of them looked rich, but their emotions were real and worthy and were being exploited by Valerie Andreas whose only gift was the gift of the gab.

For Lucy, the last straw came when, hedging her bets, Valerie Andreas made one of her non-specific statements that was bound to touch on sensitive wounds.

'I've got a baby here from the spirit world who only lived a short time. Whose mother keeps a box of little things and looks at them now and again.'

'Enough! That's enough!' Lucy could contain herself no longer. She was on her feet, outraged. All eyes in the theatre were on her as she ranted at Valerie Andreas. 'You're fooling these people! You're a liar and a cheat! You can't talk to The Dead! You're not a medium.' Then proudly, shoulders back and chest puffed: 'I'm a medium and I can tell all of you' – Lucy made a sweeping Eva Peron gesture from her position in the Grand Circle – 'that she is RIPPING YOU OFF.'

'You go, girl!' shouted Nigel, which he would later admit was both embarrassing and very outdated but well meant, because beneath his shallow persona there was a somewhat murky at times but none the less there morality. Lucy still had the theatre's undivided attention, although security were on their way.

'That stage was full earlier of spirits trying to get through and she's driven them away. There was a lad in a biker's jacket and an old lady with a flowery hat . . .'

'Come along, miss – and you . . .' A portly man in security uniform of black epaulettes and white shirt straining over a Full English Breakfast paunch was motioning to a surprised-looking Jojo who'd been sitting with her eyes shut, playing music through her mobile's headphones, and to Nigel. 'Are you with her? You're out an' all.' The security guard had Lucy by the elbow in an escort/restraint position and was manhandling her towards the fire exit. Lucy was not to be silenced.

'. . . and there was a little girl about five, blond bunches, carrying a panda and holding hands with her grandma . . .'

A man's voice shouted, 'That's our Pamela!'

'. . . and Valerie Andreas couldn't see any of them!' Lucy cried as the fire door swung shut on her words. They were on open concrete steps at the back of the theatre in an alleyway strewn with big green bins and broken wooden pallets.

'It's not the first time I've been at the trades-man's entrance.' Nigel had a rude remark for every occasion.

'What a night this has turned out to be!' Jojo was trying to put on her coat whilst juggling her phone, and her headphones had got wedged in her sleeves like the string mothers put in coats with their child's mittens attached. 'Are we going home or what?' Jojo never suffered fools (except Jasmine) gladly and her tolerance level had been reached.

'No.' Lucy was adamant. 'I want to speak to that bloody woman. She can't go around exploiting people like that. I'm going to wait here until she comes out of the stage door and tell her what I think of her *and* show her what a *real* medium can do.'

'Well, I'm not waiting with you.' Jojo was moving from foot to foot, trying to keep warm. 'It's autumn. It's cold and it's damp and I paid for a blow-dry yesterday. And trust me, Lucy, this night air isn't doing your hair any favours either.' Jojo looked at the screen of her phone as it hummed the arrival of another text. 'Look, I'll be honest, I've got a better offer here than standing by the bins with you two – but if we go home now, I'll pass on it.'

'Who is it?' Nigel was craning to look and Jojo clutched her mobile firmly in her palm and patted her finger at the side of her nose in a 'mind your own business' way.

'I can see a taxi at the end of the alley there, so what's it to be?'

Applause could be heard beyond the fire door. Somehow Valerie Andreas had staggered on to the end of her act.

'We're staying,' Lucy said firmly.

'Are we?' The cold was seeping through the warmth of Nigel's 'wine vest'.

'Yes we are. Or I will arrange for Jonathan to haunt you.'

'Great! Something else to add to my list of worries.'

It was decided. Jojo skipped off to see Who Knows Who but had let slip that he was Too Famous to risk exposure.

'Too married, more like,' Nigel whispered as she left and he and Lucy stayed where they were, stamping their feet in the cold.

It was easy to slip back into the theatre. They waited until some Polish cleaners still with brooms in hand emerged from a side exit to smoke their cigarettes and then simply pushed past them in an authoritative manner. Once inside, Nigel clapped his hands together and made little squealy noises.

'We did it! We did it! We're like Nancy Drew and the Hardy Boys!'

Before he could turn that into something lewd, Lucy said, 'You're more of a Big Softy Boy! Now shush! We've got to find the dressing room. That's where she'll be.'

It wasn't a big theatre. A hundred years ago in its heyday it would still have had only the cheapest acts to amuse the masses. Now its biggest draw was the annual pantomime when some ancient celebrity less well known than his sidekick – a novelty animal puppet – would join forces with the local tap and ballet group. Hence there was only one 'star' dressing room, and because it was no bigger than the cleaners' cupboard the door was open.

Valerie Andreas sat in front of the bulb-surrounded mirror sipping tea-coloured liquid from a whisky tumbler. The bombshell wig sat securely on a polystyrene head and the 'Psychic to the Celebs' rubbed at the thinning grey hairs that naturally covered her head. She was slipping her wide-fit feet out of her slim-fit shoes with the kind of satisfied groan that, you really wouldn't want to hear from a woman of her age under any other circumstances.

She jumped as Nigel and Lucy entered the room, little splashes of alcohol bursting from the glass, and hastily tried to shove the wig back on. Valerie clearly didn't recognise either of them as her Performance-Wreckers. As it had been on stage, her patter was slick and well rehearsed.

'If you're from the press, see my agent, and if you want a one-on-one then you need to make an appointment over the website. Or I can sign one of me pictures for a fee of two pounds . . .' Valerie Andreas did not get much further with her spiel. Lucy was advancing upon her with a murderous look in her eye.

'How much do you make? What do you charge? You're despicable! You should give back every penny you've made tonight! I came here because I needed your help—'

'They *all* need my help, darlin'.' Valerie was cocky on the surface but was backing away towards a telephone on the wall.

'I came because I've been hearing voices, seeing things . . .'

'I'm not a shrink, you know.' Then Valerie directed her comments to Nigel. 'You should get her to see a doctor. Security! Security!' She was yelling into the telephone receiver now.

'I'm going to give you some advice.' Lucy was coming on strong now like a gangland heavy. 'I want you to give up this act and stop tricking innocent people or you'll be seeing a lot more of this . . .' and Lucy closed her eyes and twisted up her face in an ugly pose of concentration. There was an awkward moment of silence and stillness and Nigel really believed Lucy was going to make the biggest fool of herself when *Whooosh!* The whisky spilled on to the table as the glass rose into the air and smashed against the opposite wall. Valerie Andreas screamed. So did Nigel. Jonathan Rayburn was back and knew exactly what Lucy wanted. Life Time be damned – there were principles at stake. The wig flew off Valerie's head, made two sweeps of the room, and shot out of the door into the face of the security guard.

'You again!' he roared, but before he could grab either Nigel or Lucy the stack of misty filtered photographs waiting for autographs were thrown into the air, fluttering to the floor like big rectangular snowflakes, and Nigel and Lucy were able to make a dash for the exit, dodging the chubby arms of theatre security and tearing down the back alley scattering the brooms and buckets of the cleaners behind them.

Meanwhile, Jonathan did his worst, scrawling 'Get Out of Here' in Valerie's gaudy coral lipstick on the dressing-room mirror and leaving a ghostly footprint in her scattered face powder on the dressing-room floor. It was worth wasting a bit of Life Time to avenge the spirit world.

That night, Valerie Andreas decided that maybe it was time to retire and spend more time in the garden. The security guard never did work out how they did it but said that Nigel and Lucy were the best act that he'd ever seen in that crappy little theatre.

'I think there's something you should know about me.'

It was Sunday night and Lucy was sitting opposite Tony Russell in another nice bistro. He was full of apologies for letting her down the night before and to his credit he did look pale and sickly, though that was the result not of a virus, as he told Lucy, but of too much beer on Saturday night and winding up in a dodgy lap-dancing bar in Peckham. At her words, he blanched even more and a look of panic crossed his face.

The restaurant described itself as an 'eaterie'. It was a 'nice' place. It was playing 'nice' mellow music by a 'nice' girl-guitarist-singer-songwriter. Amy Winehouse would be too edgy for a safe place like this. This was this year's Best Newcomer Brit Award winner with hippy hair and a two-album deal stuck in her back pocket. In two years' time she'd be moaning in the Sunday supplements about how fame had turned her head and got her hooked on cocaine but now she wanted to be taken seriously and in the meantime was hawking a solo album of political songs.

To go with the general 'niceness' of the evening, they had taken in a rom-com movie beforehand, which really only deserved to be seen on DVD. Lucy was just glad that she hadn't shamed herself by falling asleep, which she could do even when Matthew McConaughey was fifteen foot high on the screen with his pecs out.

All in all, a nice time had been – and was being – had. They had eaten a nice dinner described as 'pan fried' and 'locally sourced', although it had actually been spelt 'sauced', which jarred Lucy Diamond's lexicological sensibilities all through the meal. After all, Lucy had got As in her English Literature and English Language GCSEs. She had stared at the menu for some time and had become quite distracted, unable to take in anything that was said by Tony Russell. Was it a simple case of awful spelling? Did they intend to say it had been bought locally or that tomato ketchup had been added nearby?

Dessert plates had been whisked away and coffee ordered. Tony Russell had been attentive – doors held open, seats pulled out. Certainly, Lucy Diamond had been on worse dates – like their last one.

It was not dramatic; no Jonathan Rayburn, nor being slapped around the face by an irate ex-girlfriend, which had happened in her dating history. It was not passionate – Tony Russell had not lunged for her in the darkness of the cinema and poked his tongue into her mouth or ear. Physical contact had been made, though: he had held her hand discreetly in such a way that the contacting flesh had not been allowed to become unpleasantly clammy. He had laughed at her jokes (guffawed at his own). Admittedly, she had caught him checking his artfully mussed hair in his knife and thought him a bit of a twit, but overall it was a promising evening.

So now, buoyed by the climax of 'An Audience with

Valerie Andreas', flushed with a new pride in her own special abilities and lulled into a comfort zone by the success (and alcohol intake) of the evening, she felt the need to confess, to unburden herself to Tony Russell. After all, they were practically having a relationship and she believed honesty was the best policy.

Seeing the fear criss-crossing Tony's face, Lucy remembered her own panic when she'd heard those words uttered on previous dates. There was the memorable 'I'm a cross dresser', not to mention 'I have three children by three different women; I must warn you I am very fertile.' But the most off-putting had to be, 'It's not catching unless there is moist skin to skin contact.' She really had had more than her fair share of bad dates. Now, Lucy noticed that Tony had backed away from her slightly in his seat. How could she put it to him? How could she express what she wanted to say without sounding like a raving lunatic?

'It sounds so silly if I say it aloud, but . . . emm . . . er . . .' She struggled to find the words.

'It can't be that bad, surely?' Tony Russell tried to sound jocular, but a slight tremble in his voice was evident. The last word had a desperate note to it.

'I hear voices.' He could not disguise his alarm and his eyes widened in horror. He was a second away from calling for the bill and making a fast getaway.

'No, not those kinds of voices. I haven't explained it very well. I have abilities. Special ones.' Lucy was confusing rather than clarifying. Tony was already trying to formulate an excuse to leave before the coffee came.

'I am . . . I can see . . . and hear . . .' Now she really was rambling like a mad woman. Lucy, spit it out! Just tell him! Or don't tell him, because that would be the wisest thing of all. But she's going to, so here goes.

'On our last date . . . I was talking to someone . . . he wasn't there. Well, you couldn't see him . . .' In less than eloquent terms she told the man who thought he was the Player from Accounts all about imaginary friends, spirit voices, messages from beyond the grave and Valerie Andreas. She rounded off by giving a full explanation of their last date and reassuring him (or maybe herself) that 'I am, you know, very normal.'

Like many men, Tony Russell only ever really listened fully to his own voice. His attention had waned at some point around 'imaginary friends' and he'd only picked up a few of the main themes after that. In his head – which kept repeating heady scenes from his Saturday Night of Excess, so much more enjoyable than the rather dire film and polite civilisation of this evening – he slotted her into the neat little box of 'Hippy Chick' along with those of his ex-girlfriends who had had their noses pierced or expressed an interest in rock bands with long-haired singers. Lucy Diamond would be alarmed to know that she was turning into her mother after all. In Tony's head, that box came with the stereotypical and optimistic tag of 'very free sexually'. So when he said with an enthusiastic smile, 'It's OK. It's kind of cool. It makes you . . . unique. Different,' they were really words without meaning. He had not taken in what she said and now, with that cruel bet hanging over him with his arse of a workmate, he was just saying what he thought she wanted to hear in order to get her most quickly into bed.

Blindly, Lucy basked in the glow of his words – 'unique', 'different' – which he'd said as if difference was a good thing, not as if you wore jumpers made of home-spun yak's wool and the other kids wouldn't play with you. 'Unique'. 'Different'. She suddenly gripped Tony's arm and he jumped in shock, looking over his shoulder fearfully as though one of her imaginary friends would be there.

'You won't tell people at work, will you?' She didn't want this bandied all over the company. People who actually enjoy jobs in windowless, air-conditioned offices can have very narrow minds.

'No,' Tony reassured her. 'Your Psychic Secret is safe with me.' And he patted her hand reassuringly. What information he had extracted he didn't want spreading like a forest fire either. It was never good to be known for choosing to date an office oddball. It was best to keep her as something of an enigma – at least until the bet was won.

'This has been nice.' Lucy was being truthful and filling the silence that had settled upon them as they waited for coffee. She played with a neat little parcel of sugar.

'Yes, and you didn't feel the need to throw a single drink over me!' Tony lightened the mood. 'They're taking their time with that coffee!' Unusually for Tony, he couldn't catch the waitress's eye. 'Look – if we stand and put on our coats, they'll think we're about to do a runner and bring us the bill. You could come and have coffee at mine.' And he'd said it. Dropped the universal-coded invitation for sex into the conversation as easily as he was now handing his card to an anxiously arriving waitress.

It was a tense moment. The ball – so to speak – was in her court; or, as Nigel would chuckle, was going to be.

Should she? Shouldn't she? It was no good saying she would just have a drink and leave because that never happens. And it was only their second date. What about romance? What about rejecting all that raunch demanded by a sex-obsessed society? What about rising above the demands of the flesh? What about demanding respect? On the other hand, why not, when there is the fuzzy glow that comes after a good meal and a glass or two of the grape? He had been so sweet about the whole talking to spirits thing. So understanding. And he really seemed to like her for Who She Was.

How mistaken can a girl get?

'Why don't you come to mine?' The words were out of her mouth before she fully realised what she had said.

Lucy – what are you doing? You're giving him the message that you do this with everyone after a little light entertainment and linguini!

'It's nearer.'

And it was said without eye contact, coy and casual, and Tony Russell agreed heartily that going to her place was a Good Idea.

Then they were stepping out into the light rain and hailing a taxi and he was kissing her hand and for a moment, a brief giddying moment, Lucy Diamond felt just like Audrey Hepburn with George Peppard at the end of *Breakfast at Tiffany's*. That's the trouble with romantics. They see what they want to see.

Some time later, Lucy's living room showed what the police would call 'the signs of a struggle'. Cushions were cast on the floor, the throw spilled from the armchair. A high heel lay next to a man's single black Marks & Spencer sock.

So this is where the 'nice' film, the 'nice' meal, the 'nice' evening ends? Nice. Secretly, due to Nan Peters's lecturing, Lucy fears Nice girls Don't; but they Do, and Lucy is going to Do It with Tony Russell. To hell with romance! Sometimes you just want to kiss and touch and lose yourself in the physical animal moment.

They reached the bedroom, shedding the rest of their clothes, and metamorphosing into pale, ethereal beings in the blue-white light cast by the moon and an old street lamp below Lucy's window.

The force with which they fell hungrily to the bed surprised them both. Who would have suspected over the pasta less than two hours ago that a better feast was yet to be eaten, devoured as if they were starving hungry? An observer of this primitive scene might even think, in view of the dim and therefore flattering light of the room, that it was not Lucy Diamond from Human Resources and Tony Russell from Accounts at all. Even they did not feel like their usual day-to-day selves. He felt powerful. She felt beautiful. And if you were there, if you were watching, it's doubtful they would even have noticed because they were so lost in each other and the sheer physicality of skin to skin and mouth to mouth.

Sometimes good, even great, sex can happen with people you're not that interested in (Tony), and naked, fevered desire can be indistinguishable from the love you want to feel (Lucy). He wasn't the man of her dreams, she knew, but still the loins can respond even if the brain can't.

So unhearing, unfeeling and unseeing – except for each other – they did not notice the curtain shifting a little as though in a warm summer breeze. Moving back and forth, almost to their rhythm, gaining momentum until, accompanied by a cruel blast of chill October air, the Victorian sash slammed open and the curtains billowed over the bed like a ship's sails. This was a window that had not moved in all the time Lucy had lived here because of the multiple layers of paint gluing it shut.

'What the . . .' Shocked, the two lovers leapt apart, skin already beading into goose flesh with the cold and adrenaline.

'I'll get it.' Hair tousled, cheeks flushed, Lucy sprang up to wrestle the sash shut. Still in heat and confident in the dark, she did not care that the cellulite dappling her bottom cheeks might be visible to her guest. Just as she had rammed the sash shut in a way she hoped was sexily attractive and Tony was reaching out to pull her back down into the bed, the light snapped on and she became visible not only to him but to the ASBO kids congregated under the lamp on the corner below. A small cheer rose from the street and she instinctively crouched below the sill.

Simultaneously, a book flew from the shelf and hit Tony Russell on the side of his head. In a reflexive response, he sprang into a martial-arts pose, ready for his unseen assailant. Sexual allure was gone. He crouched with the duvet half covering his groin, semi-prepared for combat like some judo-trained Gollum.

The light was snapping on and off, on and off, speeding faster and faster towards a climax, and the bulb – an un-eco-friendly trad sixty watt that Lucy had, for a long time, been willing to blow – did just that, shattering into a crystal shower over the bed. The room was plunged back into darkness. What had seemed like the most flattering light for lovemaking now felt like a menacing gloom. The sash dropped open again with a startling bang. Lucy stood up to shut it and the curtains swirled around her like the cloak of the Scottish Widow. Her long hair, already curling and frizzing in the damp, blew across her face, spiralling wildly outwards and looking to Tony Russell like the snaky barnet of Medusa herself.

It had certainly ruined the mood.

Suddenly, the pile of working-week clothes, thrown on a chair, took on a life of their own and were flung this way and that. All over the flat, lights were going on and off, books were falling to the floor. The TV was blaring and skipping from channel to channel, and along with the chaos came the rhythmic thump-thump of Miss Crump's broom through the bedroom floor.

'What the fuck is going on?' Tony demanded.

Lucy's confident sexuality was replaced by a sense of foolishness as she rifled around through the tumble of strewn clothes on the floor to find her beltless kimono.

'I don't know. Perhaps the wiring's gone funny,' she lied, literally filled with anticlimax. Tony was scrambling for his clothes.

'Is this part of what you were going on about earlier? Your psychic-whatever? Your imaginary friends?' Tony Russell's Nice Guy persona had slipped somewhat. He was angry. Angry because all the energy previously holding the flagpole of his passion aloft had to go somewhere and it certainly was no longer keeping *that* up. And he was angry because he was scared and he didn't like to be scared – especially in front of girls. He could still remember the cries of 'Chicken!' that followed him home after he had refused to fly over the brook on the home-made rope swing, and he never did get to French-kiss Jennifer Swift, his secret first love, who had laughed louder than all the rest.

Lucy was determined to salvage something of the evening. She picked her way gingerly across the bedroom, avoiding the broken light bulb glass, to try to appease him. Around them the chaos showed no signs of abating. He was clutching the only one of his socks he could find and ramming his feet into slip-on shoes, aware that if he couldn't find a taxi home his heels would soon be sprouting blisters if he walked to the tube.

Lucy shouted above the TV and CD player and offered him a coffee, but the proposal seemed preposterous as the automatic kettle was already boiling away without signs of stopping. He snorted at her request as though she had invited him for a spot of home colonic irrigation, and ignored her when she tentatively reached out to him.

Knowing now that the evening was lost, Lucy resorted to helping Tony find his missing garments. She had never seen anyone dress so quickly in all her life. Despite the ruined ambience, Lucy had amazed herself. She had not shared the terror of her bed-partner, as she would have only a few short weeks before. In fact, the only thing she felt was irritation. After all, there could only be one culprit and it certainly wasn't dodgy wiring.

She just about managed to shout 'Give me a call soon, yeah?' as the door slammed shut behind Tony Russell. He didn't reply. No sooner had the latch clicked shut than the bedlam ceased entirely. The curtains settled back to their proper position. The sash slammed home. CD and TV fell silent and books and clothing stopped flying about. The only sound to be heard was Tony's hastily retreating footsteps clattering down the last few stairs and the slam of the front door behind him. Even Miss Crump's broom had stopped bashing against the ceiling.

'JONATHAN!' Lucy yelled in her best school-marmy tones. 'JONATHAN!' Suddenly, he was there, leaning against the door frame with his arms folded across his chest and a look of smug self-satisfaction on his face.

'What do you think, Lucy Diamond? Whaddya-think? Talk about special effects!' Jonathan Rayburn was glowing. His eyes were glittering with pride at his handiwork.

'What do I think?' Lucy was fuming, her fists clenching and unclenching, and had she not known that a punch would land on thin air she was sure she would have swung for him. As it was, she walked straight through him. His conceit dissipated and he shuddered and retched from her violation.

'Lucy, I've told you not to do that! You *know* not to do that!' He whirled around and followed her, a little paler and certainly less filled with self-importance than before, but hey! It was his Life Time he was wasting. Lucy began tidying away the debris and ignored the spirit dancing around her, trying to gain her attention, until she could stand it no longer.

'Why?' She whirled round, waving her dirty washing at him. 'Why?'

'I've told you, Lucy. I really don't like that man. I wanted to stop you doing something that you might regret.'

'It's not for you to decide, is it?' Lucy spat the words at him, shocked at her own venom. 'Just because it's over for you you have to ruin it for me! Is that it?'

'What were you doing with him?' Jonathan shouted back. 'On a second date? Do you think it would last very long after that?' Jonathan's words sounded old-fashioned, a tad fatherly, and if Lucy had had an older brother she would have known what it was to be cared for in this slightly lecturing, overprotective way. And Jonathan did care for her, this girl who was his only connection to the world he once knew and the life he once had.

'But I won't get the chance to know, will I?' Lucy was bellowing, unattractive little bits of spit flying from the corners of her mouth. 'At least you had it once, Jonathan! You and Laura had it! I've never known what it's like to be "in love" like that but I'd like to! And you come in here with all your stupid games and tricks and ruin it all. I'm thirty and a half and do you know how afraid I am that I'll never meet someone who feels about me the way that you do about Laura?'

'Haven't you heard the song "Eleanor Rigby"? Do I want to be picking up the rice after a wedding? Do I want a funeral where nobody came? And what about "Hey Jude" for a sad song? And the maudlin dirge of "Michelle"? Call it a love song? It's a funeral march! "Lovely Rita" is only about getting a leg over, isn't it? It's not a song of love and longing!'

'Don't you realise how fucking scared I am that my name – my stupid long name that was supposed to fill my life with all the power, creativity and good luck of the Beatles – is really a curse? A curse! And I'll never find that one special person to spend the rest of my life with? But you did, Jonathan! It might have been over too soon, but you did! But still you choose to come here and disrupt my life and expect me to help you. I've already made a fool of myself once in front of Tony and a whole restaurant full of people but that's not enough, is it? You want more! You want to humiliate me when . . . when I'm naked, and then you have the audacity to think it's funny. Funny! Just some private prep school "high jinks"? Well, it's not some Boy's Own practical joke – this is my life! Yours might have all gone so perfectly and easily as you so fondly remember, but mine hasn't! All this' – Lucy gestured to the flat – 'all this was hard won and paid for by hours spent in a shitty job! No expense account and days on the golf course! No cheque in the envelope from Mummy and Daddy. And you come and wreck it like some spoilt baby and then you want me to help you? After all this? The Girl with No Life should help you cos yours is over? You expect me to listen to your endless moaning? "Oh, I'm dead! Poor me! I'll never be married to my beautiful girlfriend and live in Kent and holiday in France and I'm so used to getting everything I want!" I think you've wasted so much Life Time trying to mess things up for me that you're actually behaving like one of those bloody wraiths Keith Richards was on about!'

Lucy Diamond, who all this time had been stomping around the flat trying to tidy up, realised she wasn't just shouting at Jonathan but shouting because she was sick of being disappointed and short-changed her whole life. That realisation didn't help make her mood any better and she picked up a book and aimed it squarely at Jonathan Rayburn. He tried to dodge it, but her secretly treasured copy of Jordan's life story passed directly through his head. He reeled and shuddered.

Her set text for A level, Jane Austen's *Mansfield Park*, was soon followed by the teachings of the Dalai Lama

(Jasmine again) and as each passed through a very shocked-looking Jonathan, Lucy yelled louder.

'Just get out, Jonathan! Get out and don't come back because I don't want to help you! I don't want to see you and I don't want to speak to you! I don't want to speak to your girlfriend or your dead friends. I don't want to see you ever again. So don't come back! Don't come back!' An unused Jamie Oliver cookbook hurtled through the air.

Jonathan Rayburn disappeared like a snuffed candle. Just like Tony Russell, all her passion had had to find a different outlet, but when her anger subsided she was left tearful, sitting on her knees amongst the flotsam of clothes and jetsam of books and wondering how a nice evening could end up going so very, very wrong.

11

Where better to go when you have wounds to lick and hurts to heal than home? And home for Lucy Diamond was not an eco-shack with Jasmine but up north with Nan Peters – eighty-two and fit as a fiddle as she would tell anyone she met at the bus stop. The taxi had deposited Lucy on the pavement after a forty-minute drive during which she'd heard the taxi driver's opinion on everything from green issues ('Global warming – it's a myth put around by vegetarians') to equal rights ('I wouldn't have that Heather McCartney Mills in this cab, one leg or no leg.')

Lucy had her hand on the gate, its gnarled faded-to-grey wood a familiar friend. She had swung on the gate as a toddler, much to Granddad Peters's despair when he was alive – 'Eh, lass, pack it in – you'll fetch it off the hinges' – and Nan had leaned on it to gossip with neighbours while Lucy skipped in and out of the rose beds revelling in the rare chance to 'play in the front', something considered too risky and too common to happen every day. Here she would listen as Nan Peters repackaged their lives to make them more palatable for the neighbours.

Home. Lucy always felt guilty when she thought this. Home should be with Jasmine, but despite

Jasmine's best attempts to be an earth mother she had never managed to be homely. So home was here with Nan Peters in the two-up-two-down worker's terrace in a North Yorkshire village where she'd spent the last seven years of her schooling after passing the exam for Our Lady and St Margaret's of Cortona's. Jasmine had gone off on one of her navel-gazing missions to Goa or Ibiza or somewhere, and except for her occasional visits Lucy had gained the normality she had spent her early childhood craving. A base at last, and meat and two veg instead of alfalfa and sprouting beans. And a uniform! How she loved the regulation navy blue, the striped tie, the V-neck. The normality that Jojo kicked against Lucy relished.

Our Lady's was a non-fee-paying Catholic grammar school in the nearest big town. Jasmine had railed against Lucy's going there, her objections based on capitalist brainwashing and the stunting of creativity by organised religion, but little by little Nan had won her daughter round by appealing to her bit-chomping lust for freedom. Nan had pointed out how much easier it would be for Jasmine to travel unhampered by a child, without the worry and the guilt – that even Jasmine felt – when the money ran out and food wasn't easy to come by.

So Jasmine had relented and Nan Peters made it her mission to feed up the pale vegan child and Lucy surprised them both by agreeing to stay because she was more than ready to give up the responsibility of monitoring her mother, making dinner when Jasmine was too stoned to cook and missing out on *Grange Hill* because she didn't believe in TV.

'Yes – he works abroad. In Morocco,' was the garden-gate comment to explain the fatherless child. 'Well, you've got to get work where you can . . . they'd do no good here.' Barbed comments since Mrs Haddock had a son with an uncertain future in coal. 'Oh, Jasmine's doing wonderfully well. Travelling all over the world!' Nan always declined to mention that it was mostly hitchhiking and meditating. 'We like to help 'em out where we can and we love having the little 'un 'ere. Keeps us young!'

Of course, Nan Peters knew – and even Lucy heard – the whispers of the gossips who labelled Jasmine a feckless mother which, in some ways, she was. Part of the unspoken deal about keeping the lid on a scandal in a small community was that you kept your head high and pretended it was normal and nobody actually said anything to your face and in that way you carried on until it *became* normal. Before long another scandal would come along to demand attention, and sure enough the interest in little Lucy's elusive parents soon declined when the local rector ran off with the fund for the new church bells to pay for a sex-change operation.

There was no need for a key. Lucy went through the entry to the back door, which was on the latch.

'Nan!' she called. In Ploxbury, it was fine to walk into someone's house so long as you heralded your arrival. Nan Peters's friends – like garden birds – each had their own individual call – 'Coo-eee', 'It's only me!', 'Betty! Bettee!'

Nan was at the kitchen table writing a shopping list in her spidery writing on the back of a cut-up Weetabix box. A frugal act, a relic of post-war rationing and recycling from an age before green issues were even thought about.

'Hello, pet.' She rose stiffly up as if Lucy's walking in

through the back door happened every day just like it used to. 'I'll get the kettle on.' She grabbed Lucy's face in both hands, kissing her cheeks with noisy enthusiasm. Her glasses, decades old, could now pass as ironically retro. She had a 'pinny' on and her permed hair was set into a helmet. She smelt of face powder, soap and something menthol for sinus relief.

'I'll do it – you finish writing your list.'

'You'll do no such thing. Travelling all that way. Sit yourself down. Biscuit? Cake? How 'bout a piece? Do you want a jam piece?' Piece – Nan's word for a sandwich. 'Egg and soldiers?' The menu went on and on and Lucy knew from experience that she had to eat something or the list would never end. She settled on the white bread and home-made strawberry jam. The best of comfort food.

Everything in the house was just as it had always been, although Granddad had been gone some time. That was typical of the village – widows living alone for decades into old age. Women who kept the village alive, though their husbands were dead, with their church flower arrangements, fund-raising jumble sales and informal, unasked-for neighbourhood watch.

The same teapot sat on a cork coaster at the centre of the table. It had a chipped spout, an unmatching lid and a handle fixed long ago with superglue. The new flowered Denby bought with Lucy's first pay packet sat unused on the window sill waiting for 'best'. In a throwaway, this-year's-fashion-for-home-interiors world, Nan kept things until they fell apart and were beyond fixing. But then a state pension didn't allow for throwing out the chintz in favour of minimalism and then, a year later, bringing the chintz back in.

*

'I don't know how many times I have to tell you – it's no good setting your cap at that Nigel fellow.' The teapot had been filled again and Lucy had cried a little bit over the bourbon biscuits as she'd given Nan the 'highlights' of her disastrous dates with Tony who, surprise surprise, she'd not heard from since.

She'd also made the mistake of telling Nan that she was worried about Nigel – mainly to illustrate that they were all losing their way now their carefree twenties were over, but Nan had seized on it and like a terrier with a rag she wasn't going to let it go.

'What's the point in worrying about him? It's obvious that 'e's an 'omosensual.'

'Sexual, Nan – homosexual.'

'That's what I said – an 'omosensual.'

'Sexual.'

'Don't use that sort of talk, Lucy. It's not nice.'

Lucy was about to give up and then inspiration struck. 'It's better to say gay. Nigel is gay.'

'That word had a very different meaning when I was a girl. Your granddad would never have danced the Gay Gordons with me if he'd known what it would mean one day.'

Lucy smiled to herself, thinking of a dance troupe she'd seen when out clubbing with Nigel. She was quite sure that Granddad would never have worn a leather peaked cap and arseless chaps. Nan was set on a course that couldn't be changed.

'Anyway. It's high time you faced it, love. Nigel is a fairy.'

'You can't say that these days, Nan. It's not PC.'

'Pee see? Is that something else perverted? Honestly,

I knew nothing on my wedding night. Nothing.'

'It means politically correct.'

'Politics? You mean the fairies are in on that now? They'll be running the country next and there'll be nowt but Liberace on the radio. It's all very queer to me.'

The irony was lost on Nan Peters but Lucy couldn't wait to relate the tale to Nigel and hear him roar.

'Any road up. Nigel is what he is and I have no objection to them on a one-to-one level . . .'

'It's the hordes roaming the streets that are the problem though, isn't it?' Lucy was ignored. Funny how Nan was so like Nigel when it came to enjoying the sound of her own voice.

'. . . and Iris has got one as a nephew and what he doesn't know about fancy ways of hanging curtains isn't worth knowing. But Lucy-love, you're barking up the wrong tree there. From my experience' – a life lived in the Yorkshire Dales with Dale Winton as a primary gay role model – 'there's them as are born that way and them as need the right woman and Nigel – well, as I say, he is as he is and I bet 'e wor from 'cradle.' She patted Lucy's hand. 'I just want to see you settled down with a nice fella, that's all – and you're not getting any younger.'

'Thanks for that, Nan.' As a feel-good comment it was on a par with the time Nan had said Lucy had – quote – 'lovely big arms'.

'You're too fussy, that's your trouble. There's always a complaint – his feet are too big this or he's a trainspotter that – but have you ever thought it's because you only choose to go out with the ones that have got something wrong with them? I think you've got a problem with your – what is it now? I saw it on Lorraine Kelly – oh, that's it, self-estimation. You've got a problem with your self-estimation.' Nan sat back, folding her arms smugly.

'Self-esteem. Nan. Self-esteem.' But there was little point in trying to correct her.

'Lorraine Kelly said it's why girls leap into bed with the first fella that comes along. Talking of which – what's that Joannna Gray up to?'

Nan's lips pursed. She had always disapproved of Jojo, knowing a 'rum 'un' when she saw one. Nan Peters had always been slightly suspicious of Jojo's well-to-do background, secretly worried that her own pedigree might be questioned and about Jojo's influence on 'our Lucy'. It was entirely understandable; after all, it was Nan Peters who fetched a tearful Jojo out of the cells in Richmond where she'd been marched after shoplifting in Woolworth's. She had mellowed over the years: familiarity ('better the devil you know') and Lucy's careful editing of Jojo's life had resulted in a begrudging admiration, although it was still her policy to maintain a veneer of disapproval. Secretly, Nan Peters had observed that Jojo, despite her wildness, had been a staunch and loyal friend to Lucy, but quartering by wild horses would never make her admit it.

'I bet she doesn't wait until there's a ring on her finger before she hops under the continental quilt.' Lucy squirmed in response to Nan Peters's disapproving comment, knowing that she herself didn't always care if they were going to ring her back. 'Anyway, I'm not going to lecture you.' She just had. 'Accept that Nigel is never going to be more than a good friend. Entertaining as an end-of-pier show, I'll grant you, but you haven't got what he's looking for.' Nan's eyes had a twinkle in them. She wasn't as naïve and easily shockable as she liked to make out. After all, she'd been borrowing Jackie Collins on audio tape from the mobile library for years.

'So is that the only reason you've come back home? A dead-end date with some useless fly-blow?' Lucy had never understood the term but it was always used in a derogatory sense in reference to the latest boyfriend, and of course Nan was right. It wasn't just Tony Russell causing her heartache. In fact it wasn't Tony Russell at all. And nor was it Nigel. Not really. It was Jonathan. She felt as bad about this falling out as the time she and Jojo didn't speak for a week because of . . . she couldn't even remember what. She just remembered the pain, the loss and the feeling that all was not right with the world until they were speaking again.

But how could she explain about falling out with a ghost to her ever practical grandmother? How could she even begin to describe her new-found skills? It was easy to tell Jasmine, with her slightly ethereal grasp of life, but Nan Peters? Nan with her no-nonsense approach to money, diet, education and make-do-and-mend was directly at odds with Jasmine and her airy-fairy ways. Betty Peters would have no truck with auras, meditation or the like. Even the Nazis had failed to shake her belief in the Way Things Were. 'Get this down yer and go and give 'em what for,' she told every flying officer at the RAF base as she served soul-strengthening tea as they waited for the order to scramble. No time for super-stitions, rabbits' feet or lucky angels – just Yorkshire grit.

Lucy approached the topic from a sideways angle, treading gingerly. She wanted Nan to know, wanted her approval really.

'It's Mum. You see . . .'

Nan Peters rolled her eyes. 'What now? Has she taken off for Kathmandu again?'

'No. I went to see her a few weeks ago.'

Nan took a big slurp of tea. 'Oh aye, she said you had. She called from the phone box in the week. Said that her "birth gift" to you had finally shown itself, or something. Said about you being able to contact the other side and that you were talking to a fella called Jonathan.'

Nan was looking at her over the rim of the china teacup, her gaze steady and sure. There was no look of disbelief, no head-shaking in despair. No calling for the doctor to administer a sedative. Maybe it was having put up with Jasmine for so long that caused Nan to accept the unacceptable. Lucy breathed out a big sigh. The explaining had all been done for her, and after Jasmine's description of events anything Lucy could say would only make it more palatable.

'Oh, you get that from my side of the family.'

Lucy was stacking the cups in the sink and nearly dropped them in shock.

'*Your* side of the family? The Ever Practical Peters?'

'Not Peters, love – that was Granddad's side. *My* family – the Boswells. Well, don't say it like that as though the idea of us having any gift beyond allotments is outrageous! It's because of our gifts that our vegetables were so good. And, of course, your great-aunt Phyllis had a booth at Scarborough telling fortunes, reading cards, holding séances – that kind of thing.'

'You never told me!'

'You never asked! Anyway, it wasn't quite respectable was it? I mean, going around in a turban and shawl dressed up like Gypsy Rose Lee.'

'Who was a stripper.'

'You know what I mean. Don't get smart with me. Any road up, she earned a decent living by it – reading cards, not stripping, so wipe that smile off your face – and she raised eight children on her own all right. Although one of them did get involved in smuggling cigarettes on the ferry back from Belgium and had to pay quite a fine, as I recall. Anyway, me father – who died before you were born – used to know things would happen before they did. Never did use it to predict the outcome of the Grand National, or our lives would be very different now.

'But it comes out in funny ways in our family, you can never predict how. I was no different. I used to float outside my body all the time. Got on my nerves, it did. It got so bad when I was teenager I didn't dare put me feet up. If I did I'd be off – whoosh, just like that! Well, I set me mind to growing out of it, and I did. We didn't have time for that sort of thing in the war. And they put you in the funny farm for less in those days.

'Of course it passed your mother by. She was more like the Peterses, like your granddad. Though she'd give her eye teeth for some of what my family had. I think it's been your mum's trouble in some ways – wanting to be less like the Peterses and more like the Boswells. Always dabbling with white magic here and spiritual thingybobs there, but try as she might Jasmine hasn't got it. My side were always a little more . . . colourful.

'There were rumours that way back they were gypsies or travelling side-show types settled through marriage – but mind you don't let that get out! You know what they're like round here. Your granddad always kept a neat garden and he'd turn in his grave if he thought folk were going round calling us tinkers. I could see it in you. You were always hearing voices or seeing things – imaginary friends, that sort of thing. But I didn't want you growing up like I did, always worrying what folk would think. Always worrying that there was a straitjacket waiting for you with the loonies up at Moat Hall. That's why I wanted your head buried in books at Our Lady and St Margaret of Cortona's, but I see now that times have changed. People are more . . . understanding of such things, I suppose.'

Nan was sweeping the tabletop now, wiping the crumbs into a pile to be scattered in the bottom of the budgie's cage. Lucy was left washing up at the kitchen sink with a sense that everything she had assumed about her grandmother was wrong.

Lucy could not believe what she was hearing. Nan, who was as normal as you could get, was worried that *she* would not be seen as normal, that there were secrets to hide. Nan's family, who Lucy had always thought had merely tilled the land and mined the earth, were really a bunch of vagabond horse-whisperers, palm-readers and carnival men. The moustached men standing straight-backed in the sepia family portraits, hands resting on corseted wives, were just pretending to be pillars of the community. They were actually soothsayers, herbalists and psychics.

All this time the aberrations of the past had been bubbling through Lucy's genes trying to break free. She felt that she just wanted to curl up in bed, pull the covers over her head and suck her thumb until her brain could compute all that she had just heard. It was a big deal to find out you had the gift of mediumship, but to suddenly discover that half of your family did – well, that took the biscuit. More than the biscuit – it took the whole darn Peek Freans assortment.

'So what are you going to about it?' Nan was back from feeding crumbs to Joey. 'I mean, this sort of thing doesn't matter these days, does it? No different to being homosensual, is it?'

'It is a bit different, Nan.'

'Not really. Single mums, fairies, men in dresses, psychics. Anything goes these days. And like your great-aunt Phyllis – there are worse ways to earn a living. And this Jonathan fellow your mum was telling me about, is he the only one you can speak to or are there others?'

'I'm not really speaking to him at the moment either.' Lucy gave a great big sob over the dish drainer.

Nan Peters reached for the stainless steel kettle. 'I'll put a pot on to brew. Now tell me all about it.'

When Lucy had finished, the table was littered with screwed-up tissues, bourbon crumbs and empty teacups. She sat red-eyed and puffy-faced. Nan was patting her hand and making comforting sounds like she always did.

'It sounds to me like you miss speaking to Jonathan. No different to one of your imaginary friends, is it? I don't see why you fussed so much about telling me. So long as you don't go mooning about over this one. Gay's one thing – dead's another, and you'd definitely be barking up the wrong tree with that one! It seems like he had his reasons for ruining your date with that Tony Russell. You should find out what they are. Tony Russell? Sounds like a cheap act in a working men's club, if you ask me. All flash and no substance. Perhaps Jonathan was right not to like him. Have you thought about that? As I said earlier, it's not like you know how to pick 'em, is it?'

Nan was searching through her tatty address book with its 1970s cover of psychedelic swirling flowers. It was held together with elastic bands and had postcards, old bits of paper and newspaper cuttings wedged into it. 'It's here somewhere. I put it away. I know I did. At the back of my mind I knew you'd need it one day.' She placed a square of cardboard on the place mat in front of Lucy. 'If you can't get through again to this Jonathan, and as you've said you tried, give this a go. You timed it right, all right, coming to stay just now. This is exactly what you need. Our family have gone along to it for generations. Very hush-hush it was back then when it first started, but they're bound to have a meeting tomorrow night, what with it being Hallowe'en and all. I'll make the arrangements for you to go. I'll call Barbara – you know Barbara with the hip?'

Nan and her generation always referenced in this way – Alf whose dog ate rat poison, Mrs Fellows who had the hysterectomy, Brian the one with the pigs. Who am I? Lucy wondered. Am I known as Lucy – you know, the one with big arms?

Nan was speaking on the telephone, sitting at the doily-covered table in the draughty hall. She still spoke loudly and slowly as though speaking on the bad connections of old.

'What time, Barbara? And she'll have to catch the 125 to drop off in Barrockby? You will look after her, won't you? Yes, I'll tell her.'

Lucy reluctantly picked up the yellowed calling card, wondering what she was getting herself into now. Probably one of Nan's God-bothering groups, where they'd pray for her and sing 'pop' songs on an acoustic guitar. Lucy turned it over in her fingers and read the smudged, curly script of the print on its reverse side and the words made the hairs on her arms rise.

This was no knitting-circle, Bible-bashing group with a trendy young vicar singing 'Kum Bah Ya'. This was something altogether darker. This village society seemed to have a distinctly Gothic twist.

12

The faded card, which shared brown spots of age with Nan Peters, declared that this unassuming wooden clapboard hall was the hosting venue for the Barrockby and District Society for the Academic Study of Anomalous Phenomena. Associates of the St Saviourgate Spiritualist Society. Twinned with the Swedish Spiritual Alliance. (Est. 1864)

After a jolting, painfully slow bus journey, Lucy had arrived at the hall, which stood on a particularly bleak edge of the moor. A mist was rolling in and Lucy could almost hear the mournful howling of wolves. It looked like something from *The Amityville Horror*. Lucy was feeling jittery. Very jittery indeed.

Barrockby consisted of only one street of grey, nondescript houses, a church and a pub. Garish pumpkin faces grinned and glowed from the odd window. Their bright orange glow didn't warm and cheer Lucy, not like the polystyrene coffins and cotton-wool spider web window displays of London at this time of year. Their candlelit grins seemed sinister. Mocking. They were a grim reminder that this was Hallowe'en.

Lucy felt very alone and very uneasy.

Nan Peters had refused to come with her on account of its necessitating a return journey in the dark and she couldn't risk the 'damp getting to her chest'. Privately, Lucy considered that the damp would have to be pretty robust to get through the defensive layers of woollen waistcoat, dress, bri-nylon blouse and thermal vest.

She knew what these out-of-the-way villages could be like. Backward places where everyone knew one another's ancestral histories and the gene pool was limited. 'No-neck, one-eyed places' Jojo called them and she had never looked back after the day she left.

As she stood facing the open entrance of the hall, Lucy was filled with the sense that, fifty years ago, it would have buzzed with bridge nights, tea dances and Brownie packs. But not any more. Now empty for great stretches of time, cobwebs swagged like Christmas garlands between the fifties light fittings. Out-of-date notices for flower-arranging classes, bring-and-buys and small ads fluttered on cork noticeboards. It smelled of dust, and the old caged radiators grunted out a pathetic heat. It was exactly one degree warmer than if you stood naked on the moor.

No longer grand enough for local weddings or exciting enough for the local youth, who preferred the inner warmth of cider drunk in a bus-shelter to an evening playing chaperoned pool under the watchful eye of a 'youth worker'. If it had been in London it would have been knocked down a decade ago to make way for rabbit-hutch 'studio apartments', but here, along with this dubious spiritualist group, the Barrockby Players, a pack of Scouts and Alcoholics Anonymous were enough to keep the hall in an active service of sorts.

*

Why have I come? Lucy kept berating herself as she stood on the threshold of the hall. But she knew why – to please Nan. Oh, and morbid curiosity. But now Lucy wanted to turn tail, run out of the building and leap back on the retreating rickety old bus.

Hallowe'en – a time Jasmine had always celebrated with scented candles, bonfires and rituals of the 'old ways' – had always seemed a benign occasion. A time for messing about with apple peelings looking for a lover's initials or divining the future with saucers of coins. In London, it was another excuse to get pissed, this time dressed in fake bloodstained bed sheets and plastic vampire teeth.

But here in desolate Barrockby, with a fog thickening around her, Hallowe'en felt like a very different affair and Lucy longed for the crass commercialism that the festival had taken on down south.

'Coo-ee.' A woman, way past retirement age, was making a beeline toward her. She had the bulge of tissues stuffed up sleeves at her wrist and a knitted waistcoat that must have come from the same mysterious knitted waistcoat shop as Nan Peters's. Where do old ladies get their clothes? Lucy wondered. Where are all the shops that sell comfortable trousers with elasticated waistlines in a hundred shades of beige?

'Lucy! Coo-ee! Lucy! Look, everyone, it's Betty's girl. Lucy? Am I right? You must be Lucy!'

Lucy resisted the urge to say well no other fool is going to be coming to the back of beyond in the middle of a working week, are they? But she didn't, because Lucy is always well mannered.

This was obviously Barbara. She had reading glasses hanging on a chain perched atop a matronly bosom – a

singular shelf of chest. She sported a 'comfy-fit' shoe.
She had a perm in that style favoured by the over-
seventies. But she was homely and comforting and Lucy,
feeling as raw and befuddled as she was, had the urge to
lay her head against that pillowy chest and have her hair
stroked.

Barbara did not look as Lucy had expected a member
of a society devoted to 'Anomalous Phenomena' to look.
But then, a quick glance round the room told her, nor
did the others.

Lucy was invited to sit at a circle of chairs whilst
Barbara fetched a cup of the tea being served through
the serving hatch from a dyspeptic-looking urn.

'Sugar?' Barbara offered. In Yorkshire there is always
the assumption that tea comes with milk. No good
asking for green tea – that sort of thing is blamed on the
scale in the kettle and not considered a healthy alternative. A cup and saucer were shoved in Lucy's hand,
with a shortcake biscuit and a custard cream balanced
on the saucer.

'Your grandmother's told me all about you and
there's nothing to worry about. You're amongst friends
here. You say as much or as little as you want and you
take your time doing it.'

Barbara rattled on cheerily as Lucy stole sly glances
at her fellow associates of the Swedish Spiritual
Alliance. They looked strangely normal. Average. So
ordinary that she felt she had stumbled into a staffroom
of teachers and that at any minute she would hear some
complaint about the prefects being unable to keep the
corridors quiet during assembly.

There was, she was relieved to see, no trace of tie-
dye, but there was plenty of man-made fibre. They

looked more like craft-fair goers than the village's answer to *Most Haunted*. No one appeared outwardly mad and a cross-section of the north Yorkshire community was represented by the sort of men and women who looked like they went to garden centres, rambled and shopped at British Home Stores.

Barbara was giving Lucy a potted history of the society but Lucy was so busy sizing up the other group members that she took in very little. She gathered it was founded by villagers who wished to explore things seen and experienced that common sense couldn't explain. There was something about famous witches and ghosts in the area and mention of an affiliation to a university via the patronage of a local gentleman who was once a famous playwright.

Lucy wasn't listening. Lucy was being taken over by a vain, creeping smugness because she was possibly the youngest woman present and certainly the most attractive. It was an inappropriate thought but something she tended to do in any social circumstance, rating herself against every other female in the room. She was never going to be top when Jojo was present and usually totally ignored when Nigel (honorary girl) was around. So this was an unusual and happy experience for Lucy Diamond.

There was a woman with untidy hair talking loudly about childcare issues who could well have been younger but didn't look it, worn down as she evidently was by lack of sleep and me-time. There were more retired women who obviously all went to the same hairdresser, and a sprinkling of men who were most definitely not on *Cosmo*'s 100 Most Eligible Bachelors list.

There was a lot of fleece. Zip-ups, pull-ons, every shade of green and blue. Lucy wondered what the collective term for a group of fleece-wearers might be – a flock? of A tog perhaps? Barbara interrupted Lucy's wandering thoughts by handing round more biscuits.

There were a couple of cloth-capped pensioners and a chap in rambling boots sporting a bum-bag. At least Lucy's worst fears were not being realised. She didn't have the feeling that she was going to be sucked into a brainwashing cult or that the evening was likely to degenerate into an orgy of swinging free love around a pagan bonfire – though that was sure to be happening wherever Jasmine was this Hallowe'en.

Barbara was just taking a seat next to Lucy when a moody-looking teenager clumped into the room pulling iPod headphones from his ears, swaying uneasily in his platform New Rock boots – all buckles, black leather and straps. He was the nearest thing that the Yorkshire Dales had to Marilyn Manson. A rebellious teen he might have been, but he was still very normal in his uniform of long black leather coat and black lipstick.

'Don't mind him, pet.' Barbara had mistaken Lucy's look of amusement for one of concern. Lucy guessed that his look might unsettle the fleece-wearing folk of Barrockby, but not a Walthamstow veteran. As if to prove a point, Barbara yelled across the room, 'You all right Malcolm?' The youth nodded a reply. 'How's your mam?'

He grunted something.

'Good,' said Barbara, giving him a thumbs-up and talking to Lucy from the side of her mouth like a ventriloquist. 'He's harmless. Lies around in the grave-yard in all weathers, he does. Bit off-putting at first, but you get used to him. Comes to every meeting, mind. Not that he has any, you know . . . skills.' She mouthed the word as though it was slightly dirty, as if they were talking hysterectomies and other 'downstairs' problems.

Suddenly, a woman with a short practical hair-do – the sort that people say proudly 'I can just wash and leave', as if that's a good thing – stood and cleared her throat, clattering a spoon on the side of her cup. A respectful hush descended and people moved silently to the seats, balancing cups and saucers on their knees.

'Welcome, everyone.' Her voice stood out clear and accentless in direct contrast to the broad Yorkshire tones of the other assembled members. Her confident delivery implied that she was chairing the evening's events.

'Welcome to all our regulars' – she looked around and people nodded in return – 'and to a new special guest.' Lucy looked round to see who it was and realised that everyone was looking at her. The urn made death rattles from the back of the hall.

Lucy waved her hand and said 'hello' in a way that made her look like the village idiot's less clever friend. The chairwoman continued.

'Once we've introduced ourselves to Lucy we will forge ahead with the agenda for this evening. I'll begin. I'm Marjorie and I'm a clairvoyant, the first ever lady chair of the society and official archivist.'

The next person to speak was Rambler with Bumbag. 'I'm Derek and I'm interested in UFO sightings reported on the moor.' And so it went on. One by one names were reeled off, gifts or specialist interests revealed and seats of office presented.

Lucy kept smiling (in fact, her cheeks were hurting

with the effort of it) and nodding but she was lost already. There were two Dereks – or had she misheard? – and he was Eric and which one had said he was the treasurer? Malcolm had introduced himself as the self-named Raven and this had been accompanied by a rueful smile from the chairwoman and an audible snigger from the rambler.

Malcolm's flushed, embarrassed cheeks caused Lucy to swell with maternal protectiveness. He said that he wanted to train in magic and Lucy felt sure by the way he said it that he would have spelt it m.a.g.y.k.

Amongst the 'gifted' present was a pensioner who had filled exercise book after book with automatic writing, alternating in form from childish scribble to elaborate calligraphy. 'I only use a biro,' he exclaimed with pride.

There were people who owned haunted houses or had photographed mysterious orbs of light. People who were there because grandfathers and great-grandfathers had been members before them. People who came from other counties, travelling for hours, just to attend this meeting once every three months. There was an astrologer and an old lady who claimed to have spoken via séance to fifties film star Diana Dors, her own 'dear departed' mother and Elvis Presley. There was a ripple of applause for this revelation even though it was news only to Lucy.

Then there was silence, as all eyes were on Lucy. Everyone was looking at her expectantly.

'Go on, pet. Ask me what he said. We're talking about the King here. Don't be shy.'

Lucy looked around and people nodded encouragingly.

'Umm . . . er . . . What did he say?'

'Said Priscilla was the love of his life,' and she sat back, folding her arms against her chest.

'Oh!' said Lucy, trying to inject the right amount of shock, surprise and any other expected emotion into her response.

Now it was Lucy's turn and her mouth was dry and her palms were cold and clammy. She could stand at a PowerPoint with the board of directors and utter inane blabber about stakeholder relations, but this was different.

'I hear voices.' No matter how many times she said it it still sounded wrong, and even here there was uneasy shifting in chairs and people looking at each other with round eyes. 'And I am visited by two spirits.' The group were back with her now. There was an audible gasp of admiration.

'And I realise I always have been visited by The Dead, the' – she stole Elvis's friend's word – 'the departed.' She was finding her feet now. It felt good to say it. 'And I can sense things. You know how a room feels – good or bad. I used to just think it was just my imagination.'

People were leaning forward in their seats, nodding in encouragement and agreement. They were interested, not freaked out, not pressuring her to perform, and she felt so at ease and comfortable that more and more spilled out, about Nan Peters's revelations, about Jasmine, about Tobias Godough and her other imaginary friends, about her falling out with Jonathan.

She was crying now and it all became a little embarrassing. It was a relief being able to unburden herself to people who really understood, who were like her, who were not mad. People for whom the supernatural was commonplace. People who wore fleeces. It was what she needed, what she'd been waiting for, and it came as a terrible release.

The members of the Barrockby and District Society for the Academic Study of Anomalous Phenomena were round her now, handing over more tea, sympathy and tissues, holding her hand and saying stuff like 'It's hard at first' and 'You'll get used to it' and 'It's a gift – really it is.' And they did not sound like platitudes because they were born out of experience.

'What have we got here? A newbie?'

'Oh, you made it, Simon!' Marjorie the chairwoman sounded, well, frankly a little flirty.

In the midst of Lucy's breakdown, the last member of the group had arrived and Lucy was more than a bit miffed that he seemed to be stealing all the attention. Even Raven/Malcolm, who had murmured an encouraging 'That's bum that is' (which was apparently a positive thing to say) to Lucy's confession, visibly cheered up in the presence of the late arrival and was now staring at him with a gaze of blatant hero worship.

'Sorry I'm late, everyone.' Simon raised a hand to the assembled members. No one seemed to mind. 'Hey there, Newbie. All right?' He offered Lucy a geek-speak greeting and slapped her on the back, blokey-matey style, causing her to splutter her tea slightly. Lucy nodded back self-consciously, aware of her puffy eyes and swollen nose. She was not a good-looking crier.

'Simon – we were just doing some introductions.' Marjorie played coquettishly with her long string of pearls. 'This is Lucy Diamond. Lucy Michelle Eleanor Jude Rita Diamond to be exact. Her grandmother is a friend of Barbara's.' Barbara looked self-important.

'She's developed medium powers and is finding it all a bit much. I'm sure you can relate to that. Is there anything you want to say? Perhaps you can tell her a bit about yourself?'

Lucy was genuinely surprised. Completely befuddled. Simon the Latecomer had not responded to her name in any way. Not an eyebrow had flickered. No smart-alec 'in the sky with' remark. Neither a smile nor a look of disbelief played at the corner of his mouth. She realised with a shock that she had actually grown used to the attention her name demanded and she was cross with him for not giving it.

The group were settling back down in their seats. In soft antipodean tones that Lucy would later learn were Kiwi, Simon introduced himself. He talked about being struck by lightning whilst out on a rock-climbing holiday in the Dales and thereafter being able to change the times of clocks, bend spoons and wreck mobile phones. Derek the Rambler moved his mobile phone from one pocket to the one furthest away.

Since then, Simon had remained living and working locally, unable to fly home until he ceased to be a magnetic anomaly. The group seemed familiar with Simon's story but were all listening attentively, and he promised to give Lucy a bending demonstration with the teaspoons if they had time later.

He wore the kind of clothes that grunge forgot. Faded jeans, a flannel check shirt over a slogan T-shirt and boots that could easily have seen time in Iraq before he bought them. His dress sense would have made Nigel scream in terror but he had the sort of outdoorsy, healthy, easy good looks that would have had Nigel curling up on his lap and purring. His fair hair was long enough to curl at the collar but short enough to stop him being full-on Kurt Cobain. He wasn't groomed enough to be Lucy's type. Too hippy. Too much like someone Jasmine would palm off on her. But even so . . .

Lucy realised she was staring, but looking round she saw that she wasn't the only one. It wasn't just Marjorie who'd gone all of a twitter: even mumsy-woman (she read auras but had become less capable because she was so tired and couldn't find the child care) was fluffing up her hair. Raven/Malcolm looked on with adoration.

As Simon talked, he sat in the chair leaning back and rocking, relaxed, more than a little cocky, one arm slung over the back. His legs were bracing the rocking motion of the chair. The muscles on his thighs were straining through the denim . . .

'Lucy . . .' Simon was still speaking to her. She shook herself back to consciousness and felt guilty because she'd been leering. 'It looks like you are kind of lumbered with it. So crying ain't gonna change it.' Leering *and* unattractively weepy. 'Better get used to it. Find a way to make it work for you.' Simon leaned forward and slapped her on the arm as a show of compassion. It rattled Lucy's teeth. He winked and all the ladies present heaved a collective sigh.

Yes – he was definitely too ungroomed and lacking in urban sophistication for Lucy's taste, but he could carry a faded pair of jeans, she'd grant him that.

Marjorie decided the time was right to address the agenda for the evening and between items – cake sale fundraisers, Derek's latest Lights on the Moors photographs – Lucy found herself stealing sidelong looks at the latecomer. Why? Because he was the only man of shagable age? Because she was wondering if he was gay or not because his check shirt was a little Village People? And why was she wondering whether Nigel would fancy him? Was she really unconsciously comparing every man to her gay best friend? Her gaydar wasn't shifting so did that mean Simon was straight? Her track record on predicting these things was not good. Straight or gay – did this make him more or less attractive to her? She didn't usually go for the sort of men who looked like they might enjoy camping – not the Nigel way – or was she just trying to pick faults? Maybe Nan Peters was right after all.

'He was dogging,' Simon whispered in her ear.

'I beg your pardon?' Lucy was always trying to cover up for her wandering mind.

'Dogging,' he repeated. 'The UFOs are a cover-up for his real hobby.'

Lucy sniggered a little. It was just the sort of irreverent thing that Nigel would say. It was a good release of tension and he flashed her a smile, the sort that should have been in a toothpaste-with-added-whitener ad. For a second, every gene in her body screamed to reproduce with him. Why? Lucy screamed back. Why? He's not my type. She focused very intently as Marjorie introduced the next item on the agenda.

For the next hour, Lucy was talked through evidence gathered from a poltergeist-infected house and horoscopes for the following three months. There was barely a mention of the significance of the date. Marjorie finished off the agenda with the discovery in the archive that fairy activity was reported on the moor during the late 1880s. Lucy whispered back to Simon, 'There's still plenty of fairy activity on Hampstead Heath.'

He snorted and she basked in the thrill of making him laugh. The proceedings were interrupted by the insistent steaming of the urn. Several pensioners filed out to stand under the canopied porch and cigarette smoke drifted back into the room.

Simon had spotted Lucy's squirming agitation in response to the pungent smell.

'Smoker?'

'No,' she lied. It fell out very easily as she sensed his disapproval, but then the art of guilt taught so well by the nuns at Our Lady and St Margaret of Cortona's caused her to downgrade the Big Fat Lie to a Fib.

'Well, ex-smoker.' Lucy felt the neon finger pointing from the heavens and a booming voice shouting *Liar!* 'I'm trying to give up,' she amended.

'Good girl!' Simon elbowed her. It was nice that he was so physical in his expression but boy – it hurt. She would be black and blue tomorrow. Little did she know what an accurate prediction that would turn out to be.

'How long?'

'How long what?'

'How long have you given up?'

'Oh . . . em . . . six weeks.' Oh, the guilt! Submarine alarms seemed to go off all around her. 'Three – I lapsed,' and Lucy pushed the Marlboro Lights further down into her pocket.

Marjorie cleared her throat again.

'After the break there will be a practical demonstration. Mrs Gamble' – it was the Elvis séance lady – 'has kindly brought in a genuine Ouija board dated from around the time of the Society's founding that belonged to her late mother. Anyone who wishes to stay and participate is welcome.'

Mumsy-woman was already donning a pastel-coloured storm jacket and muttering about babysitters. Barbara very loudly reminded Raven/Malcolm that since he had school tomorrow his mum had asked him to get along home as soon as possible. He scowled in reply, asked Simon if he'd be staying, found he was and was in the corner on his mobile phone negotiating extra time at the club to be near his hero a bit longer in exchange for household chores.

'Will you be staying?' Barbara handed over more tea, although Lucy's bladder was full to bursting.

'I'm afraid not. The last bus . . .'

'Simon! Simon!' Barbara's shrill voice echoed over the hall to where Simon was queuing at the hatch. 'You can give Lucy a lift home after we've dabbled with the wee-gee, can't you?' Barbara made it sound like they were testing a new window-cleaning device.

'No worries!' He waved in response to Barbara. 'I mean, she ain't pretty and she's a bit past her sell-buy date, and she does look on the verge of a breakdown, but I'll do it.'

The whole hall hushed into aghast silence and Lucy's face boiled in embarrassment.

'Oh no!' Simon realised his mistake. 'I'm talking about the car! The car ain't pretty. I meant the car. Gee, Lucy – no – I was talking about the car!'

There was very British relieved laughter all round and Simon brought additional custard creams over as a peace offering to Lucy who dodged him by escaping to the loo where she ruffled her hair up in the spotted, cracked mirror and rifled through fluff and shredded tissue in her pockets, looking for a lipstick to apply. Finding nothing but her shameful pack of ten and loose change she resorted to biting her lips and pinching her cheeks – a top beauty tip gleaned from BBC period dramas. Feeling a little more appealing she swung open the fire door and ran directly into Simon. Stuff scattered everywhere. They both swooped to pick up fallen items.

'I thought you'd given up.' Simon handed her the pack of ten that had fallen from her pocket.

'I keep them to test my resolve.' She blushed with the lie. 'Your phone.' She passed it over a little quizzically, wondering why it hadn't melted because of his electromagnetic powers.

'Oh yeah. Old habits. I keep it in the hope that it will magically work again and I'll be normal. Know what I mean?'

'I know exactly what you mean.'

'Places, everyone!' Marjorie's voice sing-songed out and Lucy scuttled over to the group. 'Oh, you're staying! I am pleased. It should be fun, and who knows? Our collective energies on this very special, most spiritual of nights may help us to break through the block to your spiritual friend Jonathan!'

The circle of chairs had been replaced by a folding card table with the baize beginning to lift – a relic of cribbage classes – and half a dozen chairs arranged around it. Lights were being flicked off until only the glow from the kitchen hatch remained. Other members had already drifted off and now there was only Marjorie, Derek the bum-bag-wearing rambler, Raven/Malcolm, Simon, Lucy, the well-upholstered Barbara and Mrs Gamble – owner of the board and hostess of séances to the stars of yesteryear. Derek was setting an outdated video camera on to its tripod. He was recording the event for the society's archive.

A more unlikely-looking bunch to be contacting the spirit realm you could not meet. Lucy had expected robed white witches like her mother's wannabe friends or a temple complete with pentagrams and crystals. Where their normality had been refreshing, comforting even, now their lack of ritual unsettled her.

Lucy suddenly had her doubts about the séance but her logical inner voice worked hard to dispel them. She suddenly remembered the dire warnings of the nuns to not meddle with things you don't fully understand, but she pushed the thoughts away. She could hear Jasmine's voice intoning about All Hallow's Eve when the realms of The Living and Dead moved closer together but, as daughters do, she dismissed her mother's words as rubbish. I am in the hands of experts, she told herself; they know what they are doing.

A bit of Gothic writing and olde-worldey dates like 1864 and we are all fooled into thinking people are experts. After all, the card said they were 'established'. It stated that they were 'associates'. They had international connections – and the Swedes are a sensible bunch, aren't they? They gave us IKEA and ABBA and they look after their old people better than Britain does. So they wouldn't associate themselves with any fly-by-night organisation, would they?

If advice could have been given right there and then, then Lucy could have been told Don't Do It. Listen to your instincts. Go home, get the last bus. Give Simon your number if you must, but make some excuse. Say your grandmother needs you. Say you're tired. Say anything, but go home.

After all, who are these people in this draughty

village hall? What are their credentials? Are they professors of parapsychology? No.

They are nothing more than enthusiastic amateurs, purveyors of fine words and keen interest. The bored, the lonely and the curious. So some claim they can see mystical lights – well, so can hippies on acid. One says she can read halos of colour emanating from people – everyone's seen that on the Ready Brek advert. What is their Health and Safety policy here? What are their precautions? Where's the priest with his chalice of holy water and his rosary? Where's the Inuit shaman to step in on this spiritual journey if it takes an unanticipated path?

But Lucy Diamond is quite liking her place of importance as the first new medium to join the Barrockby and District Society for the Academic Study of Anomalous Phenomena since 1944 and she is wanting to impress a man whom – whether she wants to admit it or not – she finds attractive. That's her vanity for you again.

And she likes the idea that they will help her to talk to Jonathan again. She wants it to be right between them. She doesn't like the idea of him being alone, drifting between worlds with the faint hope that he might run into Keith Richards, prey to the wraiths and all their misery. But, Lucy is ashamed to say, she can't remember all the words and incantations that Keith told them on that night. The spells of protection and healing that guard the channels from this world to the next. Mrs Gamble, owner of the Ouija board, is sure to know them well with all her years of experience. Marjorie must have seen them written down in her archives of material. Barbara wouldn't get involved with it if they didn't know what they were doing, Lucy convinces herself.

So Lucy feels justified in taking her seat at the table. She realises that she has thought more about Jonathan since *that night* than about Tony Russell. Though she is lacking courage, she wants to help her spirit friend. She is sorry for things she has said. She doesn't want him to come to any harm. She wants to ease her conscience.

Don't do it, Lucy, it's not too late. Run for the bus. Go home to Nan Peters and text Nigel on the way about the hunky lumberjack-lookalike. Or ring Jojo and ask her how she is, because right now she's staring at a calendar *and* her diary and feeling very unsettled.

Too late. Lucy has settled between Barbara and Simon. She's ignoring her niggling sense of doubt. She's thinking of the positive – talking spirits that everyone can hear, not just her. She's refusing the proffered biscuits and Mrs Gamble is drawing a box from a carrier bag. A battered black velour paper-covered box, held together with yellowed, brittle tape. Could this really be the portal to the other side? A means for concentrating living energy in order to contact The Dead?

Mrs Gamble has something to say now. She's leaning forward to Lucy, her mouth set, weighty with the importance of what she must impart. What wisdom of the ancients is Lucy about to learn? What mystical rituals will be passed over to her as the heir to this society's medium crown? What traditions of All Hallow's Eve will she share? Will she tell Lucy those all-important, mystical, protective, so-sacred words? Her lips are at Lucy's ear now, her hand on Lucy's own in a grip of sincerity. Lucy's head is spinning, dizzy with the possibilities, her mind open to receive . . . anything.

Absolutely anything. She's ready for this now. Lucy wants to learn. She recognises that, though she may have natural skills for connecting to the other world, compared to this woman's lifetime of work she is just a novice, an apprentice.

Mrs Gamble's words come out as a hoarse whisper as she leans over the semi-opened Ouija board. Lucy holds her breath in anticipation and is both relieved and disappointed with what Mrs Gamble has to say.

'Call me Pearl, love, and if you're not eating that Garibaldi do you mind if I have it? I only 'ad a sandwich for me tea and I'm famished.'

13

Innocent-looking things, Ouija boards. At first glance you would not think that they are devices for contacting other realms, portals to the spirit world, channels for The Dead. Mrs Gamble's board with its alphabet of Gothic lettering laid out over gilt numbers and the simple words yes, no and goodbye looks – at a distance – more like a teaching tool or a spelling quiz.

And the little scene here – chairs arranged around a card table in the unlikely setting of the Barrockby village hall – looks as if a pack of cards are about to be dealt, or a dice shaken until a winner gets to shout 'Rummikub' or 'Ergo' or some other eighties board game victory cry.

But look again and you will see that this board is more elaborate than most. Some Ouijas are home-made; girls at sleepovers, daring each other on, despite the folklore of teens sent mad or to their deaths, dabble with bits of paper on the bedroom floor. Some are mass produced – there are Ouija drinks trays, place mats or beach towels to be found in the tourist voodoo emporiums of New Orleans.

But this one, this is no kitsch keepsake. This one is centuries old. The gold lettering has not dimmed in the decades it has been kept, boxed, in repose. Wrapped in hand-stitched linen sheets – too good to be on a bed – tucked away in a drawer where curious childish fingers couldn't meddle. So the lettering shimmers still and the inky midnight background is as vivid and deep as any cloudless night sky.

Around its carefully set out alphabet, it is edged with a curling elaborate frame of gold leaf, painstakingly laid down once upon a long, long time ago by someone's deft hand. But even this border is not as it seems.

Each corner is, in fact, either a sun or a moon with a smiling impish face and lips curled slightly with malice. Eyes are cast to the side as if sharing a joke, though by doing so each avoids the gaze of the other. So moon looks to sun in the opposing corner who looks to the left to a twin moon whose gaze seeks fruitlessly, in perpetuum, that of the other sun. From each corner, clouds scud away or towards one heavenly body or the other. The billowy cumulus forms new images, religious symbols – the Christian cross, the Hindu swastika. Pagan green-man faces merge with demonic, ghoulish masks of pain or sexual ecstasy, it is not clear which. Figures tumble over one another, clawed hands grasp, hooded figures arch to and from unknown tortures and passions in a swirling, giddying mass.

It is beautiful and terrifying in equal measure. The more she looked the more Lucy Diamond saw, as if the board itself was choosing to reveal its hidden layers bit by bit. Lucy was uneasy. The disturbing images hidden within the innocent-seeming clouds had caused the hairs to rise on her arms, although it could just have been the poor draught-proofing of the hall.

'Oh, hell and darnation. Damn it and set fire to it.'

Lucy leapt in her seat, her eyes agog. Were these

Keith Richard's words of power that she had forgotten? Was Mrs Gamble using some ancient occult oath?

'I've only gone and left the glass at 'ome. Me mother always used a particular whisky tumbler and I've gone and left it on the kitchen counter. Well, there's nothing else for it. I haven't got time to fetch it. Nip in the kitchen, Malcolm-love, and see what's in the cupboard over the sink, would you?'

Raven/Malcolm nipped as best he could, see-sawing on his platform heels, and returned with a stout half-pint glass that had wandered in from the White Swan over the road.

'Was there nothing better looking, lad?' Mrs Gamble moaned.

Malcolm looked crestfallen, checking all the time for Simon's reaction. 'Just the little fat glasses that playgroup use for milk.' He spoke knowledgeably, having once been a chubby toddler running around the hall pretending to be Postman Pat.

'Well, this'll have to do, I suppose.' But she didn't sound convinced and Lucy didn't like the feeling that this was an omen that the séance should not proceed. Nobody else seemed bothered, though. Derek was in raptures, leaping this way and that, clicking away like David Bailey with his cumbersome camera and all its unnecessary accessories and testing the sound on his video camera like it was a satellite link.

'One, two. One, two.'

'Can you give me a copy of it when it's done, Derek? Reckon it'll make great viewing.' Simon actually sounded sincere and interested.

Marjorie was simultaneously warbling on about why had she never been shown this wonderful relic before and scribbling on a jotter-pad in her trained-secretary shorthand. The notes would later be typed up and added to the society archive. The others sat riveted to Mrs Gamble's potted version of the rules of Ouija, dos and don'ts and step-by-step instructions, none of which up to now Lucy had given the slightest attention because she was too busy wondering if Simon thought she was attractive despite her very unsmooth hair. Lucy Diamond's wandering train of thought really could be her undoing.

'Now we need to purify the glass,' Mrs Gamble instructed the onlookers, 'to make it pure.' Surely the last part of that instruction was unnecessary? 'Mother used to wash it in the spring on the moor. The one that spouts out of that gargoyle at the top of the churchyard wall. Since foot and mouth, the Ministry haven't let any of us near it. All ticker-taped off in yellow and black it is, with health warnings stuck on the trees. It's an outrage. Don't get me started!'

We didn't, thought Lucy. She was uneasy, and therefore easily irritated.

'Can't we run it under the tap?' Raven/Malcolm suggested helpfully.

'Don't be bloody daft, boy!' Mrs Gamble snapped to what Lucy had thought a reasonable suggestion. Simon made a shrugging 'never mind you tried' gesture to the crestfallen goth and Raven/Malcolm visibly revived with his support.

'Fire is very purifying,' offered Marjorie. 'We could hold it over the flame on the hob.' Everyone nodded in agreement.

'I don't think the gas ring in the kitchen gives out the right message,' said Mrs Gamble doubtfully.

'I've got some matches,' Lucy offered.

'I thought you gave up smoking?' came an amused, inquisitive aside from Simon. 'Another test of your resolve?'

Lucy blushed.

Matches were lit and wafted all over the outside and the up-turned inside, leaving black sooty stains on the glass.

'Oh, look at it!' Mrs Gamble wailed. 'That's no good, is it? Who'd bother coming from the other side if that was your welcome?'

'I've got a bottle of Elvic water.' Raven/Malcolm had become almost chatty since a bit of practical 'magyk' was in the offing. He produced a sports-capped bottle of filtered mountain water from his cavernous pockets.

'It'll do, I suppose.' Gratitude was not Mrs Gamble's strong point. The glass was doused thoroughly in Elvic over the institution stainless steel sink and carefully dried with a tea towel bearing Blackpool Tower and a calendar from 1978.

Once everyone was seated, Mrs Gamble rubbed her arthritic hands together. 'So are we all ready then? Anyone got a particular wish for speaking to a dear departed? We need to agree who we're asking for.'

'Elvis.' Derek could barely contain himself and his eyes glittered like a star-struck teenager's.

'No, that's a once in a lifetime event.' She shook her head firmly and pursed her lined lips shut.

'Let Lucy choose,' offered Marjorie. 'She is our guest today, after all.'

'Jonathan. I'd like to speak to him.' The words seem to have shot straight out of her unconscious.

'Right ho! Let's begin.' Mrs Gamble grasped the

hands of those nearest to her. Lucy slipped one hand into Barbara's poorly circulated grasp and the other into Simon's strong paw and the circle continued. Raven/Malcolm, looking a bit foolish, was wedged between Simon and Derek. None of them looked comfortable holding hands with one another.

Lucy's mind was still meandering. In Lucy Diamond's head, chains of thought that began with the political situation in the Middle East could end via a convoluted path at the subject of baby food. She was thinking now about the feeling of Simon's fingers, the slightly work-roughened calloused palms, and wondering what he did for work. She imagined him to be something outdoorsy, maybe a farmer delivering lambs by torchlight, and then she started to wonder if farmers all had electric light in their barns these days and if so, did they run cables underground? Or did they have generators? And could they use wind power? She had to force her mind back to the words being spoken at the table.

Mrs Gamble was intoning a simple prayer to an unspecified deity and all present were asked to imagine the table shielded in an arc of white light. She spoke of its being a special night. Of Hallowe'en being a time when the worlds of The Living and The Dead move a little closer, but of the need for vigilance. She warned of the need for protection and how focused minds and pure hearts were all that were needed to keep malevolent spirits away.

Lucy's attention snapped back and she felt a sudden chill as she recalled Keith's warnings about wraiths slipping into The Living world. She stole glances at the others, who sat fully concentrating on Mrs Gamble's words, and then felt comforted as, following instructions, they each placed hands confidently over her own on the glass in the centre of the board. Lucy, following Mrs Gamble's lead, closed her eyes and they were off.

'Is there anybody there?' Mrs Gamble's reedy voice whistled through her false teeth. Nothing. The glass did not move. Nothing stirred in the hall; even the draught had given up.

'Jonathan Rayburn, are you there?'

Nothing.

'You ask,' Mrs Gamble instructed Lucy. 'You're his spiritual channel, after all.'

'Jonathan?' Lucy sounded hesitant and not a bit like somebody who held a certificate in assertiveness from Mind Games seminars. Still nothing.

Lucy had felt sure that Jonathan would be chomping at the bit to come through, ready to beg forgiveness. Maybe he'd really taken to heart what she'd said. Didn't he realise that she could only ever be mad for short periods of time?

'We haven't talked for a while.' Lucy offered her excuses. 'We fell out, remember?'

'You don't want to go round upsetting spirits,' Mrs Gamble said ominously.

'I didn't mean to. He upset me first.' Lucy was aware that she sounded childish. 'Shall I ask for his friend? He's more experienced than Jonathan. He may find it easier to get through.' Mrs Gamble nodded to indicate that Lucy could proceed.

'Keith – Keith Richards. Are you there?'

'I didn't think he was dead—' Simon began.

'Sssshhh!' Derek, Raven/Malcolm, Marjorie, Barbara

and Mrs Gamble all hissed as with slow and faltering steps the glass began to move. Lucy could barely breathe. The glass began to move slowly but then stopped abruptly as though a heavy hand had placed itself over the top of theirs to prevent its passage.

'Ask again.' Mrs Gamble nudged Lucy and she did. She was sure she saw Marjorie nudge Derek and cast him a look. The kind of look that said, 'Look at that berk acting like she's some sort of paranormal anomaly.' She didn't need others doubting her. She was doubting herself.

Don't waver, Lucy. Not at this point. You chose to stay, remember. You have to see it through now. Don't let a single negative thought pop into your head. Remember the rules of Ouija as told by Mrs Gamble. Remember Keith Richards's warnings – 'not a trace of negativity' he said. Remember? Like attracts like. Negative attracts negative. But you weren't listening, were you? You were too busy thinking about your flyaway hair or something. In a situation as grave as this, your hair was your priority. Is it any wonder that some men think women shouldn't fly planes?

Lucy didn't want these people to see her as a fraud. She wanted them to think well of her. Dammit, she wanted Simon to think well of her. She wanted to show off her power. She wanted them to ooh and aah and even be a little bit afraid. Was this her vanity again? Where did Lucy's arrogant pride come from? Haven't we been told since nursery that such things come before a fall? Didn't Hans Solo warn Luke Skywalker not to get cocky?

'Keith Richards, are you there?' Lucy asked firmly and this time the glass moved smoothly to Yes and everyone opened their eyes, exhaled and smiled at each other with a here-we-go sort of bonhomie.

'Remember, ask him only simple questions. We don't want to tire him,' Mrs Gamble reminded her.

Lucy cleared her throat but her voice wavered. 'How are you?' It was the only thing she could think of to say. Manners are a terrible affliction in certain circumstances and though nobody said anything she knew it was a lame question, but she couldn't just jump in with a 'tell me the meaning of life' query. But the glass obliged, moving first to O and then to K, and there was even a chuckle around the table. Lucy warmed through and she asked, in what she hoped would pass as a casual and nonchalant voice, 'How is Jonathan? Still mad at me?'

Mrs Gamble hissed, 'One question at a time or you'll confuse the spirit.'

But the glass was playing ball – if such a thing is possible. OK, it answered, then swung across the board to Yes. Had she been alone Lucy would have said Why? Why is he still mad at me? It was him that started it. And then she would have given Keith a whole slew of angry messages to relay back to Jonathan Rayburn.

This was not good. This dark shadow falling across what was essentially the goodness of Lucy. There only needs to be a chink in the curtain to let in the night. The rules, Lucy, remember the rules. But you weren't listening, were you? You weren't listening to Keith that night and now, in the presence of a man you deny you find attractive but so obviously do, you weren't listening to Mrs Gamble either. Not at all.

'Will you help us tonight?'

Yes, came the immediate response. Lucy began to

frame her next question, but Derek butted in before she could ask it.

'What year did you die?' Derek closed his eyes, trance-like, before he pinned his attention to the passage of the up-turned glass again.

'Is that relevant?' Lucy asked, a little annoyed at Derek's interruption. The reply was already being pointed out on the numbers: 1 9 8 8.

Lucy nodded. She was not entirely sure, but the date seemed appropriate given the dodgy outfit Keith wore. Later, she would realise that this should have been taken as the first clue that all was not well. Did not Keith himself tell her he had only been dead three years? Was Lucy not even listening at that point?

'How did you die?' Derek asked.

'What happened to the simple questions?' Lucy asked irritably.

B-A-D-L-Y, came the response, which could be open to interpretation. Mrs Gamble interjected now. She sounded concerned.

'Ask him a question so we know it's him. Remember – bad spirits can slip in disguised as others *and* they can read minds.'

Lucy lifted her chin. 'What does Jonathan wear?' The words came out as a challenge. She was trying to think of something, anything other than the sophisticated trench in which he regularly appeared.

The glass trembled a little before moving, as though switching on the sat-nav of its course. H-A-T.

Lucy froze. 'That's not right.' She was turning from side to side. 'He never wears a hat. He's never even mentioned a hat.'

'Perhaps he's wearing one today?' Derek offered.

'Why would a spirit wear a hat one day and not another? Don't they always wear what they passed over in or their burial shroud or something? They can't change their clothes like us, can they?' Lucy was looking wildly around the group, looking for help, but her questions were never answered.

Suddenly, the ground seemed to shake, slowly at first, accompanied by a rushing sound that began as a low indigestible rumble and then became a thundering roar like a straight-through Underground train. The dust of years was blown from far corners and unreachable coving and whirled up into a tornado-style dust devil that spun across the room. The gentle draught in the hall became a wind that whipped around them. It could have come straight from the great plains of America and Lucy could almost hear Nigel's Friend of Judy stock response to any unnerving situation about no longer being in Kansas.

Every door in the hall blew open and slammed closed simultaneously with an ominous bang. Locks clicked shut. Chairs were blown over. In the kitchen, cupboard doors swung open and pale green institution crockery emptied to the floor in a tide, each piece smashing into a thousand shards. Old notices were torn from the wall by the rushing wind and swept around the room. The curtains were ripped from the poles, shredding in the violent wind, and the lights dimmed and flickered on and off.

Lucy had seen this before. Then it had irritated her, although it had also amused her in a way she had not admitted to Jonathan or even to herself until now. But now – now she was terrified. It didn't feel like a Jonathan Rayburn Special Effect. It felt too dark, too big, with its undercurrent of unsettling power. Now, a hollow-stomached, heart-stopping feeling of fear descended on her like an icy blanket.

'Take the glass to Goodbye.' Mrs Gamble's words were quick and efficient. Calming because her tone was brisk and brooked no nonsense. As if she'd seen it all before and this was the way to end this sort of 'malarky', which is precisely the sort of word she would use. 'Take the glass to Goodbye.' This time the words had an edge of panic about them.

'I'm trying, I'm trying,' Marjorie gasped. 'We must all take the glass to Goodbye.' But the glass could not be moved. With straining faces and tensed muscles, with all their will directed to the up-turned glass, they still could not move it.

Instead, the glass chose a different direction. First to the letter H, then A, then H again, then A, becoming with each move more sure of its direction, more forceful, despite the unwilling hands trying to alter its course. H-A-H-A-H-A.

'It's laughing at us,' gasped Marjorie. 'Who is this spirit, Lucy? Who have you called?' Then, out to the room: 'Who are you?' The glass changed course again.

J-O-E – a simple name. Kind-sounding. The name of good friends and benevolent uncles, of approachable rock musicians, men of the people. Surely not a name one would give to someone capable of inciting such fear, of creating the whirlwind that whipped at their hair and faces. But for ever more, for the people assembled around that rickety card table, the name Joe would be on a par with Damien or Chucky.

Above them the lights were flicking with a new madness, on-off, on-off. Lucy knew what would happen next. Sure enough, the pre-war electrics fizzed and crackled their last with small explosions of sparks. The urn, as if it had been waiting for this moment for all of its existence, exploded like a geyser sending hot water splattering up the walls and units of the neat little kitchen. Their only light now was the orange glow of the street lamp. From the floor and shadowy corners, a deeper darkness pooled. An oozing blackness that crept nearer to the little card table like an oil slick. The members of the séance huddled closer together, looking behind them fearfully like frightened gazelles stalked by hyeneas, trying with all their might to move the glass to Goodbye. The glass had different ideas.

B-I-T-C-H – one letter after another it traced its course. D-I-R-T-Y W-H-O-R-E.

'Who is?' asked Barbara, perplexed at this sudden turn of events and outraged at such filthy language in a community founded by Quakers.

'It doesn't matter who is the whore,' yelled Mrs Gamble. 'We've got an uninvited bad 'un in the room and we've gotta get it out! Don't let go of that glass, hold on to it with everything you've got in you.'

The evening was not going as planned. It was not a game any more; no longer just a hobby to while away unfilled hours. Not a subject to observe and catalogue and analyse. This was not a spirit to bring to the dinner party to amuse one's guests. This was no Hallowe'en party game to make you shriek. Nor was this trickery, sleight-of-hand entertainment to fool the ready believers. The séance now had all the features required to become a cautionary tale. Don't go dabbling in the afterlife, children, look what happened to your great-aunt Lucy – and she was one who could talk to the spirits – she was never the same again!

Raven/Malcolm made a sudden little whimpering sound.

'Oh, the boy.' Barbara's face was an agony of fear. 'He's just a boy. Don't let anything happen to him. Not the young 'uns,' and she started reciting long unpractised prayers in a barely audible whisper, invoking merciful gods and unheard of saints, pledging herself with a long and fruitful life behind her in sacrifice for the sparing of youth. An old-school willingness to give for the sake of others, so rare in these selfish times. It did not go unnoticed or ever forgotten by those cramped around the little table.

'Keep on, Raven, you can do it, mate. We need you. Hold on, mate.' Simon's words were snatched away by the wind. The boy had paled even under his heavy goth make-up but that word from Simon – mate – the acknowledgement that he wasn't just a kid, a son, someone's lad, but a mate, a peer, an equal, lifted him anew. It is only in being given responsibility that people have the chance to rise to it. Raven breathed deeply and fixed his eyes on the glass with renewed concentration. It didn't make any difference – the glass didn't stray from its set course – but he was giving it all he had.

From letter to letter the glass sped, spelling out with precision every imaginable insult, swear word or profanity. The pressure on the glass scored the delicate paper of the board, driving welts into the cardboard and smearing the gilt of the lettering so that soon the alphabet became indecipherable.

The first blow felt like a fist and it hit Lucy square in the stomach. It was unexpected and its force was unlike anything she had ever experienced. She was winded, trying desperately to get air into her lungs as though trapped under water. The second blow came to her back, as though her adversary had circled her as a predator might, seeking weak, unprotected points. She could only imagine that it was what a kick to the kidneys might feel like from a six-foot skinhead in Dr Marten boots. She slumped forward on to the card table, almost upending it. Her hand would have slipped from the glass had Simon not grasped it harder, keeping her smooth, limp fingers trapped under his own roughened ones. She struggled to breathe.

As Lucy at last gasped in air, a stench filled her nose, strong and stale, like teeth long uncleaned. It was a smell you could taste. Then blows seemed to rain down on her chest, her face, her arms, and the force pushed her this way and that like a boneless rag doll whilst the others struggled to keep her hand firmly in place. Fingers were pulling her flesh, poking, gouging and scratching. The others at the table could only watch in alarm as purple bruises began to swell and spread across her cheeks. Scratches and welts smarted and bled.

In the haze of her semi-consciousness she saw every-thing happening around her as though on fast-forward, with sound garbled and muffled. She could hear Simon yelling instructions and felt his arm clasp her back, protective and strong, but she could not respond, could not communicate. Like watching a TV through someone else's window. Even when she saw the tall, latticed windows of the hall shatter inwards, showering the table with crystal droplets of glass, she could not react. Still the brave members of Barrockby and District Society for the Academic Study of Anomalous Phenomena did not release their hold on the glass.

Lucy felt that she was in a bubble, trapped in a glass snowdome, unable to make contact with the world outside. Figures streaked past her, unknown and malevolent. They moved around at unnatural speed, zigzagging from one side of the room to the other, materialising from the gloom and melting back into the shadows. Everyone was still sitting at the table, hands clamped around the glass, so who were these faces that loomed over her, enjoying her imprisonment? The faces laughed at her in cartoon voices, each accompanied by the same acrid smell that tainted her mouth and burned her eyes. It was like stale sweat and old ashtrays. Like unwashed people and Glastonbury toilets.

One face hung over her now as a figure loomed above her, breathing out its vile vapours of hangover mornings and constipation, but the face and its odour did not seem to match. For a moment, Lucy's brain could not compute what her eyes were seeing because this spirit, this lying, malignant trickster, this apparition of everything that can be wrong in a man, was, well . . . quite beautiful.

Then, suddenly, it made total sense. It was one of the big fat tricks played by nature. The worst of practical jokes. That Which is Beautiful is Also Good. How often are we fooled by a pretty face? We are willing to believe beauty, willing to forgive, make excuses. He/she is so beautiful how can they possibly be mean/cruel/manipulating/murderous? But they are, and eventually the truth will out. It takes time, but one day the badness will inevitably seep through the cracks like pus from a sore staining a bandage. True malevolence always hides best behind a pretty mask because from there it can really do its worst.

A halo of dark curls surrounded the smooth-skinned face like a pin-up gypsy David Essex before he lost his hair. Crystal-blue eyes bored into her own, shining with a mixture of merriment and mirth at her predicament but chilling in their cold detachment, as though devoid of any human feeling. But mesmerising, as must have been Franz Anton Mesmer, the hypnotist magician and source of the word.

Lucy was caught, all right. Lucy was the fish at the end of his line, hooked cruelly for him to do with her as he wished, but with those eyes, those captivating, jewel-like eyes, boring into hers she felt herself giving up willingly.

The eyes were full of promise, full of the cheap words of flattery and soulmate love that women fall for every time, but beside this streams of images flicked like early cinema and Lucy could see the record of his actions. Women used, beaten and abused, laws broken, animals kicked and strangled. But still, inch by inch, she was pulled nearer to him, the very essence of herself leaving the solidity of her body and moving towards the icy depths of those eyes. Lucy was charmed like a Disney-cartoon Mowgli hypnotised by the flickering snake-eyes of Joe's Kaa.

In the distance, as if far away, dimmed voices called her name in panic, Mrs Gamble, Marjorie and Simon commanding her, willing her, to come back. They could not see her spirit attacker but they could sense her leaving, they could see the life ebbing from her pale body. She arched her back then, as one might when accepting a lover, but the shudder that ran through her was not one of pleasure. He was inside her now. He slipped into her physical being as smoothly as if Lucy had helped him into a new coat.

She spoke now but it was not her voice and her face contorted in ways that were not her own. Profanities tumbled from her lips, and though Lucy was a keen advocate of swearing in socially appropriate situations – in fact felt there was no substitute for the f-word in certain trying circumstances – the words did not come easily or sit prettily at her mouth.

'Dirty bitch, whore. You shall all fucking pay. Fuckin' motherfuckers.' The glass was moving in frantic figures of eight, propelled by a new and powerful force. The others were pulled this way and that, jerking and straining against it.

Then, as quickly as he had entered, he was leaving her and at the same time stripping away the last of Lucy. A body is after all just a body, as a home is just a house without its inhabitants. And inch by inch they could see Lucy peeled from her earthly form. Her body was jerking, twisting, resisting.

'Fight it, Lucy, fight it.' Simon's teeth were gritted with the effort of holding her and clasping the glass.

They say that the quickest way to someone's heart is not through their stomach, whatever surgeons and cooks might say to the contrary, but through fear. Terror. That roller-coaster feeling of death's being imminent kick-starts all those emotions that lead you to bond and therefore procreate. A sort of 'hey we're gonna die so let's have a last shot of life and what could be more life affirming than a little you know what.' After all, is that not what lies behind all those gung-ho films where hero and heroine to fall for each other as the last alien dies or the angry natives are driven back over the hills?

Not that you realise that you're thinking this, of course, but it's there ticking away in the seedy underbelly of your unconscious as adrenaline kicks in. Use it and take your next date white-water rafting.

But at this point sex was the furthest thing from Simon and Lucy's minds. She was thinking *I'm gonna die* and he was thinking *We're all gonna die.* He had thought Lucy was kinda cute but nothing more; a little eccentric with her claims of talking to the deceased, borderline mad even, but certainly no devastating beauty to blow his socks off and distract him from the mission that had led him to this out of the way wacky village society. But as he saw her now, literally fighting for her life, his heart filled with admiration for the little tigress he had not imagined would be beneath her skin. It touched on his inner hero and he just knew that he had to get this girl back. She was too good to simply let go.

'Help her, for God's sake! Somebody help her!' Simon did not know who he was shouting at. This was not a bully he could stop with humour as he had in the school playground. This was not a handbag mugger he could trip in flight like a Have-a-go Hero. For a start he couldn't even take his hand off the glass. It was hampering him somewhat. Then, in the most intelligent act of the evening, he rifled through his memories of Lucy's words and yelled, 'Jonathan Rayburn. Jonathan Rayburn. Jonathan Rayburn.'

He yelled it three times because he remembered the De La Soul recording of the song that said three is the magic number and because he had seen the movie

Beetlejuice and he thought what worked in movieland might just work in Barrockby.

Though Simon later tried to convince Lucy it was all his doing, his commanding manipulation of supernatural forces, Jonathan Rayburn would tell her he had it planned all along and that he was merely amassing his army and waiting for the moment when the malevolent spirit of Joe was at his most distracted carrying off Lucy Diamond's soul. Either way, the assembled members of the Barrockby and District Society for the Academic Study of Anomalous Phenomena were very glad to see them and had Lucy been *compos mentis* then she too would have been impressed by the arrival of the Barrockby Magnificent Seven.

Orbs of light came tumbling into the room from the very walls of the hall itself, spinning and careering until they became nothing but streaks, leaving impressions in the air like bonfire-night sparklers. They moved so quickly that it was difficult to see how many there were. Suddenly and simultaneously, they paused in mid-air as though seeking out a scent and then shot off in hunt. The atmosphere in the room changed palpably. A lightness, not just in terms of dark and shade, could be felt. There was a shift in mood like the that when Indiana Jones arrives to rescue the girl and you know the baddies will lose in the end. Their arrival should have been accompanied by trumpet calls and bugles as they galloped around the room like a spectral cavalry. Seven in total, the lights were bright one minute, watery and of indeterminate colour the next. Each orb was made up of a bubbling mass changing through every colour of the spectrum. They darted this way and that, literally chasing the darkness from the room. Plunging themselves into the darkest corners and splintering the heart of the shadow.

Lucy felt a pull, a force opposing the one trying to strip her from her very being. It was like being on the threshold of two rooms, a foot in the hall and a foot in the lounge, with people pulling you both ways. She thought she was still on the earthly plain with its vivid colour and life but that was only an impression, a sensation like a memory; her vision instead was filled with the grey monochrome of a wasteland. Coaxing, wheedling voices filled her ears – first benign then sharp and spiteful.

'Come on, come on, come with us.' Many voices were hissing, wishing her to make the final step over the threshold. 'We want you. We neeeeed you.'

The effort of resisting was proving too much. It would be so easy to simply give in, to just go where they asked. But something was stopping her. Maybe it was the assertiveness training (best course that she had ever been sent on) because actually she was holding off because she didn't want to go. She didn't want to go into this barren no-man's-land with its heavy cloud-filled grey sky, as dull as any February Sunday. Its landscape was featureless, not a tree nor a bird, just scrubby soil faded to a desolate grey stretching ahead over great flat plains.

But Lucy was used to being polite, going along with things in an effort to keep the peace, and she was so tired. Maybe if she just went for a while . . . As if sensing her slide into weakness, figures appeared, reaching out, digging their cold spiny fingers into her arms. They were repeating her name over and over, faster and faster, like biblical lepers desperate for miracles, their clothes reduced to faded rags, cobweb forms of their earlier selves. Faces were carved and careworn, lines etched deeply, sketching atrocities seen or committed, and Lucy was reminded of post-war photographs of prisoners in Russian gulags with their haunted faces, old before their time.

Standing head and shoulders over them all, colourful, clean and crisp, was Joe. Later, she would learn that he was an energy vampire – sucking from others to fill himself with the fuel for life. His beauty stood out in stark contrast to the dull ugly world around him and Lucy was drawn nearer and nearer to him. He was calling her, beckoning her, promising her safety if only she crossed over to him, and now he was begging her, those eyes pleading with her like those of a romantic film hero. She had always wanted a man to look at her that way, to whisper all those oaths of undying love, to say – as Joe was saying – that he couldn't live without her. Then his beauty faltered. Just for a second, the mask slipped, perhaps weakened by a glitch in the energy flow as he drained it from her, and she saw him, at last, for what he really was.

Old wives' tales and Christina Aguilera talk of beauty being only skin deep and reassure less attractive children that they can be 'beautiful on the inside'. Lucy saw the truth of these statements first-hand. In other worlds, it is what you are that counts, and your deeds – good or bad – are what colour you. Without Lucy's energy Joe had none. His was a deformed, ugly skull, oozing maggots and dead flesh, dropping rotten teeth and diseased skin. In places, his form oozed and bubbled, swollen and bloated. In other areas, it was wasted and withered. His beautiful, smooth hands were really talon-tipped claws, and though he beckoned to her with those same slick, seductive words Lucy was repelled.

The image had only flashed before her for less than a second, but with a jerk of panic Lucy knew where she was. Limbo – or in Keith Richards's terms Limbow. She thought of Jonathan and understood his terror, his panic, at the thought of being left in this place. His dilemma, needing to cross over to his place of light but pinned to the earth by his wish to connect one last time with the love of his life. And all the time this place, these *things*, were waiting to ensnare him if he hesitated or lingered too long. This was not the Limbo invented by bishops to coax baptism money for sickly babies out of the poor but the world between the earthly and higher plains. Nothing more than a corridor, a passing place, a celestial dead-end if you take a wrong turn, a maze from which very few ever return.

Amongst the hoarse, rasping whispers of her name she heard a clear clean voice cutting through the others. It was calm, assured, instructive. Managerial.

'Lucy – follow my voice. This way, come on now.'

Should she be suspicious? Was this another Joe trick? The carrot on the end of the stick he would beat his wife with? But she had to trust. Amongst this colourless, frightening world, the voice vibrated with life and light and goodness. It was familiar, though she couldn't quite pin it down. It wasn't easy to move towards it but the voice was persistent. Lucy fought backwards through the morass of stooped, hunched figures. It was like trying to move through treacle or run on sand with a coastal wind against you, but the voice itself seemed to lend her strength.

'Come on now, Lucy. Keep going. This way. Follow me.'

And then the greyness of Limbo gave way to the Barrockby village hall. Plunged into darkness as it was, it was still more colourful and vibrant than the between world where she had been. Lucy was easing back into herself; gentle hands were coaxing and smoothing her into her physical being. The ghostly voices in her head were driven out by a voice as silky as a young Sean Connery's.

'Lucy, it's OK. You'll be OK now.'

Now she knew the voice, abandoned herself to it. It was Jonathan and now she knew she was safe.

Around the table, they had seen the colour and pulse of life return to Lucy. All around them the wind still raged, but through it they heard a chant, indecipherable, almost monastic, calming and meditative. It was as alien to these Yorkshiremen – and women – as a yoga mantra, as hypnotic as Paul McKenna urging you to lose weight with your unconscious mind. The chant increased in intensity and as it did so the roaring wind in the hall subsided, becoming smaller and smaller until it was centred on the ceiling above the table, herded into a small clump by the magical words. It was a whirling vortex that was sucking upwards, hoovering up the darkness and taking the wind, the noise, the distant screams and the shouted profanities with it.

Around the card table, they clung to the glass and to one another as their hair was pulled upwards into comedy-style wigs. Wall notices and shreds of curtain whipped past them and were sucked into the void. Then everything stopped. The noise, the chaos, the roaring wind. There was stillness. Silence.

And then suddenly, out of an orb, accompanied by an explosion of light, Jonathan appeared, standing behind Marjorie with the light of the other six orbs behind him, a disparate band of old and young. He stood hands on hips, legs astride, a superhero, his trench coat flapping behind him like Batman's cape. A cocky Peter Pan crowing, 'Oh the cleverness of me!' But he was paler, almost transparent, and Lucy knew that to do what he had done had cost him energy, lost him Life Time, reduced any time he might have to connect via Lucy to his beloved Laura. But she beamed at him, would have run to him in an embrace, but could only say, 'I am so glad to see you!'

In answer, he sketched a Yankee-doodle-just-doing-my-duty-ma'am kind of salute and was gone, with his companions, in a flash of magnesium flare. For a few seconds there was quiet and the society members sat unmoving, still braced for the worst, their hands clamped and cramping around the glass. Raven/ Malcolm was the first to move and speak, shaking his free hand so that his fingers snapped together Ali G-style, a broad smile stretching across his face.

'That was wicked!!!'

Lucy snuggled back down under the continental quilt, as Nan Peters called the duvet, and winced as one raw, sore bit or another reminded her why she was still being allowed to lie in at nine o'clock in the morning. She could hear Nan on the phone telling the office that no, Lucy wouldn't be in for the rest of the week and yes, she'd send a doctor's note. Nan Peters's voice did not invite further questions. There'd be no miserable boss complaining about lost time over this one. Nan's instructions were followed by a list of Lucy's injuries recited in salacious detail.

The mobile buzzed with the arrival of another text from Nigel. *Bored. Come back now I need u.* Similar messages had been arriving almost every hour, and beyond the inane response of *back soon xx* Lucy couldn't even begin to explain via text what she'd been through. Nigel would turn it round anyway so that his mini-dramas of late buses and woollens washed at a shrinking sixty degrees would become more traumatic and wounding than her fist fight with a spectral being.

Lucy reached over for the steaming cup of tea on the nightstand and was reminded by twinges in her hip, back and shoulder that this was no idle sickie. She could not stop replaying the previous night's events – with added string section whenever she revisited a scene where Simon reached for her hand or lent a supporting arm.

Despite Derek's urge to blame the Armageddon-style carnage of the village hall on the local youths, they had concocted a story that blamed the devastation on the unpredictable urn which had so spectacularly exploded along with the electrics. Further questions by the parish council were to be avoided by stressing how lucky they all were to be alive and by using the phrase 'we won't be suing . . . yet.'

Not a piece of glass remained in a window. The velvet curtains hung in tatty shreds. Chairs once neatly stacked were scattered all around the room. Simon's chair had twisted and bent beneath him, possibly a by-product of his intense concentration, will and electro-magnetic force. They decided that this would be the chair to claim Lucy had been in when she took the full force of the blast – although the very human-looking scratches to her face made the whole story look less convincing.

Now the members of the Barrockby and District Society for the Academic Study of Anomalous Phenomena were bound together by a terrible secret and Lucy was secretly horrified at how easily these upstanding and respectable members of the community – pillars of the WI, most of them – had created a smokescreen of lies. Marjorie had already made appointments to interview everyone for the archive but stressed that this file would be confidential – accessible by select members of the Barrockby and District committee only. These were Barrockby's own X-files, a Yorkshire Roswell. Sadly, Derek's video camera had been smashed early on in the proceedings, but he was able to leap around the wreckage, taking still photos with his mobile phone on all aspects of the devastation.

'Further evidence,' he had added threateningly to the young locum vicar, totally out of his depth, who had arrived in response to Marjorie's emergency call.

'There's them as are born and them as are made and he were born that way and that's for sure.' That was Nan Peters's assessment of Joe, their uninvited guest for the evening. It seems that he'd been the Village Bad Boy for as long as anyone could remember. Theft, arson, sexual assault, supplying and a whole string of other offences were associated with his name, and many more besides that could not be proved. Animals, children, his wife, his mother – it seems that no one was spared his wicked ways. Nan Peters's recounting of his life made him sound like some wicked villain of a Grimm fairy tale – capable of leaving babes alone in the woods or demanding the cutting out of a rival's heart.

'His own kiddies would hide under the bed when they heard his key in the door and some say they heard his wife begging to die as he was beating her before the bobbies arrived to carry 'im off. And there's them around here still addicted to the drugs that he first sold them. There was none of that in these parts till he bought 'em along. No one grieved for 'im when his car came off the road up on 'moor – even his mother said it were a relief. There'd be no more coppers banging the door looking for him, no more money gone from her purse. Some say it was the drug dealers what did for him – he'd cheated those that wouldn't stand for it. Others say it was the coppers themselves – meting out their own kind of justice when the courts couldn't keep him off the streets. It strikes me that even death couldn't improve him.' And Nan Peters pursed her lips together, shaking her head in disgust and disapproval.

But Jonathan Rayburn and his A(ngel)-team had sent him packing and if that Ouija board was his portal back to this world then Raven had seen to it that he would not be back.

Raven/Malcolm had walked into that hall a boy with all a boy's usual worries about girls (lack of) and AS levels (looming). He left the meeting a man and no one doubted it. He had bravely torn the board into seven pieces and taken them straight up on to the dark, moonlit moor and buried them in a high, windy, lonely spot with a splash of water from the church spring (no Ministry ticker tape was going to thwart him from his mission) and an incantation gleaned from a spell in a computer-generated elfin world – real enough to those who played it. If Joe were ever to return he would be unlikely to upset anyone but a passing sheep with his evil mischief.

Mrs Gamble had gladly handed over the board and told him with uncharacteristic generosity, 'You're the best man for the job.' Even Derek had used the words

'You're a braver man than me' and if it were possible, he had walked out standing even taller and it had nothing to do with his platform boots.

Jonathan had visited briefly once Lucy was home, bathed and in bed. He had, at last, learned about the etiquette of visitation. She had cried with relief when she saw him and then she had cried with worry when she had then realised she could see through him. Right through him. He was like a net curtain version of himself.

'I missed you,' she said through a snotty ball of tissues. 'And you wouldn't come when I asked for you.'

'And you wouldn't let me through when I wanted to come. God! Women!'

'Men! You're all so pig-headed.'

'That Simon chap looks nice, though. Is he pig-headed, I wonder?'

'I don't know what you mean.' Lucy feigned misunderstanding, then softly added, 'Thank you, Jonathan. You risked a lot for me. Limbo, I mean – I know what it must feel like to think that you might be stuck there . . .' Her voice trailed off. 'I promise you as soon as we're back in London, we'll go straight to Laura's. I'm ready for it now.'

He cut her off short. 'Would you help the others first?'

Lucy looked confused.

'The rest of the search and rescue party? They're such good people. They've all fairly recently crossed over, like me, and they're all a bit pissed off about it, frankly. I said you probably would.' He held his hands up in a defensive surrender gesture. 'I know, I know. I shouldn't have. I should have checked with you first.'

Am I really such an ogre to those on the other side? thought Lucy. Clearly Jonathan thought so.

'But I thought if we were successful getting you back – I mean, I know there're lots of them . . .' He was grasping for words.

'I don't mind, Jonathan. I don't mind at all. I'd love to do it. It's the least I could do. How did you – well, what I mean to say is, why did they . . .' She, too, was struggling to find the right thing to say. 'After all, they don't know me.'

Jonathan waved a hand. 'Just call it Community Spirit,' and they chortled together at his awful pun. 'I'll help them come across to you and be on stand-by – just in case.'

'But you're already weak, Jonathan. The wraiths – what if—'

'But these are my friends, and they're good people.'

And suddenly Lucy could see again to the very heart of him with crystal clarity. To his love, his loyalty, promises kept and not broken, his morals and principles, the 'doing unto others'. His faith in Gentlemen's Agreements and Scouts' Honour, and very boldly for Lucy Diamond she smiled and said, 'I could fancy you myself, Jonathan Rayburn.' A pink blush tinted the pale transparency of his cheeks.

'Nah.' He brushed off her compliment. 'I'm not your type. I'd need to grow my hair and wear a lumberjack shirt,' and with that cheeky remark he was off, melting back into the ether.

Just that little reference to Simon and his chequered flannel shirt was enough to make her stomach flip over and she lay back on the pillows, all thoughts of Jonathan and his heroic deeds forgotten as she tried to interpret every action, every word of Simon's from the night before.

She finally had to admit to herself that she fancied him. Was he just being matey? Just helpful to a girl in need, a fellow freak? When he'd helped her into the house, supporting her, strong arms lifting her up every step and laying her gently on the sofa, was that nothing more than chivalry, or had there been genuine concern? Real liking? Did he enjoy the physical contact as much as she had? Had any flicker of enjoyment crossed his face? Or was it just her, panting away with unrequited lust?

She had just finished her egg and soldiers – the perfect invalid lunch served in a Basil Brush egg cup from a long-ago Easter – and was propped on the pillows with the tray still on her knees when she heard the doorbell. Before she had time to leap up as best she could and open the window to get rid of the eggy smell lingering in the room, Simon was filling the door frame holding a wilting bunch of flowers.

Nan Peters squeezed around him to retrieve the tray, and grabbed the flowers as she walked past. 'I'll find a vase for these. It looks like they could do with a drop of water.'

'I sometimes have that effect.' Simon shrugged apologetically, nodding at the flowers. 'It's part of my powers.'

'But they're lovely. Thank you. It's very thoughtful.' Lucy was still worrying that he would think the lingering egg odour was actually a farty smell and she was feeling embarrassed because he was here and she didn't know how to talk to him. It would be easy if they were in a bar and she had alcohol running through her veins and there was loud pumping music so that she had to lean right into his personal space and shout in his ear. But here she felt vulnerable, exposed, and not just because she was sitting up in bed in her pyjamas.

'I've just had a boiled egg.' It was an odd thing to say but she had to offer an explanation for the aroma in the room.

Simon looked a little surprised, but rallied a suitable response. 'Oh.' He paused. 'I had a sandwich for my lunch.'

They lapsed into silence and he perched uncomfortably on the edge of the bed, crossing and uncrossing his legs and shifting around whilst Lucy bobbed about as the old bed shook and wobbled. She began to panic. Any more of that and Nan would be through the door wondering what the dickens was going on. She fumbled for something to say.

'What did you have on it?'

'On what?'

'On your sandwich?'

'Erm. Cheese . . . and some salad.'

'Nice.'

'Yes, it was.'

Silence again. Tumbleweed passed through the ghost town of their conversation. Then they both began talking at once and then they didn't stop. First they went through a blow by blow account of the previous night. Nan brought tea and biscuits, and they were still talking it through. Then she took the tray away, barely noticed by either of them, and they were talking about their childhoods. They say that the odds are in favour of relationships where there are similarities. Obviously a shared love of *You've Been Framed* is not enough to sustain a lifelong marriage, but true similarities of politics, upbringing, levels of education – all the books, research and experts are united in the view that it helps.

Not that Lucy had taken any notice of such things before. She felt that was dull, unromantic, dating agency advice. She much preferred to think in One True Love, united again across time, Twin Soul stuff. But as Simon talked, revealing his early upbringing at the hands of devoted followers of self-sufficiency on a communal smallholding on North Island, she felt a prick of recognition as though here at last was someone who could relate to the humiliation of being made to wear coarse jumpers of hand-spun wool, dyed by woad in the traditional urine-in-the-bucket way. Here was someone who knew the wonderful delicious pleasures of wandering over moor or field all day, all night if you wanted, but also knew the contradictory pull of wishing that someone cared that you were gone. All the freedom of the Famous Five but with chickpea salad where there should have been ham sandwiches and lashings of ginger beer.

Here was someone else at last who knew the inverted worry of wishing your parents would smoke less dope and being glad when they grew out of it. Simon described perfectly the push-me-pull-you of loving and admiring the unconventional wacky upbringing while actually wanting to be made to do homework. They laughed and they talked, Lucy leaping forward, despite her aches and pains, to sit cross-legged next to him, grabbing his arm and shouting 'Oh my God! Yes! That happened to you too?' as he recounted the horrors of parental nude sunbathing.

He was thirty-two. He had been struck by lightning. He was beginning to harness his powers so at last was able to drive a car. He had never really got used to living in a city and made no secret of his awe that she could survive in London. He wrote a little, he said, but did not say what and she didn't press him in case it turned out to be poetry. Bad poetry that he might make her read that would break the spell of her attraction to him. He worked outdoors felling trees, laying hedges, and keeping as far away as possible from anything electrical that could be broken just by his being around.

'So no internet porn for you!' Lucy found herself saying, and he looked a little shocked at her quip.

He did not own a suit. He had a limited interest in tapas – too much like Mom's kitchen experiments. He did not drop any designer names of anything into the conversation. He was unlike anyone she'd ever been out with. She had to find out if he was single.

Lucy's phone vibrated with the arrival of another Nigel text. She picked it up and read it without even hesitating in their conversation and gave a little rueful smile when she saw Nigel's message. *If you don't come home the puppy gets it.* Simon interpreted the scene. 'I bet your boyfriend is worried sick about you,' he said, nodding towards the phone.

'I haven't got one.' Then, with faux coyness and eyes turned back to her phone, directly avoiding any contact, 'I bet your girlfriend won't want you to go to any more meetings after this one.'

'Oh, I'm not seeing anyone right now,' he said simply. Result! And they looked at each other, holding the other's gaze for a fraction of a second too long and then looking away with the heat rising on their cheeks. It was all so Celia Johnson and *Brief Encounter*. So understated, innocent and restrained that Lucy could have had a bonnet strapped to her head and a heaving bosom as he crossed and uncrossed his riding-britches-clad legs and adjusted his frilly Darcyesque shirt.

It was a meeting of hearts, heads and minds, not loins. Though if he kept looking at her like that the loins were sure to follow. It was the exact opposite of the World of Relationships according to glossy magazines, with their Orgasmic Sexual Positions of the Month and Anal, Anyone? articles. And she liked it. (The niceness and innocence thing, not the up-your-bum sex thing.)

It felt natural and right, wholesome but not twee. Like home-baked bread and honey from the hive. It was as good and real and right as a clean body unscented with man-made chemicals masquerading as Magical Mango. A night of drink-fuelled coupling couldn't match the buzz she was getting from this.

It was at that point Nan Peters chose to bustle into the room. 'Is he staying for dinner or am I making up the spare room?' One of her not-so-subtle phrases to intimate that his visit had gone on rather too long for her liking.

Simon made his apologies and got up to leave, while Lucy tried to communicate with her grandmother using eye movements alone. She wanted to say, 'Nan, how could you embarrass me like that? He was leaving anyway and we weren't doing anything. Naan' – in a whiney teenage voice – 'I want him to stay longer.'

'Don't go back to London without saying goodbye,' he managed before Nan Peters ushered him out of the door, and from his pocket he drew a pre-prepared piece of paper bearing his address and telephone number that fluttered down to the bed like a butterfly.

So he *was* interested. Lucy lay back on the pillows, clutching the scrap of paper feeling very, very pleased with herself. And it didn't occur to her, not even once, that it was a little bit odd that someone with alleged electromagnetic powers should have a landline.

Back in London in a ridiculously expensive, minuscule flat with the right postcode and a gloss white, genuine marble-topped kitchen, Jojo was looking from her phone in one hand to a plastic stick shaped like a coffee stirrer in the other. The phone was smooth and cold like a pebble in her palm. Reassuring and as steady as a rock. She was willing it to ring and it to be *her* rock – Lucy. She toyed with the idea of pressing speed-dial, but did not really know what she would say or how she would begin if Lucy picked up.

Life for Jojo Gray was rarely problematic. There were hiccups but not downward slides into misery like Nigel's. Things were overcome, sorted out. And then there was the trust fund to help with many of life's problems, and everyone acknowledged that Jojo was like a cat – she could fall from the tallest of buildings, twist, turn in mid-air and still land on her feet, needing nothing more than a shake of an elegant paw before she was off again. Work had never been an issue either – she was an arch political player. She knew how to work a room at any function. She had a dozen outfits for any required occasion and a million snippets of small talk to match. She knew who were the right people, she knew how to say the right things to the right people and she never let little things like loyalty or obligation get in the way of getting ahead.

But in the last month everything had changed. Lucy and her mysterious, unsettling new powers. Nigel becoming more of a recluse with each passing week, and now this. Why did things have to change? Why couldn't everything just trundle on as it had before? Why did life have to go and get complicated?

And where was Lucy when she really needed her? Back 'oop north'. It never did feel quite like home for Jojo. She was born to be a Londoner, and it's not as if her parents were there any more. They'd taken off with their money (her inheritance) to Alicante and would be drinking wine and playing bridge on the terrace of their villa at this very moment. And what could they do for her now anyway? There would just be recriminations and Dad's endless You-had-all the-advantages-I-never-had-and-you-go-and-waste-them speeches.

She could ring Nigel, of course, ask him to come. Churn it all over with a glass of wine – a small one – but this wasn't something she felt she could share with him. This was all too feminine. Too girly. Too 'lady parts' for Nigel to stomach.

Jojo looked from the phone and back to the stick. It was one thing to hold a white plastic stick shaped like a coffee stirrer in your hand if, in the other, there was a latte, but it was quite another if, in a little plastic window, a line on the stick was quite clearly turning blue.

15

Nigel couldn't relax in Walthamstow Heights these days. Any creak or sudden noise caused him to leap for cover. Jojo had no patience with him. 'It was a spiritual visitation, Nigel, not Vietnam!'

They were glad to see Lucy back, although she looked like she'd been in an East End pub brawl. She was partway through telling them about the Magnificent Seven and how Simon had taken charge of planning the visits with pinboard and map when Nigel's phone sang out with his latest retro ring tone – Power Rangers.

'Those outfits!' he sighed, thinking nostalgically of Blue Power Ranger in particular. It was another of his aunties, and after several 'I know . . . I know' type comments he said, 'I wouldn't believe it myself but I'm looking at the proof,' and handed the phone to Lucy. She had to go through the whole tale again, starting with Jonathan Rayburn's first visit and ending with a catalogue of her injuries.

By the time she got off the phone Jojo and Nigel were deep into a film on True Movies – something about a homeless mother battling her own mental illness, trying to change the law and taking on a multinational company over pollution. Lucy stood in front of the television to get their attention and insisted on no more interviews.

'You're gonna have to get used to it,' Nigel said through a mouthful of crisps (prawn cocktail) and dips (mango chutney), an eye still on the TV. 'You'll have your own cable show soon. I know it. I can see it now: *High Spirits with Lucy Diamond.*'

'I wouldn't want it.'

'Why ever not?' Nigel was incredulous.

'You're making me feel sick.' Jojo had her hand over her nose and was opening a window as far away from Nigel as she could get.

'I've got to put something in my mouth if we're not smoking!' All of them had made a pact to give up for their very different and undisclosed reasons.

'There certainly could be a publishing deal in it, though.' Jojo straightened her back into work mode and her friends glimpsed the work-shark of steel within.

'So what have you guys been up to?' Lucy was trying to change the subject, to get the topic away from herself, even though she'd spent the last two and a half hours talking about her plans – building up a client base, looking for premises and going part time at work. If Lucy had been paying attention to the subtle signs her friends were giving out, the lack of eye contact, the non-committal 'dunno, nothing much' replies, the evasive responses that became questions to direct attention back to her, then she would quickly have sussed out that 'stuff' had been going on. But she didn't. In short, Lucy Diamond was not being a very Good Friend. But then who can blame her with a new sixth sense to cope with and her mind distracted by a man who could bend spoons?

She thought that she had been subtle about mentioning Simon but clearly not. Nigel had started a little game of 'Simon Says' in a childish, whiny voice, and although he might have intended to be amusing, Lucy was irritated with him.

'Simon says . . . will you get your knickers off?'

'Simon says . . . I'll show you mine if you show me yours.'

All that innuendo and she'd not even kissed the guy.

Lucy had of course done a little more than kiss Tony Russell but he had not seemed remotely pleased to see her or looked in any desire of a rematch when she bumped into him at reception. One minute he was chatting away to the pretty gossip behind the desk, spiking up his hair in the reflection off the glossy surface, and the next he was backing away as though Lucy was contagious.

'Now I'm sorry to hear you've been poorly, Lucy.' His hands were raised in front of him, karate-style again, ready to ward off any attack. Unconsciously he flicked a crucifix from under his shirt and simultaneously his eyes were darting all around reception, looking for signs of the supernatural. 'And I don't want to upset you or any of *your friends*' – he looked at her meaningfully – 'but please don't come near me.'

'I wasn't going to. I was just dropping these disks off. I'm having a few more days' leave, that's all.'

'Yes, good. You take all the rest you need, Lucy. Have a good long rest.' He was talking to her as though placating a venomous snake and taking careful, measured steps toward the lift. Suddenly, the receptionist's computer blinked into colourful life with a musical Microsoft herald. It was too much for the strained nerves of Tony Russell and he burst through the fire doors, making his escape in blind panic.

'What's up with him?' The receptionist was agog. Lucy shrugged her shoulders. The girl continued, 'I reckon all that hair product he uses has gone to his brain. I've always said anyone who fancies himself that much either doesn't have a very good mirror at home or is tapped in the 'ead, and now we know which one it is.' And so would the rest of the office by lunchtime.

So now Lucy was shutting up the flat, kissing Jojo and Nigel bye-bye and taking the train back north. She had a week off work of one kind and it gave her time to work in another – to make her visits to the loved ones of the Magnificent Seven. Simon had offered to meet her at the station and personally drive her on each of the house calls she had to make.

She was very grateful. Any visitation or channelling was very tiring and the thought of legging it up and down the country by public transport was not inspiring even if Lucy did have a debt to pay to each of her rescuers. Simon had been very helpful, and very organised. He'd produced a spiral-bound reporter's notebook for Lucy to log notes in and a hand-held tape recorder that he said he could no longer use, as well as his pinboard plan to develop an order of visits. Funny, really. Such skills of investigation, organisation and analysis seemed wasted on a farm labourer.

Carly. Sweet fifteen and never been kissed. Most unusual considering the part of Leeds she came from, where most girls have at least one baby on the way by that age. But then leukaemia doesn't tend to enhance your social life. While other girls were drinking cider on the park swings she was hooked to a drip in the General. As the others hung around in the Headrow Shopping Centre, she was trying to find the energy to reply to the texts that arrived with almost clockwork regularity to keep her in the loop. Proving that given the worst of circumstances, even wayward hoodies can rise to the occasion.

Carly had appeared with Jonathan, clinging wide-eyed to his arm like he was a favourite uncle, wearing her favourite nightshirt fronted by a cuddly rabbit. She was gamine-thin with a Girls Aloud attractiveness that given time and enough spray-tan could have bagged her a footballer had she lived. She'd never had a period, the drugs robbing her of one curse as she grappled with another, and she'd never been on a date. Plenty of boys-as-friends, she explained, but no boyfriends. So Carly was relying on Lucy to deliver a message from this place where text and MySpace, Bebo and Facebook could not reach.

'No message for your parents? Your sister? Your best friend?' Lucy had asked. Carly shook her head.

'No. We had plenty of time to say all the things we wanted to say before I went, but I didn't have the courage to say this then. So you can do it for me now. And I want to know *exactly* what he says because I'm too embarrassed to be listening in when you tell him.'

So a good fifteen years after it was seemly to do so, Lucy found herself with the bittersweet task of sitting outside a sixties-built secondary school with a *my mate fancies your mate* missive. She sat with Simon in his vintage Morris Minor, the only car robust enough to stand his electromagnetic presence, so he said, and with electrics simple enough to fix. They had a flask of tea and a carrier bag of sandwiches and pork pie – courtesy of Nan Peters – and sat nervously behind newspapers waiting for the school bell to toll the end of the day. It was a kind of psychic stake-out.

'I've gotta say, Lucy,' Simon said in soft Kiwi tones, 'I'm not really very comfortable sitting outside a school like this. I'm sure the police would agree that it's not really something a man of any age should do.'

'We're OK,' said Lucy. She was too keyed up about the task in hand to care. 'There are lots of parents in cars. We just look like one of them. We don't stand out at all.'

Simon shifted in his seat. He wasn't so sure. Neither was the lollipop lady. She had been eyeing them suspiciously for some time. A distant bell rang, and Lucy checked her watch.

'Right on schedule! So stop worrying. We'll be done here in a minute.' They could see teenagers beginning to spill from every exit, forming groups, kicking bags or each other along the path, mobile phones at the ready, texting or calling people they had been sitting next to less than five minutes ago.

'And this kid we're looking for – remind me what he looks like,' Simon asked as the first pupils began to emerge from the gates.

'He has short, dyed, dark hair with a long fringe and Carly said he'd be in a blazer with the sleeves rolled up and his trousers worn low with some sort of against regulations belt.'

'Thought so,' said Simon as it became obvious that every second student piling through the gate fitted that description.

Despite having longed all day to be free of school, the teenagers showed little sign of going home, and were forming clumps outside the gate, lighting cigarettes and playing tinny music from their mobiles.

'You wait here,' said Lucy, and before Simon could protest she had leapt from the car and was halfway across the road. Simon felt the cold eyes of the lollipop lady fall on him.

Lucy gave her description of the wanted boy to the first group of youths she could find who looked vaguely Carly's age. As soon as she began talking, others clustered around and pressed forward, oozing eau de Monster Munch, Lynx and Impulse.

'Who wants to know? What are you? The police or something?' A girl whose blazer lapels were covered in band badges and whose very non-regulation earrings hooped low, almost skimming her shoulders, appointed herself as spokesperson.

'No.' Lucy could sense a rising hostility and blurted out, 'I'm a friend of Carly's in Year Ten.'

A stony, unbelieving silence descended over the group and in a split second, without a word passing between them, they synchronised – shoulder to shoulder – into a gum-cracking, arms-folded, hips-cocked defensive force to be reckoned with.

'Carly's gone,' said Miss Badges, her scraped-back ponytail wobbling this way and that. 'And if you really was a friend of Carly's you'd know it and I ain't never seen you before. Not 'ere and not on Facebook.'

Her friends were murmuring, nodding their agreement as other youngsters pushed past yelling endearments like 'Oi! Wanker!' Lucy was glad that she had not chosen teaching as a career. She would not want to be quizzing this lot over late homework and lapses in uniform.

Simon's car was also attracting interest, and not because it was a fine vintage specimen. Possibly tipped off by the pursed-lipped lollipop lady, a vigilante group was forming. As texts passed faster than the speed of sound, other kids were stopping to look at the odd little car with the driver that nobody recognised. An SMS Chinese whisper of two and two added to make five began and a group message had been fired with the ominous words picked out in capitals: NONCE ALERT!!

The vigilantes were now twenty strong and growing. Simon was oblivious; he was craning his neck to see if Lucy was safe but his actions gave him the unfortunate air of a dirty, ogling old (he was over thirty so therefore deemed almost pensionable) man. To the assembled under-sixteen jury 'looking funny' was enough to find him guilty as charged.

Meanwhile, Lucy, surrounded by a sea of blazers, was doing her best to defend her own case. She was being grilled about her knowledge of Carly and she was unable to say where Carly had lived, who her form tutor had been and what pets she had owned.

'Well then,' said Lucy's badged interrogator, 'seems you ain't no friend of Carly's after all then, are you?' And she clicked her fingers and wobbled her head, copying the sassy black girls from American movies.

Lucy tried to ignore their unhelpfulness and the rising panic that this was all getting a little bit out of control. All those years protected in a precious all-girl grammar school had made her afraid of kids like this. *I am an adult, I am an adult*, she reminded herself.

'I have to speak to Tom Evans. Carly gave me a message for him and asked me to give it to no one else.'

Lucy hoped that, to this rabble, she sounded PE-teacher confident rather than supply-teacher shy.

'What? Tom Evans the geek?' said a spotty-faced youth with his sports cap perched on the back of his head and dodgy teeth that suggested a diet loaded with fizzy pop. The boy's name seemed to act like a password on the previously hostile girl with the badged blazer and hooped earrings. She grabbed Lucy's arm and dragged her away from the rest of the group, whose attempts to follow were met with a glare. They backed off like cowed dogs.

She dragged Lucy over the road to the other side of the ice-cream van queue. Lucy couldn't help but note it was doing a roaring trade. She was always looking for alternative careers.

'What did you say? Say it again and tell me what the message is for Tom or . . . or I'll shank ya.' The girl shook Lucy's arm to force the secret out of her. Lucy didn't believe the threat for one minute, not when it was so obvious that her words had seriously rattled the girl. She felt fifteen again. It took her straight back to when the sixth formers had tried to get her to say whether or not it was true that Jojo had lost her virginity to the captain of the rugby team from St Symphorian's following a successful home win. Jojo had, of course, shagged him but her virginity had been lost on that particular playing field a good while previously. It had never been found.

Lucy didn't give in then and she wasn't going to give in now. 'She asked me to give Tom the message and no one else.'

'Listen, you – whoever you are.' The girl was angry now. Her fingers dug into Lucy's already bruised flesh but tears were filling her heavily kohled eyes. 'I am . . . was . . .' She corrected herself again and this time sounded certain and sure. 'I *am* Carly's best friend and I don't know what you are doing here messing with us but—'

A sudden roar distracted them both. Even the ice-cream queue had broken away to observe events, although one tubby youngster was quick enough to slip in his order of a double whippy with flake. This noise was different from the familiar shouts of 'United!' and 'Twat' – the usual school-gate chorus. This was repetitive, aggressive and getting louder by the minute. This was a war cry.

'Nonce! Nonce! Nonce!'

Simon's car was surrounded by a gang of angry-looking teenagers who were rocking the little Morris Minor from side to side in rhythmic time to their chant. The angry mob was spearheaded by the lollipop lady, who had abandoned her post and was whacking the bonnet of Simon's car with her lollipop stick. A permanent marker had been produced and 'paedophile' was being spelt incorrectly along the grey flank of the car.

'Simon!' Lucy could see his face, a picture of panic, at the steering wheel.

'Is he with you?' The girl looked at Lucy with a mixture of fear and disgust. 'I might have known . . . You pair of sick freaks.'

Lucy could never imagine that her next words would have the effect of a badge-carrying TV cop.

'It's not what you think. You've got it wrong. I'm a psychic . . . a medium.' She groped for the right words. 'I'm a ghost whisperer.' She hoped that some reference to Jennifer Love Hewitt's glossy series might cross the cultural divide of their different ages. 'He's just my . . . boyfriend,' and Lucy winced as she said it, it sounded so weird.

The girl stared for a fraction of a second that lasted far too long for Lucy's comfort and Simon's predicament. She swung her head from Lucy to the little car being buffeted by the baying gang and then back again before bellowing out a lie in a voice that drowned out all their chanting.

'Oi! That's my fuckin' cousin!'

'Shit,' someone shouted. 'Oh, shit! He's one of the Cartwrights.' They all knew the Cartwrights. It was not wise to upset (even fictitious) members of that extended family. The crowd dispersed almost as quickly as it had formed. Kids muttering pleas of forgiveness melted away. Attention spans had been filled anyway, and the lollipop lady returned to the crossing without an apology for dents caused, growling in an ominous Scottish brogue, 'No smoke without fire.'

Simon, still hyperventilating, groped in the glove box for a restorative Murray Mint.

'You were saying?' Sasha Cartwright's mouth was set in a hard determined line, though she waved a goodbye and managed to flash a smile to some departing friends.

'I told you. Tom Evans. I need to give him a message from Carly, and I've been asked to give it to no one else,' Lucy repeated.

'You already said that. She only told *me* about Tom, you know. Only me. Swore me to secrecy and I promised her I'd never tell a soul and I didn't. She fancies him, doesn't she?' The hard little face became relaxed and warm.

Lucy's heart tugged a little at Sasha's use of the present tense and she mirrored it. 'Yes, she does and she wants me to tell him. She wants to know what he says.'

'How do I know I can believe you? You didn't seem to know anything about Carly.'

'I don't.' Lucy was honest and told Sasha the little she knew and how she owed Carly a debt of gratitude for stepping in to drive out evil Joe.

'That's just like Carly . . . oi, fuck off!' She punched a boy who had accidentally banged into her in the arm. 'She hates bullies.' The irony of her statement was lost. 'That's Tom there.' She pointed towards the sound of a fire exit slamming shut. 'He always comes out a bit later to avoid getting stick off the others, innit,' she added in self-conscious street-talk. 'Tom! TOMMMMMM!' she yelled in a voice that nearly made Lucy's ears bleed.

The boy looked up. He matched Carly's description perfectly. He raised his hand to acknowledge he'd heard and as he lifted his head and started towards them Lucy felt a jolt of recognition. He looked artistic – carrying his GCSE artwork in a plastic folder – and poof-gentle. He was beautiful against the grim backdrop of the crumbling inner-city comprehensive, carrying the polyester uniform like public school flannels. He looked like someone you could share the innermost secrets of your soul with and that hair – that floppy fringe. He could be Nigel and poor Carly could be barking up a very wrong tree, eternally longing for something that could never be returned.

'He's n-n-not . . . erm . . .' Lucy wasn't sure how to say the word.

'Gay? Of course not.' Sasha was disgusted at Lucy's old-world approach. 'Just because he's clever doesn't mean he's gay. Why do all you people think that? God – you old people are so lame. The other boys don't like it but the teachers say he'll go to university one day.' Sasha puffed her A-cup chest in reflected pride and glory.

Lucy resisted the urge to issue dire warnings about student loans whilst her inner gaydar waited on stand-by. Not that she could ever vouch for its reliability.

'Sasha – whassup?'

Tom Evans was a dreamboat but he didn't know it. He was the living British embodiment of *High School Musical*'s Troy Bolton. In the last few years, as puberty kicked in, he'd swapped glasses for contacts, grown out of his pre-adolescent puppy fat, and emerged a butterfly but without any awareness of his new Adonis self. Lucy could see why the other lads ostracised him. What chance would they stand with the girls when Tom Evans was setting the standard? He did not share the brutish, belching, leering qualities of the other boys who had gambolled out of the gates around them. So, the easiest way to crush him was through mockery and bullying. He was charming, mannered, mature and – judging by the darkening above his upper lip – he could grow a moustache. The testosterone was coursing through him. The gaydar gauge did not register a reading. His eyes had even unconsciously flicked over Lucy, appraising her, but then so did Nigel's before he savaged her dress sense.

How do you begin to tell a fifteen-year-old boy that you have a message for him from the other side from a girl who fancies him? It was bad enough first time round, waiting for their reaction and then having to edit it into a palatable form for your friend. Harder still when you're the other side of thirty and therefore nearly dead in their eyes. Luckily, Sasha did the talking via lots of 'you know', 'like', 'I said to her' and 'whatever'. Lucy just hung around trying not to flick her hair and turn her toes in, all the time feeling a crush coming on.

'So Carly was really interested in you and everythin' but what with the . . . with being ill and that' – Sasha still couldn't say that word, that killer of her best friend, leukaemia – 'she couldn't tell ya and then she didn't think that you'd be interested in her and then – well, then it was too late, weren't it? So what we want to know and Lucy here is gonna tell her is . . .' Sasha paused dramatically and cracked her gum, 'if Carly wa˜ here would you go out with her' – crack went the gum – 'or not?'

Tom was well within his rights to look as astounded as he did. Although he'd taken the whole thing about this woman talking to Carly from beyond the grave in his stride with typical adolescent insouciance, so much so that Lucy had almost expected him to shrug his shoulders and say, 'Yeah. And?'

What he couldn't believe, what was causing him to gape and roll his eyes and repeat 'Really? Really?' was that Carly had wanted to go out with him. Carly whose passing was lamented by all the boys. Carly who wore the shortest skirts with the longest legs and the sweetest smile. Carly who came to school until she could no longer stand. Carly who, in his sketchbook, he had captured more vividly than life in that pre-death phase like the consumptive muses of the pre-Raphaelite masters he so admired. Carly, who he thought would never look his way because he wasn't loud enough or G-Star enough, because he was just 'the geek'. The speccy fat geek. Or at least had been. But Carly fancied him.

The hot girl. The one they all wanted to go out with fancied him. Carly. Fancied. Him. Had fancied him? Still fancied him!

'So?' Sasha was cracking her gum impatiently. Loyal, fierce Sasha who, just a year from now, would name her first daughter after her best friend. 'Would you go out with her or not?'

'Result?' asked a considerably calmer Simon who had had time to reflect that he'd rather take his chances with evil spectres from the other side than school-age British youth with all their potential for binge drinking and gang-banging.

'Result.' Lucy Diamond smiled as she slid into the front seat. Smiled because she could see to the place above our world where we, The Living, like to think they, The Dead, are sitting on clouds with harps looking down on us and she had seen a pretty, skinny girl in her favourite nightshirt and a pair of novelty monster-feet slippers jumping up and down and high-fiving a sandy-haired man in a raincoat.

The Morris Minor with the bashed-in bonnet and the blacked-out graffiti limped all the way home.

16

'Thanks for offering to do all this driving.' Lucy and Simon were sitting outside Nan Peters's. It was late. It was dark. The car had that fetid, damp smell that old cars have when two adults have been cooped up with a decaying packed lunch for a long period of time. Condensation was already clinging to the windows and it would only take minutes before the windows began to steam and the neighbours started talking. It was an awkward moment.

They had spent a lot of time in each other's company, first planning the trips and then on the long drive to and back from Leeds, but there had been no physical contact. Sure, there had been plenty of invasion of personal space – Lucy had brushed sandwich crumbs off his chest, he had wiped pickle off her sleeve. They had also leaned against one another, shoulder to shoulder, elbow to elbow, as they planned their route on the pinboard map. But beyond that, nothing. He had not held her hand or snaked an arm around her shoulder. He had not casually brushed his crotch against her in a tight space or leaned into the Kiss Zone from which there is no going back. All the things he had not done hung in the air around them and it was the most erotic experience of her life.

Lucy could almost not bear it. Even his gear changes as his legs arched, or the flexing of his forearms as he turned the steering wheel, became pant-tinglingly exciting. She was developing an unhealthy fetish for the lumberjack shirt. How long before she was sneaking into Millets and sniffing sleeves? She could barely concentrate on their conversations even though the talk – and most important the silences – seemed to flow naturally between them. The signals were all there but there was no action and Lucy was trying to ignore the doubting, nagging voice that dredged up memories of that first year of university and her painful, unrequited love.

Over and over she replayed her memories, looking for patterns that might be repeating themselves, just as Nan had warned, but she had to admit that even then, even with Nigel's dazzling conversation and perfect grooming, even when she was left breathless and longing for his company, there had been something missing. Something she couldn't quite pinpoint, something that gave her feelings towards Simon more of a spark. What was it? She followed the thread of her emotions like a diver groping for a tether line under water and found it took her to an area that, if contracted, yoga teachers call the mula bandha. In other words, it took her to her loins, her genitals, her front bottom. What she felt for Simon was different. Different because the added ingredient was sex.

Yes, she had been crazy about Nigel. Loved him. Loved him still. She loved the feel of him, the smell of him and how he looked, but it was more like a crush, like the way you might admire an older girl at school or Jennifer Aniston to the point of wanting to *be* her and being borderline *Single White Female*. But sex doesn't enter into it. It's never part of the equation, and even dredging the darkest corners of her mind Lucy could not find a single sexual fantasy about Nigel.

Yes, she'd kept his pants that time and that might seem a bit weird but it was more about keeping a part of him so that she wasn't so . . . so . . . alone. It could have been a shirt he left behind. It just so happened it was pants, that's all. Being cuddled by him? Yes, she liked that. Feeling connected, belonging, brotherly, familial? Yes, all those things. Having Nigel fill the great big emotional void left by a mother who needed mothering and no brothers or sisters to share the load? Yes! A million times yes! But sex? Sex with Nigel? Boingy-boingy, squelchy, orifice-filling, 'Do it to me now, big boy' sex? Yuk. No thanks. It wouldn't be right. It would be nothing short of . . . incestuous. Wrong. Unnatural. Perverted, even. Maybe her gaydar worked after all.

But sex with Simon? Yes please. Yes please with knobs on and a cherry on top. God! Even that sounded filthy and erotic. Yes, she could easily imagine sex with Simon. Sex with Simon in the car, on the moor, up an alley, in a bed, on a table. Sex clothed, sex unclothed. Sex in the dark at night, sex in the day with light, sex lit by candles. Sex underneath, on top, from behind, up a wall. Sex, sex, sex, sex, sex. Bring it on.

But then the doubts started. Why hadn't he made a move? Did he not find her attractive? They laughed together, talked constantly. It felt like they were connected. There was a bond there, but did he just view her as an amusing friend? Or was this part of the respectful waiting game that she had so longed for and never experienced? Should she start stripping flowers of their petals for *loves me, loves me not*-style fortune-telling? Couldn't he sense the gusset-wetting lust she exuded for him? Was it just part of his electromagnetic skills that he could actually exert sexual power over women, turning normal, average (romantic!) girls into sex-cats on heat? Lucy had decided that she could not bear the not-knowing any longer. *She* was going to make the move, leap in mouth puckered and arms outstretched, and hang the consequences. She'd just have to deal with the rejection if it came, but in the meantime, if he lacked the courage, lacked the conviction, it would be down to Lucy to force his hand. As it happened, she didn't have to.

The awkward moment hadn't passed. Lucy scrabbled around the floor of the car picking up old bits of tin foil, sandwich wrappers and fruit juice cartons. It gave her something to do, cramming all their rubbish back into the carrier bag. It meant that she could stay in the car longer, put off the moment of parting and procrastinate a little longer about when best to lunge for him.

Simon coughed gently. 'I don't mind driving. I mean it's fun, isn't it? Driving, talking – oh, and thank your grandmother for the sandwiches. It really was a top lunch.' Barely were the words out before his mouth was suddenly on hers as if he had to act in that moment, at that instant, or there would be no other chance.

It was not an easy kiss – though it did hit the right spots. Kissing in the front seat of a car is never easy. There are gear sticks, handbrakes, contraints of space and issues of positioning, but as their mouths touched and their tongues met it was a pleasingly similar modus operandi they adopted as their kiss.

Ears bubbled from the raised blood pressure,

occipital lobes flashed visions of lights and stars, and all sorts of rockets, sparklers and Catherine wheel shenanigans were happening in undergarments. It's amazing what a bit of increased blood flow can do.

Simon leaned over her, one hand holding the side of her face, the other on her arm. The Tesco carrier bag of old crusts and sandwich wrappings crinkled and crackled between them – an audio representation of their sexual chemistry. Her one free hand brushed the soft stubble of his cheeks and raked through his hair. Her other arm was kind of left out of the party, pinned awkwardly between them, still clutching some orange peel. It doesn't happen like that in the movies. Despite that, for a first kiss it was a wow.

He broke away from her to breathe, his pupils wide, black, druggie-huge in their desire.

'I shouldn't have done that. I'm sorry,' he said before leaning in again for the kill. The windows were steamy now. He kissed her mouth, her cheeks, her hair, her neck. 'But Lucy, I really, really' – he was kissing her between words – 'really like you. I mean you're' – his lips were on hers – 'so different, so brave' – he was nibbling her neck – 'funny and pretty.' Lucy made little moans of desire.

'I want you,' she whispered. 'I've been dying for you to kiss me.'

He pulled back, looking genuinely surprised and pleased, then leaned forward to kiss her for what felt like the longest time. It was Lucy who broke away eventually.

'Oh, God! I'm all juicy.'

'What?' If this was sex talk, it wasn't working for Simon.

'The bloody apple juice – it's leaked through the bag. I'm really sorry but I'm soaked through.'

'Jesus Christ! What is it?' Simon screamed. Through the misty windows an unearthly visage had appeared. It was tapping on the glass with a hand that looked like it had passed Snow White the poisoned apple.

No, it wasn't Madonna. It was Nan Peters. With hairnet but *sans* teeth, witch-like as she clutched a broom. It never became clear why she had felt the need to bring a cleaning implement to the car door. Perhaps to protect her granddaughter from any amorous advances from Simon. Maybe she liked sweeping the path in the dark.

'Are you coming in, Lucy? You'll catch your death out here, else.'

Lucy leapt out of the car looking guilty, dishevelled and like she'd wet her pants. A dark semicircle of damp stain had spread from her crotch to halfway down the thigh of her jeans. It had not gone unnoticed by Nan 'I wasn't born yesterday' Peters.

'What's been going on here?' Nan looked from Lucy's trousers to Lucy's face and then to Simon.

'I spilt juice from the packed lunch—'

'Which was lovely, Mrs Peters. Really lovely, but don't worry about making one for tomorrow. Lunch is on me!' Before there could be any protest or risk that the Morris Minor might get thumped again, he gunned the engine and sped off down the wet road.

17

It was a modest house. 1930s bay-fronted semi-detached in one of the cul-de-sacs of similar houses that can be found all over Britain. A child's scooter lay in the drive, bikes lay on other driveways. Weathered basketball hoops were nailed above garage doors. A sleek tabby cat peered round a wall as Simon shut off the engine.

It felt like a safe, sound place to live. Urban enough to be within a short drive of an all-night chemist, but the sort of place that might just hold a street party given a suitable jubilee. It was the kind of place Lucy had longed to live in during Jasmine's wandering years.

Lucy, smart and neutral in black and beige, bruises and scratches masked by foundation, knocked on the door. Signs of life were in the house. A babble of television, shrill childrens' voices coming from the garden beyond and cooking smells creeping round the jamb.

Now footsteps were heard on laminate and she braced herself for the introduction, the appropriate opening.

'Hi there, I'm a psychic . . .' Too American, too double-glazing salesman.

'Hi, I'm Lucy Diamond.' She was liable to get a door slammed in her face for that one. Too showbiz, especially when followed by 'and I'm a psychic'. She needed something that sounded professional, expert even.

'Hi, I'm an afterlife facilitator.' Too noughties office speak.

'Hi, I have a spirit guide who . . .' No, no, no. Too new age and dangly crystal. Damn! The latch was being turned. Shit! Everything she'd practised sounded too rehearsed, too glib and slick, too impersonal. She wanted to sound sincere, to make this a good and meaningful experience for the family who lived in this house.

The door opened and a man in his early thirties clutching a tea towel faced her. He looked too careworn for his age. His skin hung from him as if his very being had shrunk within the casing of his body. Lucy felt the same oppressive crushing of grief in her chest. It was becoming a familiar empathetic response. She understood it now. It was a tap into the other's unhappiness, and she knew that this would be a strong connection. She had no choice now. She launched breathlessly into her rehearsed speech.

'Here's my card.' Between bouts of French kissing that really ought to be left for teenagers to do in public, Simon and Lucy had printed fifty cards in the motorway services in the interests of looking professional.

The man took it as if he couldn't care less and was too tired to fight against offers of cleaning products, cheaper electricity or new religions that came knocking at his door. Lucy gabbled a little speech about what she did and her connection with Jonathan and finished off with '. . . and I have a list of items to give to you passed to me by my friend from your wife Claire.' She breathed then and waited for the disbelief and the slam of the door in her face.

'You'd better come in. Though I haven't got long, the kids' tea is nearly ready.' So it had been as simple as that. What she didn't realise at that point was that the young father in front of her had barely heard or understood a word she'd said.

As she crossed the threshold she turned back to give a thumbs-up to Simon, who was waiting in the car. It felt good to know he was watching her back, supporting her, encouraging her. It felt good to know they could repeat last night's snogathon any time they wished and they had at almost every traffic light, lay-by and road junction. Their journey time to this place had to have doubled. Her face was smarting from the friction of his stubbled cheek against her own. She closed the door behind her.

The long through-lounge started at the bay window at the front and ended at a double set of sliding patio doors at the back. It gave a clear view of a neat garden dominated by a timber Wendy house which was surrounded by gaudy plastic flowers, windmills, a slide and a swing. Two little girls were running in and out of the play house, laughing and chattering in their inappropriate party clothing.

Lucy felt her throat tighten with emotion. The smaller of the two was wearing a tiered silk fairy dress, wings and wellingtons, and the other had fallen into the dirt in a sparkly Monsoon creation, stripy tights and baseball boots. Her long hair knotted around her as she fell. Neither was over seven years old.

They were exactly as little girls should be, happy, beautiful, entirely unselfconscious and unrestrained. It didn't seem possible – it certainly didn't seem fair – that they had lost their mother Claire in a road accident barely six months before.

Their father Mike – a solid name for a steady, dependable man – was towelling his hands over and over even though they were long since dry. The happy scene was almost too much for him to bear.

'They're beautiful,' Lucy whispered, her voice hoarse as she tried not to let tears prick at her eyes. Mike started a little as if only just remembering Lucy was there.

'You said you had a list of Claire's? Did she leave it on her desk? Emm . . . er . . .' He pulled the card from the top pocket of his shirt. 'Lucy . . . I'm sorry, I don't recall meeting you. Did we meet at the Christmas party?' It was obvious that she had only gained access to the house because he hadn't fully read the card. Hadn't taken in her spiel. Lucy took a folded piece of A4 from her pocket and handed it to him wordlessly.

'She loved lists.' He smiled. 'Shopping lists on the fridge, Christmas present lists, lists of things to do, places to go, jobs for me.' He unfolded the paper. 'You must be mistaken. This isn't her writing.' He held the paper out for Lucy to take. She braced herself to deliver her explanation again, but at that moment a muddied Monsoon princess and her fairy companion came running into the room, already asking a question before their father was even in sight.

'Daddy, we really need a—' They skidded to a halt as they saw Lucy and looked fearfully at their father. Strangers had come to the house before and stood there with solemn faces.

'Oh, I know you!' said the fairy in wellingtons,

breaking into a smile. 'Mummy told me you were coming. Daddy, this is the lady I told you about. Have you got our letter for us? Is that the letter? Can I see it, Daddy, can I see it?'

'The lady was just leaving and this letter is not for you,' Mike said in a voice more stern than the one they were used to. As their faces crumpled so did he, almost crashing down on to the nearest sofa, overwhelmed with the grief and responsibility and the holding it all in. In an instant, the girls were at either side as though aiding a shaky foal to stand, as though they could pass their abundant energy into his shell and keep him going a little longer. Little hands held his rough unshaven face, soft arms snaked around his neck and shoulders until the three were intertwined and they were rocking back and forth for comfort. It was not clear who was rocking whom. Lucy didn't know where to look. It was a moment to which she didn't belong.

'Stop saying it, love. Stop saying it.' Mike's voice was softer now, controlling the pain that wanted to burst from his chest. The three were still rocking and he spoke into their hair. 'You know it makes me sad when you say it and I can't help that and I'm sorry but Mummy can't come back. I told you that. You can't come back from heaven. She would if she could. She would if he could.' He buried his face.

Lucy felt she should leave. Anyone else would politely say *I'll let myself out*, but she had a job to do. A difficult job. As were all her taks for the Magnificent Seven. But she had a responsibility, a debt to pay, obligations to fulfil, though she shifted uncomfortably, crawling with the embarrassment of her intrusion, coughing gently to try to get his attention.

The bigger girl spoke. 'But Lottie can see her, Daddy.' She sounded like a little mother herself. 'She told you this lady would come, don't you remember? Lottie said a lady would come with the name of a bug.'

'Lottie says a lot of silly things—'

'I said that Mummy said the lady would have a bug's name,' protested little Lottie, her voice loaded with hurt that she should be doubted.

Lucy spoke as softly as she could to correct the little girl. 'A Beatle. Almost a bug, Lottie, so you're right. A Beatles song. My name is like a lot of Beatles songs. I'm Lucy Michelle Eleanor Jude Rita Diamond. All names from the Beatles songs.' The girls fixed on their father in smug triumph.

So much sadness. So much pain. Little ones don't deserve to lose their mothers. Mothers don't deserve to be robbed of the chance to see their children grow up. A man in the prime of his life does not deserve to be crushed under the weight of loss. However you explain it – fate, kismet, the will of some god or another – it does not make much sense.

'Say it again!' Mike raised his head. It was good to see her name could still raise a quizzical smile, albeit a weak one. 'Those songs have been going around my head for days.'

Lucy saw an opening and dashed for it. 'That's no coincidence. Claire will have prompted that for you as a message. Has the radio been coming on by itself, or tuning in to a different station?' Lucy saw him pale. It was true. Claire had been toying with the electrics after a crash course in Nuisance Visitations from Jonathan.

'Who are you again?' said Mike, fumbling in his pocket for the card she'd given him.

Lucy sat down uninvited in the nearest chair, her rehearsed speech forgotten. She went on instinct. She went – as Jasmine would put it – with the moment. 'You'll just have to suspend disbelief for a minute or two. Just hear me out.' She talked with lots of hand on heart gestures, arms flapping this way and that. Mike listened. Lucy continued, 'Let me make this clear – I want no money from you, or . . . or anything else. I just want to give you the message from Claire. You know, your daughter has a gift. Like I did as a little girl. She may grow out of it but at the moment she can channel Claire. Claire only has a limited time here before she has to fully cross over, but she gave me that list to help you. She told me, through my guide Jonathan, what to write.'

Lucy picked the paper up from the rug where it had fallen and as she straightened up she came face to face with Claire, looking deliriously happy up there on the mantle-piece in her wedding photo. Her eyes were locked on to her new husband, who gazed back in adoration, and her veil was flying in a June breeze. Their whole lives stretched lazily out before them at that point. Who would have guessed how short their time together would be?

Then another photo. Claire, smart and made up, arms around her girls in a family portrait. They were who she lived for, cared for. Her family were her whole life. She missed her family so much, and they her. Claire couldn't let go, not yet. Like Jonathan, she was risking Limbo, eking out a few, precious last moments of being around her family. Lucy knew that Claire hung around the house as often as she could. She was not ready to cross over. Not when the ironing pile was taller than her elder child and Mike was only just about treading water.

Lucy's voice was coaxing, gentle. 'Read it, Mike. Please,' and then, smelling the beginnings of a burnt dinner, she disappeared into the small galley kitchen to take pots off the hob, turn the fish fingers over and give this little broken family alone-time. Eighty-seven points were on that list, ranging from the mysteries of the airing cupboard to the times of swimming classes. There were instructions for the storing of her wedding dress and the division of her grandmother's jewellery between her beloved girls. There was advice about packing for holidays and dealing with playground tiffs, and instructions for a conservatory to be built on the patio. She could hear Mike and the girls talking. There were tears and little chuckles and a groan from the girls which must have been the reminder to brush their teeth.

She looked around the bright kitchen with its magnet-covered fridge, children's paintings on the wall and chock-a-block noticeboard. There was hand cream by the sink, lipstick in the weighing scales. Small pots of herbs wilted on the windowsill and Lucy poured water into their dry soil. Claire was and would always be a part of this home, but with the list in her husband's possession she would be able to find a little peace. Keith Richards had promised to help her cross over. It was reassuring to know that there were good guys on the other side too.

Claire had thought of everything, from where Mike could the find the Sellotape to promises to her girls that she hadn't deserted them, would never have gone if she had had a choice. For electrician Mike, along with her unending love, were instructions to pick up the stiffening brushes and hardening paints and return to his watercolours – a talent he could share with his daughters. Finally, there was her blessing; that he could, if – and only if – the girls were happy, move on, meet someone new although he must never, ever succumb to the charms of predatory single mum over the road Stephanie Johnson, who had always had her eye on Mike's wages and cared more about her nights out than if her kids were safe in.

'Gimme some credit here, Claire!' Lucy heard Mike say and she knew instinctively what he had read. Then, finally, Claire's wish that sunflowers be planted every year and that be her memorial. No stones, plaques or benches in a City of The Dead graveyard; just bright, living flowers with their faces turned to the sun, watching over her children as they played.

'Do you believe, Mike – the list? Everything?' Lucy asked tentatively, joining them back in the sitting room.

At least he was honest. 'I don't know what to believe.'

And that was when Lucy decided to leave. The dinner had been saved. He had her card if he needed her, but most important of all he had his girls. And he still had Claire, for a little while at least, because she wasn't going to cross over until Mike knew how to make the girls a proper packed lunch. It was a funny business, this going around helping people, interfering with their lives, passing on the love, changing a big or a small part of their lives, then moving on.

'How d'you feel?' Simon asked a visibly drained Lucy as she got in the car.

'A bit like Dr Quinn, Medicine Woman.' Before she could explain, she fell into a deep sleep and didn't wake up again until they were past Sheffield.

*

The bungalow had not been easy to find. The two stone lions ostentatiously flanking either side of the gate and the three-tiered fountain topped with Cupid should have been distinctive landmarks but this was Solihull, affluent suburban Brummie outpost, and every other front garden had the same. Or more. There were flag-poles and sundials, Grand Design-style modern water features, telephone boxes, and every other architectural status symbol you could think of.

Keith Richard's home, he had proudly declared, had been 'done up a bit'. This was an understatement. The drive had been block-paved and landscaped with alpines, the windows had been latticed and double-glazed, and a feature window complete with incongruous galleon had been added. The rest of the bungalow had been dormered, extended, tiled, insulated, damp-proofed, dado-railed and laminated throughout. Even the garage was a pristine, ordered, shelved, shining example of what happens when someone with a good pension has time on his hands.

Keith's widow answered the door with a flashing smile, exuding verve, a walking advert for the benefits of cod liver oil tablets. She was the epitome of the word 'trim'. Her figure was neat – maintained, Keith told Lucy, by 'Popmobility' classes. Her hair was neatly shaped into a bob of 'halo' blond. Like her home, she'd been 'done up a bit'. A facelift, ten years ago, still gave her a freshness most women in their late sixties would lack, and her maintenance schedule of 'mannies and peddies' kept her groomed to the same standard as the bungalow.

Mrs Shirley Richards had been raised in the era when it was your duty not to 'let yourself go'. It was an era when hair was styled and didn't budge for a week and film stars didn't slop to shops in tracksuits. She blamed the hippies for all this *'au naturel'* nonsense. She would no sooner think of not putting on her face than of letting the weeds push through the cracks of the crazy paving.

Even with Keith gone, especially with Keith gone, she had put in her heated rollers and not missed one rehearsal of *Oklahoma!* with the Solihull Players. Yes, she would have preferred to lie under the quilt with matching valance and curtain tiebacks and howl with grief. That was to be expected, but even then – *especially* then – she had gone through her morning stretching routine. 'Use it, or lose it, ladies' as Flair, her ex-Gladiator aerobics instructor, extolled.

Even at its worst, when the platitudes of friends sounded hollow and the words of that trendy female vicar didn't mean a thing, she still put on her 'powder and paint'. Even then. It was some consolation that Keith had died in the traces. Shirley knew as a busy person he'd be glad of that, although it did upset the little pack of Brownies he was guiding around the Trust's Baddesley Clinton at the time.

It hadn't been their choice to live without children, but they filled their weekends with clubs, societies, committees and institutions. It had not been easy to break into the ranks of the Solihull WI but she had succeeded where others had failed, and now her days without Keith could be filled with flowers to be arranged, bring-and-buys and singalongs with 'old dears' in the residential home.

There was always plenty going on. Their friends kept the invitations coming – cheese and wines, Murder

Mystery evenings, Pam Ayres at Warwick Arts. It wasn't hard to find things to do. It's just that she missed Keith being there to do nothing with.

Shirley, her tracksuit and gilet in matching tones of raspberry and pink, stuck on her happy face and opened the door wide, singing out, 'Helloo.' It was a direct contrast to the stereotype of the chain-locked suspicion of the average pensioner. But this was Solihull, after all.

'Rotary bric-a-brac all present and correct, sir!' And she mimed a salute and clicked her slippered heels like the Andrews Sisters did when they sang *Boogie Woogie Bugle Boy*. She was finally letting go of some of Keith's clothes, part of the process, she had been told, and they were neatly bagged next to the box of long-unused sherry glasses and a still-boxed Chopomatic salad slicer that had never been much good.

'We're not Rotary.' Lucy hesitated. 'I've brought you a message.' Simon stood alongside her and solemnly handed over the carefully chosen bouquet. Shirley stepped backwards, her hand on her chest. The fragile cheery façade that had been endlessly papered and plastered over the three years since Keith's death cracked and she sat down heavily on the fortuitously placed telephone table in the hall.

She took the flowers carefully, her fingertips brushing over the mix of freesias, narcissi, lilies and gardenias, and pressed them to her face, breathing in their heady scent as though it was oxygen. Her voice was cracked and hoarse when she spoke.

'Oh, Keith. It's been a long time coming,' and the tears slid down her cheeks in an unstoppable stream.

*

One pot of tea and a plate of triangular potted salmon sandwiches later Simon and Lucy were waving goodbye to 'Auntie' Shirley. She'd been great company and an impeccable hostess. They were stuffed and had laughed until their faces hurt and she had been so grateful for their bouquet. It seems that Keith had long ago, when they were inseparable newlyweds, promised to send a message to Shirley from the other side using the language of flowers if he died before she did. And at last, he'd succeeded. Shirley Richards would never feel quite so alone again.

'It's good, this, isn't it?' Lucy smiled happily at Simon. They were back on the road and partway to their next visit, with an overnight stop in a hotel en route. 'Better than Human Resources. I think I could do this as a full-time job. I need never work in an office again. You're so lucky working outdoors and being able to decide what you do and when you do it. Is it something you always wanted to do?'

Simon was concentrating on the road. 'Mmm . . . sort of.' He didn't elaborate.

'You said you wrote stuff too. Is there an inner creative trying to burst out? A Nick Hornby flowing from those workman's hands?'

He snorted a rueful little laugh. 'I wish.' Unusually for them, he said nothing else.

'So what sort of thing do you write?' Lucy pressed.

'Oh . . . mmm . . . all kinds of stuff.' He looked from his rear-view mirror to his side and back before indicating and pulling past a lorry.

'Have you ever had anything published?'

'Yeah – not long ago. Oh, shit – I've got my foot to the floor and I swear that bastard van is speeding up on purpose!' The little Morris Minor rattled scarily at its top speed in the middle lane. At last, they pulled past the lorry and were back in the elderly driver/cautious mother/vintage car lane. By then, Lucy's mind had forgotten that topic of conversation and returned to the toe-tingling, gut-churning potential of giving up work.

'Could you earn money from your gift?'

'Writing?'

'No, your electromagnetic thingy powers.'

'Oh.' He sounded distracted. 'Who'd want to pay to see a few spoons bend or a watch stop? It's not exactly a gift, is it?'

'What do you mean? It's fascinating! We're marvels of modern science, we are! I'd love to see what you do. After all, you've been trailing me around watching what I do. Oh, no!' Lucy slapped her forehead with her hand. 'I've been so self-obsessed. Since that night at the village hall it's all been about me, hasn't it? I mean, I haven't even really asked about what you do. We've talked about everything else but . . . Right, that does it! I want a full demonstration of what you can do when we stop tonight.'

'Baby – you're gonna get a full demonstration of what I can do all right.' He squeezed her knee and Lucy smiled; then his tone became serious. 'Maybe not tonight. I'll be pretty tired after the drive and I need to save my energy. Know what I'm saying?'

'OK – fair point. Tomorrow then – after breakfast, before we set off.'

'But then I'll be tired for the journey and what if I screw something up in the hotel? Look – not tonight or tomorrow but soon. Let's get your visits over with first. But don't go building it all up. It isn't that exciting. I think my powers are on the wane anyway and they're not like yours. Mine are pretty useless – a second-rate magician could do them – but yours? How do you do that, Lucy? I always used to think that mediums, psychics, whatever, were tricksters, con-artists or the deluded – that it was all tricks of body language and suggestion. But you know – that night with Joe, the orbs and everything . . . I still can't make sense of it and I was there. I saw it! We all saw it! If we could just present some scientific proof . . . Anyway, let's not get too serious. Not today, not tonight.' He grabbed her hand and kissed it. 'What you do is awesome. You give people hope, reassure them and make them feel that – you know – death is not the end. That's pretty cool, Lucy.'

'Yeah – I'm a kind of Cosmic Counsellor. The Dear Deirdre of The Dead!'

'You're the Agony Aunt of the Afterlife,' added Simon.

'I'm the Problem Solver of the Passed On.' They were laughing. They were pretty hysterical considering they were such poor jokes, but they were pleased with the good turns done and giddy about the night to come. And still Lucy hasn't learned that pride comes before a fall.

18

Nigel was revelling in it. He was reading aloud from the article for perhaps the fifth time. It's a wonder that the other customers in the waffle shop hadn't raised a petition to get him to either shut up or get out. Lucy and Jojo weren't listening to him now, they were tucking into hefty doses of maple syrup and slurping orange juice, but he didn't care. He liked the sound of his own voice far too much. Jojo had given up trying to get the magazine off him. She didn't want to read Lucy's article again. She wanted to read the story entitled 'My 5-stone tumour had hair and teeth'.

The magazine was a weekly tabloid of soap operas, crosswords, confessions and C-list celebs. They should have bought Nigel a subscription. '"Psychic Saw Through my Love Rat Hubby,"' he began again and settled himself down for another telling. 'Listen. Listen. This is my favourite bit! "The dubiously named" – let me say it again. "The *dubiously* named Lucy Diamond claimed to have a message for bereaved Liverpudlian single-mum Shannon Stewart but it seems that the senseless psychic" – I'm going to get a T-shirt printed for you with that on – "may have got it lost in translation."'

He was off again, chuckling and holding up the dodgy photo sitting squarely in the middle of the two-page spread. It had been taken by Shannon leaning over the balcony of her council maisonette on a mobile phone as Lucy was leaving. It added twenty pounds and made Lucy look like a *Crimewatch* extra. The borrowed fleece found on the back seat of Simon's car did not do her any favours. Her face was squinched against the drizzling rain and it all conspired to give her the look of a shifty, murderous Bill Sikes.

He pointed to the caption running underneath. ' "Medium: Lucy Diamond" – in that fleece. Honey, you gotta be a Large! The only good thing is that no one will recognise you from this. I mean, a fleece, Lucy? A fleece? Have I taught you nothing? Is this the real you? Has there always been a Cotton Traders girl itching to get out of her Karen Millen? They say there's no such thing as bad publicity.' Nigel started again. 'Whoever said that obviously never saw this photo.'

Lucy was not happy with Nigel and she was not happy about the article either. The editors had filled in Shannon's embellished truths with downright lies. At best it made her look like a bumbling con-artist. She just hoped that people she cared about, the Barrockby and District Society for the Academic Study of Anomalous Phenomena, for example, or Keith's widow, or Mike and his little girls, if they saw it, would know it was fabricated.

But still Lucy berated herself. The message had been simple enough: 'I've always loved you, Hayley, and I'll never forget that time we had in Rhyll.'

It was only when Lucy got to the end of the sentence that she realised she wasn't standing in Hayley's flat and that judging by the look on her face Shannon had never been to Rhyll. But Shannon knew someone who had and she got on her mobile phone straight away to find out where the bitch was and told everyone exactly what she was going to do to her when she got her.

Even the right message had not been well received: 'Shannon, give the children my love and I'll see you on the other side.'

'On the other side? On the other side?' Shannon bellowed. 'I feel like topping myself just so I can give 'im what for.' She was furious and she didn't hold back. The air was blue and Lucy was glad that the children – a boy and a girl both under five – were in the other room watching an old *Teletubbies* DVD.

It had been an easy enough task and a simple enough mistake to make. Little did Lucy realise that she had started a feud that would last generations and end with her mug-shot alongside an advert for tea bags.

She could hear the words of Nigel's patron saint, Cher: 'If I could turn back time . . .' It wasn't her fault. It was the estate's. Every eighties block of flats looked the same and none of them had a complete name sign. Every one had had letters removed or rearranged for comedic effect. The Cilla Black Towers had now become 'liCk Balls ere'. Even the amusement arcade in the graffitied strip of shops had not been immune. Happy Amusements had a more earthy tone once the a,m,u and the final t and s had been removed. Clearly there was talent on that estate being wasted.

It hadn't occurred to Lucy that one of her spirit saviours might be a two-timing rat (as the tabloids would put it) with a wife and kids in one block and a pregnant mistress in another. Funny how someone can be a good soul and an arsehole at the same time. Naïvely, she thought Hayley might be his sister, or a friend. Not that it can have been easy to live with Shannon. She was a bit of a chain-smoking harpy, to say the least, but she was loving to her children and judging by the tattoo spread on her chest she had obviously thought a lot of Ryan.

Scouser Ryan Stewart had provided the muscle on the night of the séance and Jonathan had freely admitted that he had provided more than enough energy to give the final KO to Joe. Ryan had appeared to Lucy with a cheeky grin and chunky jewellery. Tattoos snaked up his arms; he had spiked-up hair and sand-stained steel-toecapped boots. He had been a builder until the head injury that cost him his life.

'Well, would you wear a hat with hair as good as this?' He'd winked, looking more like a hen night's idea of a builder than a real brickie. It wouldn't be hard to fall for someone with that patter and confidence. Lucy should know.

Nigel was still quoting from the article. Unfortunately, the by-line didn't clarify that this quote was Shannon talking about Hayley. It was picked out in bold print next to the lumpy, fleecy picture of Lucy Diamond.

' "No wonder the cow cried so much at the funeral. She sat in my house, eating my food, knowing all the time that she'd been having it away with my husband."

'And she's not the only one who's been having it away, is she?' innuendoed Nigel with a wink and a face to rival Kenneth Williams, at last shuffling the magazine into the pile of glossy supplements and dodgy mail-order brochures that spilled out of their Sunday papers.

'Aren't you eating those?' Jojo had her mouth full and was eyeing Nigel's untouched waffle brunch. 'Because if you don't want it, I'll eat it. No point in letting it go to waste.'

He pushed the plate towards her with instructions that she could have half.

'This giving up smoking is no good, is it? Jojo is eating like a horse and I'm into a full-on diet and detox now.'

'Diet? Detoxing? Did you get alcoholic poisoning or something?' Lucy asked between mouthfuls.

'No. Haven't you noticed? It's ever since that woman at the Psychic Fair.' Jojo speared a waffle from his plate. 'He's been paranoid about his health ever since.'

'No I haven't. Anyway, there's nothing wrong with looking after yourself and getting rid of toxins, because if you carry on stuffing your face like you've been this morning, Jojo Gray, then the only clothes that'll fit you will be Lucy's fleece.'

'Do I have to say it again? It was Simon's.'

'Haven't you got a photo of him or something? I want to see how many heads he's got.' Nigel was using that peculiar tone of his again.

'No. I can't use my phone around him. He can't be around technology. I told you that too. Several times.'

'What is he? A vampire?'

'Oh, yes.' Jojo perked up as if only really paying attention for the first time. 'Simon! Are you going to tell us more?' She was beckoning to the waiter for more maple syrup. True to stereotype, that was a cue for Nigel to start quoting lyrics from the musicals. *Grease*, to be exact. Lucy was Sandy to their singular Pink Lady and T-bird. They badgered her to tell them more and Lucy did.

She told them everything, but without the gynaecological detail. She didn't retell their lovemaking as slapstick comedy with inappropriate farty noises and strange requests because it wasn't. She gave them the facts but didn't dwell on faults or freakish behaviour that should get Simon sectioned. She didn't even mention doubts because she didn't have any. It was a first.

Initially, Lucy and Simon hadn't planned to do any overnight stops, but as the petting in the car got heavier and their bond closer, and because a newly mature and finally self-respectful Lucy Diamond didn't really want their first time to be in the back of a Morris Minor, she suggested they amend their route. Simon wasted no time in saying 'Leave it to me' and Lucy did; though later she would ask herself why she didn't question how a man who could not use Internet, telephone or mobile – as was claimed – could book a hotel so quickly.

Still, she had to admit he did a good job. After leaving Shirley Richards's bungalow they'd headed north, and one motorway, several A roads and a few villages later they were on a very dark and narrow country lane twisting this way and that. Lucy was spooked. 'Are you sure this is the right way to the hotel?'

'Who said anything about a hotel?' Simon smiled in the dark and Lucy was gripped with fear, worrying that she had once again totally misjudged a character and that she'd be found dead in a ditch tomorrow morning.

Suddenly, they turned into what looked like a field entrance. Each side of the trail was lit with tea lights in jam jars and twinkling fairy lights along the hedgerows. Ahead a domed tent – part canvas, part geodesic dome – looking like a mini-Eden Project glowed welcomingly in a far corner. It looked how Jasmine's eco-idyll should, without the heaps of crap waiting to be recycled and pale vegan children staring from behind bushes. The air was crisp and cold but the puffs of wood smoke promised a warm retreat, and the smell of coffee wafting on the air made it obvious that a pot was warming on the black pot-bellied stove that could be seen within. A double bed laden with organic cottons and sheepskins dominated the centre of the oak-floored dome.

Lucy had a sudden panic about toileting, with visions of sneaking out to the hedge in the bitter cold of morning, but later found a delightful flushing lavatory that had many eco credentials but looking or smelling like Jasmine's earth closet was not one of them.

'Do you like it?' Simon had looked nervously at Lucy, who had not said a thing but an open-to-interpretation 'Wow' after they'd parked the car. 'Wow' could actually mean 'Wow it's wonderful' or 'Wow – a fuckin' tent in November, you idiot!'

They'd explored the dome together. There was a little kitchen area with a basket of food including a hot casserole in a rustic crock pot and crusty bread. There was champagne in an ice bucket, and in a corner screened by muslin a claw-footed bath waited to be filled. Rose petals had been scattered over the bed. At each revelation, each surprising extra, still Lucy's response had been just 'Wow.' Simon needed confirmation. He'd held his breath.

Lucy had loved it. It had all the romance she'd ever wanted without the schmaltz. She didn't really want cards with poems by Patience Strong or red roses or teddy bears grasping hearts that said 'I wuv you' – Nigel would behead something like that if he found it in her flat, anyway. What she did want was right here in front of her – thoughtfulness, respect, and a hero who would hold her tight when the village hall was falling to pieces around their ears.

It was cold outside but they were cosy within. The home-cooked food had been fabulous. They'd played cards in front of the fire and drunk the champagne far too quickly from nerves and a feeling of celebration. They'd compared the eco-dome favourably to their parental dwellings and lounged on the big leather bean bags, stomachs full of organic chocolates and delicious bread, and pretended that the big double bed was not there, waiting, beckoning with all its loaded promise and potential for disappointment.

'I brought you here because I really want to get to know you better, and you to know me,' said Simon, swishing down a flute of champagne and avoiding her eyes, vulnerable as he exposed his thoughts. 'I've been here before – with some mates' – a quick reassurance – 'and it's good, you know – stripped back, raw. I've always wanted to bring someone special here, someone who would appreciate it and share it with me. I'm glad you like it, Lucy. I hoped you would.'

She crawled over to him, flopping down on to his bean bag, which squished and remoulded underneath them. She kissed him lightly on the cheek and chin. He groaned with the weight of her on his stomach. He still wanted to talk.

'I mean, we don't really know each other, do we, Lucy? Not really. I mean everything is right so far but I want you to like me for me, the real me without any pretending. And here you can't escape yourself. You can in a city or surrounded by other people but here you can't dress yourself up and be something you're not. Out here there's no escape from yourself – no TV, no phones, no music, no radio, nothing.'

It was all very philosophical stuff. As though he was building up to a Big Point, a climax. Thanks to Lucy he never got there.

'You must have learned a lot about yourself after the lightning strike.' She thought he was talking about his problems with technology. She was wrong.

'What? Oh. Oh, yes. Let's not talk about that now.' He went quiet then, as if there were things he wanted to say but couldn't. As if her interruption had stopped him going down a path he really wanted to explore. It seemed entirely feasible at that moment that he was going to say that he was falling in love with her, but he didn't. Instead, he rolled her over and on to the rug, struggling to lift her and carry her, not so much an officer and a gentleman as someone trying to dispose of a corpse. Lucy struggled and giggled, shrieking at his attempts to lift her until finally he heaved her on to the big brass bed. Talk-time was over.

There are lots of different ways to have sex. There are the senseless rutting animal shags, born out of need for release rather than mutual liking or respect – rather like Lucy with Tony Russell. There are the sympathy shags or the It's Friday Let's Get This Out of the Way lazy fucks of the long-time married. There is the seeking self-esteem intercourse, the revenge coupling, the angry screw, the power (over you, over him, over someone else who's not even in the room) mating, the friendly fuck, the accessories bonk requiring whips, handcuffs and assorted household items. There are ways of having it off, getting your leg over, shafting, humping, that are funny, dirty, annoying, sweet, hot, boring or disgusting.

There are lots of different ways to do it, and sometimes there is the coming together – pardon the pun – that is so right, so faultless and mutually pleasurable, so perfectly seamless in the moves from one place to another, that it is like an expertly choreographed erotic dance. Hands move smoothly over flesh that gives itself readily, eyes lock hungrily and swap secrets with one another. Hips move fluidly in rhythmic time and bodies fit together as though moulded especially for one another. Fingers are kissed and licked, bodies slide over one another, and the touch on neck or fingers or hair is sublime.

A way of being together where it's difficult to tell where bodies end and begin. Where lips and hands seek union so desperately that a touch is like volts of electricity applied and a kiss becomes a marrying of minds. It becomes more than the act so basely depicted in porn films and magazines. It becomes a meeting of souls, a magical joining capable of changing tides, history or the world itself. A spiritual, mythical thing that explains why Romeo and Juliet did as they did, why Arthur's Guinevere slept with Lancelot, why Cathy couldn't give up Heathcliff, why Brad left Jen for Angelina (though that then went wrong), why Jude cheated on Sienna with the nanny – or maybe it can't explain that, but you get the picture.

When union is like that, euphemisms such as 'the beast with two backs' or 'how's your father' do not apply. It can only be love-making because that is exactly what it is. This was one of those nights.

*

'That good, huh?' said Jojo, looking peculiarly proud and admiring when Lucy had finished telling her tale.

'That good.' Lucy smiled, her stomach flip-flopping as she remembered in luscious, juicy detail every second of that night.

'Eugghhh! You make me sick.' It was good to know that even with giving up smoking and the my-body-is-a-temple stuff Nigel was still Nigel after all.

Still, they were all done now. All the messages of the Magnificent Seven delivered. Well, sort of. Of course she hadn't done Jonathan's but that didn't count. That was special. Different. That needed time and special handling . . . it needed channelling, a direct line. She had to prepare for that one.

So back to London and on with life as before. Although this time she was actually writing old-fashioned letters to Simon and he to her. Never had the arrival of the postman been so much fun. They were talking about Christmas; he could not even think of going home to New Zealand yet. He was saying things in the letters like 'I would love to show you North Island' and 'You would love my parents'. They were good signs. And he was a good writer: his letters were filled with funny observations and references to books and films and they started swapping silly items like car air-fresheners, sachets of sugar or boring postcards.

OK – they hadn't all gone as planned. (The meetings not the letters, silly.) Better to dwell on the positives: Carly, Claire's little family, Shirley Richards. The magazine article had been overly negative anyway and had not mentioned Ryan's actual message to his wife, which when you ignored the adultery was actually quite loving.

And OK, the octogenarian major's message hadn't been received well either. He had organised Jonathan's campaign against Joe. Drilled them all in military manoeuvres and tactical advances, but his message had not pleased his widow. It seems that he'd been met at the metaphorical pearly gates by his mother and was overjoyed at the reunion. Not so Mrs Major, who expressed such a dislike for a mother-in-law who had made her life a living hell of unreasonable demands (she came on their honeymoon and every holiday thereafter) and bitter asides ('it's a pity you lost your looks so early') that the prospect of sharing an eternity with her seemed to be more like damnation. Lucy tried to persuade her that the other side was a place of forgiveness where there were no bad feelings, but the major's widow was not convinced and said she really did not want to die now. At eighty-two with a heart condition the odds were not in her favour.

OK, OK – Lucy hadn't quite delivered that other one in Manchester. Maybe she'd not done her best, still mooning around as she was from the night before on a big brass bed in a funny domed tent in the middle of nowhere, but if someone won't take your calls and asks their doorman to eject you from the premises – well, you can't do any more. Anyway, she had written the message on a scrap of paper and got Simon to shove it, with one of her cards, through the brushed steel and cedarwood letter box of the elegant loft conversion before they both ran away giggling like school kids.

She often wondered what the young theatre director had made of his message from his deceased older male lover. Lucy was just glad that she hadn't had to deliver it face to face after all. Was it an issue of interiors or toupees? The message had simply read: 'I know you like it but that rug really doesn't work.'

It was that half-light creeping through the curtains as night slid into day. Lucy had just done her dawn zombie walk to the bathroom and leapt back into the warm cocoon of her bed in Walthamstow Heights. Wrapping herself up in the duvet, she was delighted that it was Saturday and that there were still more hours of sleep to be had. She quickly slid back into her dreams, illogical scenarios involving camels and baskets of fruit, and then on her Caribbean beach she could hear the shuffle of Nan Peters's slippers over carpet and feel the familiar weight as someone sat down heavily on the bed.

It was a nostalgic dream. A scenario played out over countless mornings before school. The gentle shaking. The 'Wake up, Lucy-love. Wake up' followed by the old groggy protests: 'Ten more minutes, please. Ten more minutes. Need more sleep.'

The dream was so vivid, she could almost feel the lumpy springs of the old bed in her bedroom, hear Nan's familiar wheeze and groan as she raised herself stiffly up.

'OK. Ten more minutes, sleepyhead,' and Nan's knotty arthritic fingers tousled already messy bed-head hair as her cold lips pressed a kiss on Lucy's forehead, leaving the scent of old Coty powder compact and Ponds cold cream.

Lucy smiled and drifted back off, grateful that she could sleep longer and basking in the affectionate gestures. And the dream stayed with her. The comforting presence of her grandmother lulling her off to sleep as though she were a little girl again.

She was woken by the incessant ringing of the telephone. Too early to be Jojo or Nigel, and it wouldn't be Simon. It seemed to ring more urgently than usual. Its tone was tainted with anxiety so that before she was even fully awake, before she answered it, she knew, and the cold realisation that it hadn't been a dream at all hit her in the stomach and spread down her legs and up into her chest like molten lead.

They say the advent of grief can be like being struck by a car or a steam train. They say you can't quite accept what you're hearing at first, that you can be happy, sad, hysterical, numb, and all are accepted emotions of loss. They say a lot of things about those early moments, the first few hours, days, years when you lose someone you really, really love. There are experts on bereavement, counsellors, people who've been there, who know the pain.

But what no words, books or observations of others could ever explain to Lucy Diamond is how much it just really, actually, deeply, physically, emotionally, spiritually hurt.

19

Lucy had never arranged a funeral before. Never had to sort out the practicalities like death certificates and funeral directors. Women's magazines were full of articles about orgasms and covering pinboards in pretty fabric but where was the real advice – 'Putting the Fun into Funerals', 'Crafty Catering for Wonderful Wakes', 'Casket Chic – Dressing the Deceased'?

Lucy was up and down between Yorkshire and London for days. There were insurances to deal with, phone calls to be made, clergymen to speak to – and then there was Jasmine.

Jasmine did not take the news of her mother's death well, but then who does? Again, it fell to Lucy to do the strong stuff, be the support, make the travel arrangements because Jasmine kept wailing that she was going into free-fall and yelling for Bach Flower Rescue Remedy. It was not an easy time.

Luckily, Nan Peters was on hand to help. Lucy hadn't so much lost a beloved grandmother as gained a rather interfering spirit guide. There had barely been time to cry. But then there had barely been time to think.

'Stop the tears, Lucy-love. It's just part of life, death,' were Nan's sage words. Lucy just wished there was someone earth-bound who could help take charge of it all.

Nigel hadn't wanted to come to help as he'd been frightened of Nan Peters when she was alive and the thought that she was around and invisible was too much for him to bear. Jojo had sent lots of supportive texts but had been feeling off colour with a tummy bug she said, so was keeping away. Poor thing – it seemed Jojo had not been feeling right for weeks now. Eating for England one moment and then going all pale and nauseous the next. However, both had promised to support Lucy on the day and were coming to the funeral.

But Simon had rushed to Lucy's side whenever she was in Ploxbury and held her as she howled, dry-eyed. He didn't stay overnight with her in the little terraced cottage but he was there with hot food and an arm round her shoulder when she needed it and he ran endless errands while Lucy made the arrangements for the funeral. He even helped her put together the 'words' to summarise Nan's life for the church reading. Those few paragraphs seemed woefully inadequate to represent all the years of love and humour, struggle and sacrifice and long-forgotten youth.

Nan Peters had her own ideas for the funeral and her instructions were very exacting.

'Don't let your mother get involved,' was her dire warning. 'I don't want any of her Viking funeral pyre nonsense or wicker coffins. I want a plain casket, a memorial service and a trip to the crematorium. And don't bother saving the ashes. You never know whose you're getting from that municipal furnace. I'll be put to better use around the roses in the Garden of

Remembrance. Now, the buffet. No salad – it'll get stuck under everyone's top set. Just a bit of garnish. Ham and potted beef will be all right – no need to go over the top. I mean, they'll be coming to pay their respects, not get a free lunch. I've no doubt your mother will make some of those tutu things.'

'You mean tofu, Nan.'

'You know what I mean. Now, how many do you think will be coming? Not many if the number of funerals I've been to in the last five years is anything to go by. You're better off dying young if you want a big send-off. You'll remember to take the cards off the wreaths, won't you? Then you've got to send thank-yous. On good writing paper, mind. No he-mails or he-shes or whatever you call that computer speak. I've got some Basildon Bond in the top drawer of the bureau in the front room that should do you. Did I tell you I've met that Jonathan of yours? Came and introduced himself he did. Lovely fella. Ever so polite. I can see why you like him. Is he gay?'

'No!' Lucy was instantly transformed into a stroppy teenager.

'Well, I'm only asking because you do know how to attract them. So Jojo's coming, is she? Remind her it's a funeral and not a fashion parade. And Nigel, you say? I didn't know him that well but it's very good of him to come, I must say. Perhaps he could arrange the wreaths as everybody leaves the crematorium. He'd have an eye for it being the way he is, and those funeral directors – they sling them down anyhow. They're no more than dressed-up hod carriers.'

Lucy couldn't remember the last time she saw her grandmother so enthusiastic. She was always at her best with a 'do' to arrange and said she wouldn't dream of crossing over to the light until it was done. Births, marriages and deaths are the milestones of life, or were for Nan Peters's generation. Such things are inconveniences to our modern living. Now we have women returning to the boardroom barely having passed out the placenta, and internet pay-per-view funerals so that you don't even have to leave the office to see off a loved one. Deadlines, performance management and the newest season of *Big Brother* have become the big issues of the urban dweller, eclipsing the real stuff. The stuff even our most primitive ancestors knew had to be celebrated if any sense was going to be made of existence.

These days, the workplace is more sympathetic to time off to attend auditions of *Pop Idol* than to attend to a sick, dying or dead relative. However, thanks to Tony Russell, the weird bruising and her erratic attendance, Lucy's paymasters were so convinced that she was in the grip of some sort of breakdown that they were happy for her to have more time off for the funeral. Lucy's workplace hadn't always been so easy, not like Jojo's. She, of course, could call the shots and pass off a bit of a jolly up north to a cremation as work-related and still claim expenses.

It was Destination Funeral. The journey had Road Trip stamped all over it. It started off optimistically enough, if that's possible when a cremation is the goal. The sun was shining – the sky was a clear-visibility blue. There was water in the windscreen washer. It was to be a leisurely drive, not the white-knuckle ride that Jojo was usually guilty of, and they had agreed to factor in plenty of stops since Jojo now seemed to have some sort of bladder infection and was constantly going to the loo.

The sat-nav confidently pointed the course with the reassuring voice of Austin Powers: 'Take a left, baby, yeah!' There was a car-picnic of M&S's finest pre-packed sarnies, fruit and a multipack of organic exotically flavoured crisps that had probably been hand cooked by monks to a crispness that removed the top layer of skin from the roof of your mouth. They had glossy magazines including copies of *Hello!* and *Heat* – juicy bits to be read out to the driver and surgical enhancements of the stars to be critiqued by Nigel – 'Holy St Kylie! You've gone too far!'

Despite the solemn circumstances, they felt young, they felt free. They felt just like the Supergrass song until they realised that if you could remember the song's release you were neither of the above.

'I'm Thelma.'

'You're Louise.'

Jojo and Lucy argued and Nigel was smug, knowing that they could not dispute that he was Brad Pitt, but they were happy to be together again, though Jojo looked decidedly green when Nigel opened his chicken Caeser wrap and she had to open the window.

And there was the inviting prospect of the Boyfriend. They were finally going to meet Simon. Jojo and Nigel couldn't wait to get together to analyse and assess and decide the odds of its lasting, but meanwhile there was chat, upbeat banter to take Lucy's mind off the task ahead of her and lots of swapping of funny, sentimental stories about Nan Peters between Jojo and Lucy.

'Remember that time she called the police out looking for us because we were so late coming home? And they asked for a description and once she'd finished describing our miniskirt and over-the-knee sock ensembles the police said, "And, madam, you're still wondering why they're not home?" '

'And when she used to order baguettes from Greggs and call them a "bag of teats"?'

'Best cook in the world, though,' said Jojo, suddenly wistful. 'Her apple pie.'

'Her lemon meringue.'

And then they fell silent.

There is nothing upbeat about losing someone you love, no matter how good their 'innings'. The world somehow will never look the same again. Everything will be viewed through a lens of loss, the lack of them. All the weddings they'll never go to, the new-born babies that they will never hold, the new homes and holidays they will never see. And the things you will never hear them say again. Death is no picnic even if M&S are involved.

Nigel filled the silence with a complaint about leg room, shifting around in his seat and trying to pull his jeans from their uncomfortable resting place.

'These jeans are riding up higher than Simon Cowell's. I wish I'd worn my Diesels – by the time we get there I'll be cut in two!' Later, he would focus his complaining on Jojo's creeping-higher speed. 'We've got plenty of time to get to Yorkshire. I feel like bloody Dick Turpin here with you racing your way up north.'

Still it was comfortable, reassuring, to hear Nigel's cynical commentary on everything from Justin Timberlake ('logically you wouldn't but you want to anyway') to the highbrow topic of politics ('the trouble is there are no fit politicians. If there were I think I could get more aware. Know what I'm saying?').

So it had started off well, and even the unanticipated (unseen by sat-nav) road works had not dented their spirits. They had a competition of car flirting in the traffic jam, winking and lane-hopping away from vanloads of workmen, lorry drivers and lonely road reps. Nigel was the winner, of course, the uncrowned King of the Road. They pulled faces at bored children in front of TVs in their 4 x 4s. Nigel made an ingenious mask out of a magazine head-shot of Posh Spice and waved royally as they crawled past other drivers. How they laughed.

Then the creeping traffic crawled to a standstill and they sighed, but Jojo was able to turn off the engine and flick through a magazine and Nigel opted to be DJ on the in-car MP3. Then people started getting out of their cars to stretch their legs and the traffic news said there had been a terrible accident and the threesome thanked their lucky stars that they hadn't been in it. An hour passed, but they weren't worried. It was frustrating but they had plenty of time.

'It doesn't matter what time we get there,' said Lucy, ever optimistic. 'The funeral isn't until eleven tomorrow. We've got plenty of time.' Famous last words, as the saying goes.

You see people huddled on hard shoulders, all of their luggage stacked behind the crash barrier, and you may think *Poor souls, I'm glad it's not me* or *Close shave* as the tattered blown-out tyre becomes visible or *Idiots – don't they know how to change a tyre?*

You see the driving rain from the cloud that came out of nowhere on a beautiful clear winter morning and think *If only they had packed an umbrella or a blanket or even a decent waterproof coat that wait before the*

recovery service arrives would be more comfortable.
Then in seconds you've moved on and you're that bit
further on towards your journey's end and the people
sitting on their weekend bags on a sopping wet
embankment are forgotten.

It doesn't occur to you that they will be there for
hours because it's an unusually busy day due to
unforeseen accidents and gridlocked traffic jams and
tow trucks needing repairs. You never ponder about
whether they will be late for their important appointments, wedding or funerals. You never think about their
smart-occasion clothes getting soaked through in the
driving rain, streaks of dye running through pressed
shirts and dry-clean-only wool-mix suits losing never-
to-be-regained shape.

Funny how a five-hour journey can turn into an epic
trek of gap year proportions. In the time it took the
three mourners to get the key in the front door of Nan
Peters's house they could have flown to South America.
The cloud that had dogged them on the side of the M1
had clung to them like a cartoon depression, so that
even as they humped the sopping luggage from Simon's
ancient Morris Minor to the front door rain hammered
down on their backs. This journey would go down in the
myths and legends of their friendship – along with the
time that Jojo had wet herself – and would be retold
with only minor embellishments for years to come. Oh,
they would laugh about it in the future. Right now, they
don't feel like laughing but one day they might.

'Remember that time . . . and Jojo's RAC membership had run out . . . and the heat had caused the rear
right-hand disc to melt . . . then the next tow truck
driver was drunk and drove off the A road and into a

ditch . . . and we were in the back of beyond . . . and we couldn't get a taxi . . . and Simon drove to get us and we had to sit all cramped together with the cases on our laps . . . and by the time we got there it was half past four in the morning' and so on.

But right now they weren't laughing. Right now, in the early hours of the morning, wet through, starving, exhausted, with just a few short hours to sort out a funeral buffet, they weren't laughing at all.

Y ou can throw a buffet together in a very short space of time with the right amount of potted meats and pre-packed Scotch eggs. It helps if it's not designed for the smoked salmon and blini crowd, because their tastes can be a little more judgemental. Likewise, you can speed-dry an outfit using a hairdryer and a two-bar electric fire if you're persistent enough, and an artfully tied neckerchief can hide unwanted scorch marks.

It is also possible to attend the funeral of your most beloved relative and not take in a word that is said to you or about your loved one. All of the above are survival techniques and mechanisms that Lucy relied upon on that day.

In some ways the funeral was the easy bit. The cremation was a piece of cake – there was something wildly exuberant about the way the casket disappeared behind the curtains just as Frank Sinatra belted out the last few bars of 'My Way'.

'Make it "Disco Inferno" when my time comes,' Nigel requested as the velvet curtains slid shut. The hard part was afterwards. The send-off. Taking care of distant relatives and being hostess under the watchful, judging eyes of Nan Peters's Widows' Posse – Widdas with Attitude. That included the unibosomed Barbara whom Lucy had not seen the séance at Barrockby village hall.

Trying to butter an entire white sliced loaf whilst chatting to Nan Peters who (ironically) wouldn't go away and simultaneously keeping an eye on Jasmine who was wafting around the house burning herbs and reciting Celtic verse for the Journeys of The Dead. That was the hard part.

Lucy designated the job of Jasmine-watch to Jojo and got her to make spot checks on Ert because he had taken up permanent silent residence in the garden arbour where he sat rolling spliff after spliff despite the chill. Nan Peters was not at all happy about it, but then she wasn't happy that he was here at all.

'What's your mother doing bringing 'im 'ere? He's about as useful as patio windows on a submarine. He's making the whole house smell like a Moroccan brothel! And they're sleeping in my bed! Together! Really! Your mother has the morals of an alley cat and you can tell her I said so.'

'I'm not going to bring it up today, Nan. When this is over I'll channel the two of you into a nice little chat. Jasmine's having a hard time getting used to the fact that she's now the matriarch, that's all.'

Nan snorted derisively. 'Matriarch my eye! I notice that it's you setting up the spread. Oh, tell her to stop all that chanting – it's upsetting Mrs Braithwaite from next door. Put on Radio Two, for pity's sake. I always have Jeremy Vine on at this hour.'

Nigel appeared flushed-cheeked with an empty platter, fresh from avoiding the advances of a tipsy comb-over. 'We need more sarnies. It's like a bulimic convention in there. I know that they're on pensions and all that but I swear that they're tipping plateloads into their handbags for later. Lucy, you're at risk from cramp in that forearm with all that spreading, but if they don't get more ham, things could turn really ugly.'

The doorbell rang and Nigel as 'Funeral Monitor' made a dash to answer it whilst dodging the pinching fingers of the sex-pest in tweed and carrying a tray of small glasses of sweet sherry. It was Simon, looking uncomfortable in a shirt and borrowed suit. Jojo, Jasmine and Nigel all stood in the hall, gaping.

There are 'fine words and grand gestures' as Nan Peters used to say. Easy for a rich man to throw money at a problem or for people like politicians to drone on about all the great and good things they intend to do. But it's the actual doing that counts, the small actions, the little things, stuff that doesn't cost. It is by seeing what is done that the real character judgement of a man (or woman) can be made, and Simon turning up in Lucy's hour of need said it all. It made her heart swell and tears cloud her eyes.

'Anything I can do to help?' he offered.

'Keep that Australian Uri Geller away from my cutlery,' Nan warned.

Mrs Braithwaite appeared with an armful of crockery. 'Lucy-love, I thought you should know, that effeminate lad's put out Betty's wedding china on the buffet. I don't think she'd be happy about that. She saves that for best.'

'Don't I know you?' Nigel made a beeline for Simon and coquettishly flicked his hair around, almost upsetting the tray of sherry.

A familiar figure in a National Trust name badge and slacks appeared, unseen by the others, in the doorway adjoining the hall. 'I know it's not a good time, Lucy, but I really need to talk about Jonathan. I'm very worried about him.'

Walking directly through Keith Richards to get to the kitchen, an old man in a faded green suit brought a plate of half-nibbled sandwiches to Lucy. 'Olive can't have potted salmon. It brings her out in a rash.'

Jasmine wandered past wafting burning sage, intoning, 'I was made from the ninefold elements, from fruit trees, from paradisiacal fruit . . . by the wiseset druids I was made . . .'

Lucy gripped the kitchen counter top for strength and carefully put down the spreading knife. She felt as though her head was in a vice. She counted to ten very slowly before she turned round.

'Don't worry, Mr Harbottle, I'm making another round or two of ham. Mrs Braithwaite, the good china is fine. Trust me, Nan told me herself that I should use it today of all days. Simon – thank God you're here – will you help Mrs Braithwaite to put the china back?' And from the side of her mouth, 'Nan – can't you come back later?'

'Why? I'm enjoying myself, and if strangers can turn up at my funeral' – she gestured to Keith – 'I don't see why I should leave.' Keith momentarily vanished, clearly to avoid any sort of phantasmal fight.

What Lucy didn't realise was this was just a warm-up, a prologue, a prelude to the main event. The best – as Frank Sinatra also sang – is yet to come.

Finally, the pensioners were sated on ham and Lucy could turn her attention to making endless pots of tea. Ert remained in the arbour where he was assisting a member of the retired to re-pack a pipe, probably not using tobacco. Nan had floated off to watch over her wake and hear what her friends and relations had to say about her. Jasmine was discussing organic gardening with the allotment holders of Ploxbury who, of course, had been doing this for years without realising that the middle classes had a name for it.

Jojo was listening attentively with her feet raised on the pouffe, seeking solace from high heels inside the warmth and comfort of Nan's slippers. Simon was collecting up cups and saucers for the next round of tea that Lucy was preparing. As she worked in the kitchen, Lucy's hair was escaping the tight chignon she had wound for herself over the steaming kettle. She had been aiming for sophistication – it was forming a halo of fuzz.

It felt good to not have to care. She didn't feel that Simon would judge her for her inability to maintain straight hair at a funeral. He'd seen her at her worst – bloody and bruised from Joe, hollow-eyed and pasty with grief – and still he came to be an unpaid skivvy at Nan's 'do'. He didn't have to say he cared about her and send compilation tapes of Mariah Carey or *Now That's the Very Best Love Songs for Lovers in the world . . . Ever!!! Number 242*. He was letting Lucy know how he felt loud and clear.

Nigel wandered into the kitchen. He'd been deep in conversation with Simon for a while but had disappeared off upstairs a short time ago. He was back now holding a magazine, looking very serious and a little distracted.

'Simon seems nice.' It was the first time he had ever said anything positive about a boyfriend of Lucy's. He was standing very close to Lucy now, almost touching her. She 'scused past him to reach the teaspoons.

'There's not many blokes would come and do a Help the Aged bit like he's done today.'

'Except for you, of course.' She kissed him on the cheek as she swept past with the tray. He was still in the kitchen when she came back. Loitering would be a better word to describe the way that he was skulking around the sink. Lucy boiled the kettle again.

'How long have you known him now?'

'Simon? Less than a month, really. It seems longer, doesn't it?'

'Mmm, s'pose it does. It's difficult to really get to know a person in that space of time, though, isn't it? And he's a bit like you, is he? Supernatural powers and all that?' Nigel was obviously driving at something but Lucy couldn't tell what. She dried her hands on the towel and leaned against the sink.

'Electromagnetic powers,' she corrected.

'Must be hard to get around avoiding all things electric. What's his work again?'

'Outdoorsy stuff. Hedge laying, dry stone walling. Whatever comes his way, I guess. What's going on here? What are you getting at, Nigel?'

Slowly, Nigel passed over the magazine that he had in his hand. There was none of the usual merciless piss-taking. He looked worried, sorry about the Pandora's box he was opening.

'I think you should see this before you go falling head over heels.' He actually sounded concerned. It was already open at the page he wanted her to see.

It was a glossy men's magazine, the sort of lad-mag that has graphic pictures of war-wounded opposite articles on mixing cocktails. They had bought it for the journey to Ploxbury because they wanted to see the air-brushing on a bikini-clad soap star who was known for her sixty-a-day fag habit and her penchant for face fillers.

'Nigel. How is this relevant?' Lucy's eye had been drawn to a feature box concerning impossible sex positions as animated by Barbie and Action Man.

'Not that. That. I said that I knew him from some-where, didn't I?' Nigel was pointing to a two-by-six column. Not huge in the scheme of things, but signifi-cant. It was called 'Mumbo Jumbo: Kiwi Simon's Adventures in the Paranormal'. A photograph of the columnist wearing a novelty turban and looking camped-up mystical clutching a crystal ball was alongside.

'He looks just like Simon,' said Lucy vaguely as the truth slowly seeped into a place where she finally had to acknowledge it. She couldn't ignore it. It *was* Simon. Simon the Myth Buster, writing for his monthly column exposing dodgy tarot readers and mocking Roswell believers. This was his 'writing a bit', was it? Not dodgy poems at all but a sceptic's column in the national press. She scanned the article, lighting on words like 'pseudo-psychics', and absorbed the top tips about tricks used by 'mind-readers'.

Then she came to the little précis about that night at the Barrockby and District Society and Lucy's throat tightened as she read things like 'case of mass hysteria brought on by dodgy wiring', 'it was impossible to work out how the sensory effects had been achieved' and '*conveniently* all photographic equipment had malfunctioned as the séance got under way'.

Lucy felt dizzy and sick. This shouldn't feel worse than her grandmother dying but coming on top of that stress it certainly did. Human nature being what it is, her first instinct was to shoot the messenger.

'Why are you showing me this now?' She turned on Nigel, wild-haired and wild-eyed. He was saved by Simon returning cups and crummy plates of best china.

'Showing you what?' Simon had detected the edge to Lucy's voice and was instantly protective. It was too late for that now. He saw the open copy of *Wasted* in her hand.

'Oh, shit,' he said.

'Oh shit indeed.' Lucy's voice was hard and brittle.

It's funny how pensioners have to have the telly up really loud and can't hear a simple statement like 'The gas man's here', but give them a four-letter word at a funeral and their overly large ears (these and noses keep growing throughout your life – start keeping a graph *now* to note your changes) prick up like tracker dogs' on a scent. There's nothing the elderly like better than a good row at a special occasion. They mobbed the kitchen. Nigel went into NYPD mode.

'There's nothing to see here.' They ignored him and he was slightly grazed in the crush.

'I can explain.'

'Can you?'

'It's not the way it seems.'

'Isn't it?' Lucy had the moral high ground here and Nan Peters's mourners knew it although they knew nothing about why. Jasmine and Jojo pressed into the kitchen to see what the fuss was about and Lucy passed the open magazine to Barbara, jabbing at the article for her to read. Barbara reached for the bifocals resting on her chest.

'This is your writing, is it? The little bit you do on the side?'

'Who's his bit on the side?' shouted a slightly deaf Mr Harbottle.

'What are you, Simon? Who are you?' Lucy didn't care that she had an audience. 'Because this article seems to be some sort of investigation to expose me as a fraud. Just tell me who is the truthful one out of the two of us?'

'I was going to tell you—'

'What, before you ripped me to shreds in print or after?' The funeral guests' heads were twisting this way and that like the crowd's at Wimbledon.

'It's not like that . . .'

Jasmine, having taken in the sudden down-turn in her only daughter's love life, explained it sadly away to Jojo.

'It's her karma. She's paying for a previous incarnation. She was probably an adulteress.'

'Oh, shut up,' said Nan Peters, securing a ringside seat. No one but Lucy heard her. Barbara, having finished the article, suddenly struck Simon with the rolled-up magazine.

'Ow. Barbara – let me explain . . .'

'You've tricked us, you double-dealer.' Barbara hit him again and the other retired folk all murmured along in support, although none of them really had a clue what was going on.

'So were you struck by lightning?' Hot angry tears were sliding down Lucy's face as she began her interrogation.

'No.'

'And you can't bend spoons?'

'Sort of – well, cheap ones. There's a trick to it. No. No I can't. Not really.'

'And the mobile phones?'

'Done with magnets, but I didn't deliberately try to mislead you.'

'What about the chair in the hall? All twisted and mangled. How did you do that?'

Simon shrugged. 'A fluke. It was old and broken to start with and there was some pretty weird shit going down that night anyway.'

The pensioners gasped in disapproval at his language.

'The flowers? The wilted flowers you bought me?'

'They were the last ones left in the village shop.'

Lucy roared in rage and joined Barbara in physical abuse. She slapped him on the arm.

'And are you the product of hippy parents? Do you even know how to build a dry stone wall? Did you go to that tent just with "mates" or is it where you take all your conquests? Are you even from New Zealand?' Even the people in the know had trouble keeping up with that one.

'Yes. Uhh . . . yes. Shit!' The pensioners reeled again at his profanity. 'I've forgotten the order of the questions. Look, Lucy – hear me out. I'll be honest with you.'

'There's a first!' She was full of bitterness.

'I'm not a dry stone waller really – though I have been while I've been up here. It was part of my cover because I'm a journalist and my series – that was not an easy job to secure, by the way. Journalistically, that was a coup. A big leap for my career. Anyway, the job involves being a sceptic about the spiritual trade and stuff. I was supposed to infiltrate the Barrockby and District Society, being the oldest club of its kind in Britain, and sort of dish the dirt on their secrets.'

'You pig!' Barbara threw herself into the violence demanded by the situation and set about Simon with the magazine again. He fended off her blows.

'But if you read the article properly I do say what good, genuine people they are and that it can't be explained by all the cynical theories, and' – he raised his hand to defend himself again – 'and I've learned so much. Ouch, Barbara, stop it. Please. Ow. Especially from you, Lucy. Stuff that's remarkable. Ooof – Barbara! Stuff I can't explain. Ay – that hurts!'

Keith Richards materialised again. 'Is this a good time, Lucy?'

She rounded on him. 'Whaddayouthink?' she snarled.

'I'm really very worried about Jonathan,' he began and then he took in the red eyes and blotchy face of the tearful Lucy, and Barbara beating Simon around the head and shoulders with a magazine.

'It'll wait,' he said tactfully, wringing his hands together, and was gone.

'Just go,' Lucy shouted.

'Read the article properly, Lucy. Please just read it again. It's my job to be a sceptic but I do say in the article that I can't explain what I saw. Can't we talk about this?'

'Get out. Leave me alone. Just leave. Go.' And the throng of mourners manoeuvred him towards the door as he shouted above their perms and thinning thatches.

'Please let's talk about this, Lucy. I didn't want you to find out this way. I tried to tell you at the tent, I tried. I just couldn't get it out. I wouldn't have wanted you to find out today. Lucy – I thought we had something good—' The door slammed shut and everything that Lucy thought she believed about love and romance burst like bubbles in the air after him.

'What a to-do,' said Mrs Braithwaite.

'What a bloody liar,' said Barbara. 'You're better off without him, love.'

'Oh, Lucy. I wish I could give you a cuddle.' Nan Peters's heart ached for her beloved granddaughter.

'Your nan'd turn in her grave.' The allergic-to-salmon Olive Harbottle spoke as a harbinger of doom.

'She was just cremated.' Lucy was incredulous.

Suddenly, the back door crashed wide open to gales of laughter and Ert, carrying over his shoulder a very stoned pensioner who had a ganja-filled pipe still hanging from his lips, tripped and spilled his cargo on to the floor. The old man sprawled tittering anew at the hilarity of it all.

'Any more sandwiches, Lucy, please?' asked Ert, a picture of polite Swedish manners. 'I think Mr . . . um . . . Norman here is a leetle tired and maybe hungry. It is the Munchies, I think.' That was one way to describe it.

'Anyone for sherry?' Nigel trilled, trying to lighten the mood and searching desperately for ways to hint that the party was over. He poured himself a large one and pushed an even larger one into Lucy's hand. The tray passed around. Lucy boiled the kettle again, partly for something to do and partly to turn away from everyone watching her.

Nigel tipped the last of the Harvey's into a mug for Jojo. She pushed it away. She looked suddenly very tired.

'Have it,' he insisted. If he was coming off detox, he wasn't doing it alone.

'I don't feel like it.'

'Come on. It's not as if you're driving, is it? It'll steel your nerves.'

'My nerves are fine.' Jojo was tetchy.

'Well, just a small one,' Nigel cajoled.

'I don't want one.'

'Of course you do. You always do.'

'I've given up drinking.'

'Yeah, yeah. 'Course you have.' Nigel's loud sarcasm was drawing attention. Nan Peters's friends and family braced themselves for another showdown.

'Nigel, don't you get it? I don't want a drink.' Jojo was getting louder to emphasise her point.

'Why ever not? What's the matter with you?'

'Because I'm bloody pregnant, that's why.'

The kitchen fell to silence, broken only by embarrassed coughs. An old man placed his sandwich back on the plate as though his appetite had been turned.

Jasmine was ecstatic. 'Oh, blessed be!' She showered Jojo with kisses.

Mrs Braithwaite – predictably – had something to say on the matter.

'Well I can't say that's a surprise. I should have expected it off one of your friends, Lucy Diamond.' By her tone you would think that it was Lucy who had somehow miraculously got Jojo pregnant.

Nan Peters's lips were compressed into the tightness of a cat's back passage.

'She always has to be the centre of attention, doesn't she? She can't let you be dumped or my funeral pass without wanting everyone to look at her.'

'I dumped him, Nan. I was the dumper here.' Lucy sank down on to a kitchen chair exhausted, looking at Jojo, who was gazing at her beseechingly. It all made sense – the sickness, the appetite, the making Nigel carry her bags yesterday. How could she, Lucy Diamond, have not known what was happening to her oldest and best friend?

'And I've got a lump on my testicle.'

The teacups certainly rattled to that one. Everyone turned now to look at Nigel. Later, he said it seemed like the right moment to disclose something that had been preying on his mind for a long time, but at that point Jojo was staring at him aghast.

Talk about stealing thunder.

I t was the sort of road that Lucy loved to stroll along on winter evenings. Terraces but *very* expensive terraces. Georgian, black railings, and – best of all – at dusk the lights would be on and the interiors lit up. A chance to peep into people's lives so different from her own. Homes with interiors that occasionally were photographed for glossy magazines or rented out to BBC productions.

From where Lucy stood she could see expensive artwork, 'statement' lights and 'design classic' chairs. Christmas was beginning to stain the good taste of the neighbourhood, but the style-conscious fought back with ironic inflatable Christmas trees, expensively crafted wreaths and colour-coordinated décor. There were actually secret anti-tinsel police in this neighbourhood, and you'd be hauled off to a gulag if anything so vulgar as a clockwork Santa strayed into your house.

The people who lived in these houses, with their newsreader good looks, did non-specific jobs in the non-specific 'media' or were 'something' in the City. If they looked out and saw Lucy now they would think she was a nanny on her way home or one of the waitresses from the myriad of little coffee shops and delis that seemed to spring up on every corner. They would know that she did not live here, that she was just passing through.

London dusk: streaks of red and orange made more vibrant through the lens of pollution cast warm, glowing-ember colours on to the white plasterwork of the houses. The steps going up to the front door of each house reminded Lucy of her favourite Shirley Hughes illustrations: fat toddlers sitting next to geranium-filled pots on the porch, gurgling babies in prams at the foot.

She thought then of Jojo swelling steadily in her Soho flat. Now past the sickness phase and blooming, all thick hair and happily piling on the pounds. She'd swapped her addictions to cigarettes and Chianti for a craving for anchovies and cheese. Nigel felt it was only a matter of time before she started eating coal. Would the pristine flat stay so minimal and chic with a toddler around? How would Party-Girl Jojo cope with a crying baby in the middle of the night, all alone?

The father of Jojo's baby probably lived in a street like this. He was married, he was successful in publishing and he had other children and a 'life' that he did not want to leave. He'd made that much very clear. Not that she'd asked him to. Not that she loved him. It had been 'one of those things', she said. Fate. And who knows if she will ever meet the right man anyway? She'd always wanted children and she'd look better pregnant at thirty than forty. It was the start of life, not the end.

'It's only pregnancy,' she said, 'It's not as if I'm dying, is it?'

This was not a tactful thing to say in front of Nigel at that point. Poor Nigel. Lucy had never seen him look so scared or vulnerable or unsure as he did before going into theatre, and not the sort he'd always yearned to be in.

Lucy and Jojo definitely had the cheap seats for that production, surrounded as he was by a layer of aunties, nieces and his mother, who crossed herself all the way to anaesthetics. Still, it had explained so much. His moodiness, his not wanting intimacy. His depression about life being *so* over. Even his dislike of youth, because he was staring into the demise of his own. Why had he left it so long? Why hadn't he told them? Perhaps he was more of a man than they had realised, after all.

He'd tried his own range of self-medication – booze to forget, sticky patches on the soles of his feet to draw out the toxins. But, he confessed, he felt it was somehow his fault. A plague sent as a punishment for his sins. Funny how early lessons of faith and belief stick even in the face of science and modern thinking. Like legions of dads, uncles and brothers before him he'd ignored it and hoped it would go away of its own accord. Now it had gone away. Past tense.

The surgeons had cut it out and stitched him back and the girls had visited every day bringing him baskets of organic fruit, rubbing alcohol cleanser on to their hands and bleach-wiping his bed and floor against MRSA. He was at home now, waiting impatiently and irritably for his results. He was the worst of demanding patients.

The lowering fog was creeping into her clothes and mussing up her hair as usual. Best to get this over with instead of standing around getting cold, Lucy thought, mindful that she would not be looking as cool and professional as she had hoped at Laura's door but clammy and more like someone who should be selling pegs or lucky heather.

This wasn't going to be easy. She was glad of all the experience of those warm-up meetings with the Magnificent Seven, thankful for the support of the Barrockby and District Society for the Academic Study of Anomalous Phenomena, and truly understanding of what it was to lose someone you loved so much, someone so irreplaceable.

Nan was gone now, crossed into the light, tired of living, exhausted by her visitations, with promises to return from time to time. The silence she left behind was deafening. It was best for her to go. Best for her to be at rest, at peace, but the heaviness on Lucy's heart was draining. She understood now Jonathan's urgency to connect back to the girl he loved. She recognised the sorrow that had been in Laura's eyes as her own; eyes robbed of their smile and weighted with grief. And she hated Simon even more for adding to the pain that she already had to bear.

As she studied the house numbers she could see a few anxious faces at windows; possibly cheap-labour nannies wondering if she was Immigration or the Neighbourhood Watch wondering how the riff-raff had managed to slip in.

Jonathan and Laura's home had its own grand entrance though they only had the two upper floors and the small landscaped 'city' garden. Two square galvanised containers containing bay trees flanked the door. Simple yet chic. Clichéd but tasteful. And still too expensive for Lucy to introduce to Walthamstow Heights. They'd only get pinched anyway. Even these were chained to the wall.

She climbed the steps and pushed the doorbell. If she hesitated she would only change her mind, and a shrill ring echoed in a corridor. Lucy's heart beat faster as footsteps approached on what was sure to be a beautifully restored tiled floor. In panic, she felt like she'd forgotten something and realised with an adrenaline jolt to her chest that it was Simon. On all her visits before he'd been there, pepping her up beforehand, offering what she had thought was moral support and had only later realised was journalistic interest.

She masked the feelings, pushing them away to review later, and focused on Laura's blurred approaching silhouette. Lucy's heart beat faster as keys, locks and chains were negotiated. Friendly, homely London!

'Yes?' The enquiry was polite but suspicious. Even soul-sapping loss, no make-up and hair thrown in a ponytail could not dim Laura's looks. Wafts of subtle, expensive fragrance poured from the door. She managed to pull off classy in yoga pants and a simple T-shirt. Still a luscious, edible Nigella to Lucy's Fanny Craddock.

Lucy cleared her throat. 'I left a card yesterday?' She raised the end of the sentence into an antipodean-style question and annoyed even herself by doing it.

'I'm afraid we don't deal with door-to-door trade enquiries. Thank you.' The voice was cultured, educated, assured. The door began to shut.

'No. No, I'm Lucy. Lucy Diamond.'

Laura's face was blank.

'We met on a train once . . .'

Laura's face showed no recognition but was hardening into a mask of disinterest with each nanosecond. The door was being closed millimetre by millimetre.

'I put a card through the door yesterday.' Lucy's words tumbled out hastily. 'A white card. I'm a medium.'

For a fraction of a second the door stopped and Lucy blurted most unprofessionally, 'I know it sounds crazy, but give me a minute!'

Clunk. The door shut and the chains and locks were swept back into place. Lucy pressed the bell button firmly. She couldn't give up. The last time she saw Jonathan he had barely been visible. He'd stopped her from being dragged into Limbo and she sure as hell wasn't going to let it happen to him. She heard Laura's steps retreating down the passage and saw her shadow move away.

Lucy felt very uncomfortable about what she was about to do. It did not fit with her way of doing things. She put her finger on the smooth round ceramic of the door bell again, pushed it and kept it there. She paused momentarily when her finger began to throb with pain but then repeated the process all over again.

The trouble with modern decor is that no one has net curtains any more. Even muslin drapes are passé and interfere with the clean lines of modern design. Consequently, from the fine drawing rooms the view to the street is uninterrupted and the little of life that is played out in plain view draws as much attention as it would in any suburban cul-de-sac. A few yummy mummies who had walked to the local shops for organic produce and were power-pushing their Bugaboos back home took in the unseemly spectacle of Lucy refusing to give up and go away. Her insistent ringing was failing to get any results. She was gonna have to bring in the big guns.

She hadn't wanted to call on Jonathan too early; he

was too weak, too defenceless. Keith Richards had warned her; one visit too many and he would never have the strength to cross to the light at all. Lucy leaned against the hand rail of the stone steps and concentrated her thoughts. Jonathan was there, within seconds, flickering like an eddying candle, a pale and sickly version of his former glorious spirit-form self.

Now, Lucy was standing in the street, appearing to the onlookers as though she was talking aloud to herself. Ah! Care in the Community, they reasoned to themselves. That would explain the hair and last winter's coat. Shame, isn't it? Best not catch her eye.

So focused was Lucy that she didn't care about the attention she was drawing. After a quick chat, she returned to pressing the bell, Jonathan at her side. It took only three more long pushes for the door to swing open to a sudden halt on its chain.

'I don't know who the hell you are but go away. This is exploitation, trading on people's troubles. I don't know how you've found out about me but this is sick! I'm giving you one last chance to go away quietly before I call the police.'

Laura was angry, livid, but Lucy wasn't looking at her. She was watching Jonathan, watching his eyes soften and his whole being yield to Laura's presence, colour rising to his cheeks. Not for the first time, she wondered what it would take to get someone – a decent, honourable someone like Jonathan – to look at her like that. Did you have to be breathtakingly gorgeous like Laura? Are only model-beautiful girls allowed happiness? And again, she had to push the thoughts of Simon and the all-too-brief happiness she'd felt out of her head and get back to the task in hand.

'Laura – it's not as crazy as it seems—'

'How do you know my name?'

'Jonathan told me. He's told me many things about you and I can prove that I can talk to him, but only today. Today is our last chance.'

Laura cut in with a cynical, 'And I suppose you want a substantial sum of money to make your connection. No thank you. Go away.'

The door slammed shut again.

'For God's sake, Lucy – do something.' Jonathan was doing his desperation hands-through-the hair thing.

'Think of something yourself!' Lucy retorted, equally frustrated. 'You're the one who could get to the other side of the door, not me.'

'I'm calling the police!' came Laura's voice from the passageway.

'Tell her about the fish,' Jonathan blurted.

'OK, OK, but I can't think while you're talking to me.'

Oh! A schizophrenic! That explains it, the Neighbourhood Watch self-taught psychologists decided. Not that it made them feel any easier.

Then Lucy gingerly lifted up the letter box flap and yelled, 'Your goldfish is called Al Pacino,' thus confirming what the observers suspected. She was clearly nuts.

She could hear Laura on the telephone. She couldn't see her because of the bristles of the draught-proofing but she caught snippets like 'obviously mentally ill' and 'harassment'.

Lucy lifted the flap again. 'Your goldfish is called—'

'I heard you the first time. Anyone could have found that out.'

'This is good,' said Jonathan. 'She's actually engaging

you in conversation. It's the foot in the door, Lucy. You've got her attention. Keep going.'

Lucy racked her brain for the other facts given in Jonathan's brief and she stooped to the letter box once more.

'Your first date with Jonathan was ruined because it was also Naked Night for the University Rugby Club.'

'Listen, Ruby Tuesday, or whoever you are – the police are on their way!'

'No, I'm Lucy Diamond. Wrong name, wrong band. That was the Rolling Stones.'

'Whatever. You people will do anything to make money. For all I know, you've been listening at the back door and tapping the phones. I'm going to press charges!' Through the assertive threats, Lucy heard the catch of tears in Laura's throat and knew that a tiny part of her wanted to listen.

'I don't want any money.' Lucy's back was beginning to ache from conversing through the letter box, bent double. 'If you like I won't even come in. We can do it all here on the doorstep. You don't even have to take the chain off the door. But I have to give you the message or Jonathan can't rest.'

'Go away!' Laura's tears were coming thick and fast now and so was the law. Sirens were getting nearer.

'Laura – please trust me. Jonathan is here.' Only he wasn't on Lucy's side of the door any more.

His voice called out from the passageway as Lucy was looking round for him, up and down, left and right. It added to the look of craziness from the point of view of the people who were watching from behind their restored Heritage sash windows or keeping a safe distance behind their cars.

'Tell her I'm going to give her a sign and I'll fiddle with the electrics.'

'OK. OK. Laura, your lights are going to flicker now – it's Jonathan doing it.' The passageway lights flickered and dimmed on cue. Laura began crying anew. She sounded genuinely frightened. She was keeping her line open to the police.

'I think that there are two of them. I think that one might be in the house. Stop doing this to me,' she screamed down the passageway. 'You're sick! You're sick. These are cheap tricks!'

In desperation, Jonathan flickered the lights with more vigour. Laura wailed.

'Stop it, Jonathan,' Lucy reprimanded him. 'You'll wear yourself out and it's obvious that she doesn't like it.' At those words, a police car drew level with the bottom of the steps – a miracle in itself to find a parking place – and Laura screamed louder than before.

'Don't you dare say his name. He was mine, mine. Not yours. You didn't know him. You didn't know him at all. He was mine.' Her sobs engulfed her. When someone is gone there is so little of them left to cling on to, and hearing this stranger using his name so intimately, as if they were workmates or dinner party companions, was too much for Laura to bear.

The police, having heard this screamed exchange, took in the situation and made an instant assessment. Two women, a man's name . . .

'We have a domestic in Denbigh Terrace. We are going to attempt to defuse the situation. No back-up needed.' The uniformed young man stood hesitantly at the bottom of the steps trying to decide when it would be best to intervene. It would be a cliché to say he could barely grow a beard, but true. Policemen really are getting younger and shorter. He didn't like domestics of this nature. He could deal with stabbings and bomb alerts, but two women having a barney over some bloke? The only time he'd been injured on the job was when he tried to break up a jealous cat-fight outside an Ilford nightclub called Dirty Stopouts. No wonder the counter-terrorist division had a shoot-the-women-first policy. He pushed his female colleague forward.

Faces still craned from windows, although as a scene it was pretty boring. They had been spoilt by so many film crews and paparazzi chasing after the Swingers' Set of Sadie Frost and friends. It didn't look like this was going to end in murder, so with only one eye on the proceedings they could still tuck into their tapas and flick through catalogues from Cath Kidston to plan their Easter glamping trips to Cornwall.

Others in the street showed no sign of moving. More had joined them. Muttering 'How awful!' to one another was the nearest they got to community spirit and it actually felt quite nice in a Londoners and the Blitz, Keep Calm and Carry On kind of way. If it went on much longer they'd be stringing up bunting and passing around their organic, locally sourced flapjack.

Lucy had her ear pressed to the letter box and somewhere along the corridor she could hear sniffling. She had clocked the police arriving and like a streaker at Twickenham she made one last attempt to cross the pitch.

'Oh, Laura. I'm so sorry that this is upsetting you.' The policewoman was at the top of the steps now but

Lucy's conciliatory tone made her hang back. Always best to let the public solve these things for themselves. 'I know what happened on the day Jonathan died. The day he got run over. I know you had an argument and that's what he wants to resolve with you. He didn't mean what he said—'

A Geordie accent cut in, drowning out Laura's reply.

'Sorry to interrupt an' all that, but can you have a word with her?'

Lucy turned to see a man in his early twenties standing next to the policewoman, all sportswear and cheap trainers. The only thing missing was a 'tinny' of strong lager. He looked like the sort of lad who is lured by the bright lights and cheap promises of London and ends up sleeping rough and living off his wits. He shot Lucy a big smile.

'Got someone's attention at last!' It was a familiar opening line. The policewoman was oblivious to her Geordie sidekick but it was him Lucy addressed.

'I'm kind of in the middle of something here. Can you wait a while?' She knelt at the front door, trying to find a comfortable position.

'I don't know these people,' Laura wailed from within.

'Sorry, Laura, I didn't catch that. Say it again. I'm only here to help,' Lucy cajoled.

'I know, miss,' said the policewoman gently, having noticed Lucy's comments directed to fresh air, 'and we want to resolve it as soon as possible. Perhaps we can do it over a cup of tea.' The tone was the one reserved for people who soil themselves and wear their trousers high on their waist and above their ankles. She was a picture of patience and understanding as she waited for Lucy to respond.

'Just tell her' – he flicked his thumb towards the policewoman – 'where my body is and then she can get a promotion and me mam and sister will know what's happened. They know I'm missing, like, but I was such a pisshead . . .'

'Lucy – time's running out here.' It was Jonathan's turn to speak through the letter box from the inside. 'Tell that self-appointed pisshead to piss off.'

Lucy was shocked. She couldn't recall Jonathan expressing such aggression before. It was like hearing Julie Andrews talk dirty.

'Eh, mate, just let me say what I've got to say, will ya?' the Geordie pressed on. 'This bobby 'ere nicked the junkie that had me wallet and if they find my body sharpish the imprint of his boot will match the one on me fuckin 'ead.'

'Look, mate,' Jonathan spat back the word, 'just wait your turn, will you?' He was on the street side of the door now and jabbing his finger into the collar bone of the new spirit arrival.

'Calm down, mate. It'll just take like two minutes of her time. She's not your own private fuckin' psychic, you know.'

To do Jonathan justice, he did try to calm it all down.

'I understand your predicament, but I've waited a long time for this and Life Time is running out for me.'

'But at least you weren't murdered. I mean it's your silly fault if you weren't looking where you were going when you crossed a friggin' road—'

The Geordie did not have time to finish his sentence. Jonathan – all wispy like a comedy headless horseman –

swung a punch at him, but growing up on a Newcastle estate equips you admirably for such things and the Geordie dodged the blow with ease, taunting Jonathan with, 'Is that all you got?' He followed his taunts by bouncing around on his feet and chanting, 'Come on, then. Come on,' and beckoning with both hands.

Lucy was on her feet now. 'Stop it! Stop it!' she cried, trying to get between the two warring spirits, neither of whom the policewoman could see. Juliet Bravo took a step back, away from Lucy.

'Might need the men in white coats for this one,' she shouted back to her colleague, who was already radioing stuff about sedation and straitjackets. Meanwhile, Lucy was having difficulty calming Jonathan, who was wasting the little energy he had left by fighting in a very ineffective Queensberry Rules way.

His opponent was giving street-fighting swipes and kicks that were passing directly through Lucy as she stood between them. Summoning all her energy, inhaling deeply and rolling her eyes back, she pushed out and the two spirits were flung apart. The policewoman retreated a step further.

Quickly, Lucy yelled through the letter box, 'Laura, I'm going to tell you about a ring!' It was rash, it was cutting to the chase, but she had to keep her attention. To Jonathan she said, 'You – cool it. Take time out. And you—' Lucy swung round to face the young police-woman and started giving out her orders like a maverick crime-solving DCI or Helen Mirren pretending to be one. Lucy expected to be obeyed and it worked and she was. Her words had the policewoman scuttling down the steps to her partner well and truly spooked out. 'You arrested a junkie recently and he had a wallet that wasn't his on his person. It belongs to a chap from Newcastle who hasn't reported it missing because he is dead and I will tell you where you can find his body and how you can get a promotion if you just let me say what I've got to say and you' – the Geordie was still there, scowling at a slightly punch-drunk Jonathan – 'will get your turn when I'm done.'

Laura was sitting on the floor listening to the commotion going on outside. God knows how many people were out there and what was going on. She sat in the doorway of her lounge – their lounge, hers and Jonathan's – her back against one side of the frame, a thick architrave to match the 'wealth of period features', her feet against the other. It was the safest place to be in an earthquake, she'd always been told, and right now she needed to feel safe because though her house wasn't tumbling down around her ears, her world was.

She was out of sight of any eyes that might peer through the letter box or faces that might press against the front window, but she couldn't help but listen. Yes, it was crazy talk, but just hearing someone talk about Jonathan filled her with pleasure. The thing with losing someone is that after the funeral no one wants to mention their name for fear of causing pain. His parents had stayed an entire weekend recently and though they had all talked about him they had done so indirectly, roundabout, as if to say his name aloud would make the unbearable situation they were already in much worse. As if the pain *could* be any worse.

You lose someone but life goes on and others believe that because you are 'young' and still bothered by the pressing concerns of career and mortgage it will somehow be easier. Even Jonathan's mother had tentatively hinted that she knew of a nice chap Laura might like to meet. Does it make it easier if you can be sure, be certain, that they loved you?

She had always thought she knew Jonathan; that he was as dependable as a Labrador and as loyal as a St Bernard looking for survivors in the snow. Now she wasn't so sure. His last words to her had been so angry, so lacking in the respect and love he usually showed her. Everyone has those rows, friends said, but then everyone else's partners were still alive to say that they were sorry. Laura couldn't rid herself of that nagging doubt, that fear that came as she remembered their last exchange – would Jonathan have left her by now?

Blowing her nose on the nearest handy thing representing a handkerchief – a piece of kitchen roll – she considered how easy it would be to let that mad-looking woman with the fake name in and hear a few ambiguous vagaries and empty platitudes that a hopeful desperate heart could interpret as it wished. The commotion continued outside. It sounded like the pseudo-psychic – didn't she read about one of these in an old trash mag at the hairdresser's this week? – was even having a go at the police now. Leave them to sort it out.

Then the voice came echoing down the hall, something about a ring. Laura's first thought was: how had this woman got her telephone number? But she was shouting something else now. Laura should just go to the back of the house and not listen at all, but there was his name again.

'Jonathan is telling me about a picture that hangs over your bed . . . a Jack Vettriano print . . . will you let me speak . . . I told you, time out.' Laura peered from her hiding place and saw the woman through the glass making those T shapes, one hand on top of the other, but couldn't see to whom. Who was her accomplice? 'Oh, he also said – and apparently I have to tell you this – a curse on the National Gallery for not recognising Scotland's greatest artist of these times. Happy now?' Lucy added as an aside.

Although Laura had almost stripped the skin from the end of her nose on the kitchen roll she couldn't help but snigger through her tears. That was actually something Jonathan would say. Those were his words. The woman was yelling something else through the letter box and against her better judgement Laura found herself crawling a little further from her hiding place to hear.

'He said that he wrote you a message on the back of the print.' How could she possibly know this stuff? Did anyone beside herself know about it? Wasn't it their secret? She hadn't even touched the picture to read the message since the day he'd nailed it in place. The girl was still talking.

'He said that he bought you that picture because the girl reminded him of you . . . blimey, Jonathan – some of those prints are a bit sexy. I'm not sure you should be telling me this . . . oh yeah, I know the print . . . with a deck chair . . . yeah, she does look like Laura.'

Although all this was yelled through a letter box, it had stopped sounding so crazy and threatening. It was true. Real. Was this still some sort of hoax or was this someone Jonathan knew, to whom he'd given intimate details? After all, some men have cyber-affairs these days, are unfaithful in words via a chatroom. Laura cried silently into the 'thirst pockets' of her kitchen towel. Had she ever known this man at all? The girl outside was still speaking. Wasn't she cold yet? Bored? Didn't she want to give up and go home?

'Laura, he said he had it framed to match the mirror over the dressing table and the message was . . . Hang on, I've only got so much short-term memory . . . Did you? Oh, that's so sweet . . . Oh, you are an old romantic . . . No, ignore me, I'm only crying because I'm feeling a bit sorry for myself . . . Yes, Simon . . . No, he's a lying shit and I hope I never see him again . . . Laura, sorry about that. Listen – he says you know it's there and that you both said one day your children or grandchildren would find it and it's the date you met . . .'

Laura moved further along the passageway, crawling quietly like a Ninja art thief trying to avoid being picked up by the lasers. It felt like a mad thing to do but this wasn't a regular sane sort of event. What was coming next? Would this Lucy Diamond girl really know? Would she get it right?

'. . . and some of the lyrics of "Wonderwall". "Wonderwall"? You don't strike me as an Oasis fan. But I'm glad it's not Westlife. I would not be on my hands and knees shouting through a letter box, risking arrest if it was!'

Then Lucy chuckled, like she and Jonathan were sharing a big joke together, and Laura felt a searing jealousy that this girl was talking to Jonathan as easily as if she was standing next to him. The things she said, the way she responded to Jonathan's perceived impatience, the easy banter – it's how people were with him. It's how he was. For a moment she could believe he was here, alive, and this crazy, unreal, mad situation felt a whole lot better than the heart-dragging awfulness of his not being.

The young bum-fluffed policeman was having none of this solving-murders-the-psychic-way rubbish. They must call the station at least once a day, these crazies. Attention-seeking, that's all. That's not to say the force didn't occasionally . . . well, there were rumours . . . but it was all very hush-hush and last resort and though they had a couple on the books, they didn't always get it right. They were no more successful than your average copper. He was up those steps like a shot and bandying threats around about 'causing an affray'. With this crowd watching, in this neighbourhood, there'd be complaints ahoy. They'd be on to the Chief Inspector moaning about police incompetence and how they pay their taxes. Honestly, he could do without it on a night like this. It was right parky now the sun had dropped.

'Laura, I will have to go soon. The police are here, as you know, and I understand why you called them . . . but there's one more thing . . . please, officer. I'm nearly done . . .'

She was quite polite really, Laura thought. Quite personable-sounding, in fact. Almost normal.

'Jonathan wants you to go to the bedside table on his side of the bed and pull the bottom drawer out.' Lucy couldn't hear a thing inside the flat. Maybe Laura had gone upstairs or gone out of the back door, but she had a job to do and at least the pre-school age policeman had bent the rules to let her say her piece so long as she promised to go along quietly afterwards. 'There's a gap at the bottom and if you feel at the back, he says there's a box there . . . with the ring I told you about.'

Lucy's voice became a bit wobbly and high at that point. She could imagine Jonathan and Laura having a country wedding in a village church, all marquees and vintage cars, drunk uncles and aunties in best hats, and it would never be. And then the thought that it might never be for her either settled like a piece of ice in her chest, so that when Lucy spoke again her own tears, tears for herself and the end of her fling with Simon, were trickling steadily down her cheeks.

'It's there, he promises me it's there, and now you'll know he loves you. He always did and he's sorry for the things he said but if you know that he loved you . . . sorry, *loves* you so desperately and always will . . . then he can go. He can let go . . .' Just as Lucy's voice finally broke into sobs, the door opened wide, unrestricted by chains, and Laura, sobbing prettily – unlike Lucy with her mascara-streaked cheeks – held out her left hand, fingers spread. Three huge diamonds glinted in their platinum surround, catching the last few dying rays of the sinking December sun.

A gasp went round the little clutch of onlookers, whether at the accuracy of Lucy's predictions, at the size of the diamonds or the situation's romantic conclusion, but whichever it was, spontaneous applause rippled round the group.

Jonathan's sparring partner was now pumping his hand and saying, 'Well done, mate. Congratulations.' Jonathan was beaming from ear to ear and the policeman and woman were asking the crowd to 'move along, please'.

Two young women who had once been strangers were standing on a doorstep together. Lucy was holding

Laura's hand and moving it this way and that. They were laughing together and crying as they watched the diamonds glint in the weak, watery, winter light. It was drizzling. Dusk had settled on London and the sun had entirely fallen out of view.

You would not think an attic flat in Walthamstow could be a spiritual epicentre, a portal between worlds. The only 'touch of mystical' really were the lumps of crystal or feng shui ornaments sent periodically by Jasmine to promote love, healing or some other ethereal, airy-fairy idealistic quality that didn't seem to apply in E17.

Jonathan and Lucy could have chosen a different place for the crossover but Lucy wanted to contain the episode, minimise the chances of bad spirits sneaking in. At home she could be at her most positive, her most secure. That had to be a good thing. Jonathan's goodbye to Laura had drained them both. It would not have been a good time or place to do it there. It was an odd 'gooseberry' teenage feeling, reminiscent of hanging out with Jojo as she snogged some boy or other, as she passed on all of Jonathan's compliments and words of love to the fragrant Laura. Jonathan had said that in his old life, his earthly form, he would have found the spectacle arousing. Men – dead or alive – are simple consistent beings, especially when it comes to a fantasy lesbian scenario.

'I suppose this is it, then?' Jonathan shifted uncomfortably from one foot to the other, his hands in his pockets. He was looking at the floor, avoiding Lucy's gaze altogether.

'I suppose it is.' Lucy was fumbling in her pockets too. She was looking for something to blow her nose on; she already wanted to cry but all she found was an old hair bobble, a sticky lolly stick and a very used tissue almost entirely shredded. It would have to do.

He was hologram-faint, his outline blurring at the edges. There was little substance of him left, his very spirit weakened and sapped by living in Limbo for far too long. The self-assured man who had expected Lucy to jump to his commands had gone. Today, he was seeking reassurance.

'So you just command me to go into the light, it appears like a long tunnel or shaft and I walk to it and whoosh, they beam me up like *Star Trek*.'

'Something like that. I mean, some of the ones I've dealt with' – she tried to sound experienced, knowledgeable, an old hand at this medium game – 'don't need the command. It just all happens very naturally. Very, very . . . organically.' They both shuddered at the New Ageiness of her words. Both of them knew she'd only done this a handful of times, and then the spirits themselves had known more about what was appropriate etiquette for the other side than she did.

Jonathan liked her new confidence. It made her shine from within. No longer the mousy office worker you would walk past in the street. Like anyone who's been through a trial, a test of endurance, Lucy had found parts of herself that she never knew existed. She walked taller, she no longer bowed her head. She greeted each day by looking it in the eye, and today he was very glad that she did. Despite having lived his whole life being sure of what he was doing and where he was going – be it his Duke of Edinburgh Awards, managing his team or staking Laura as his own – now he was filled with doubt, now he felt out of his league.

Lucy went on, 'I think it's an instinctive thing. You knew not to turn to the light last time, didn't you? So this time, because you want to go, you'll know. Keith says he'll be waiting for you. The only thing is, it's all in the timing. The rift between the two planes can't stay open too long or negative energy could find its way in. You won't be able to hang around. Once it comes, think of it as the eight forty-five at Paddington and keep your eye on getting a seat. If those automated doors shut no one's getting on, and just like the old British Rail service you never know when one will come again. Anyway, there'll be others waiting for you, won't there? Grandparents, favourite aunties? And what of the others of the Magnificent Seven? They'll be there. You'll be fine.'

'Easy for you to say. You're not the one dying here.'

Lucy coughed uneasily. 'Jonathan, you're not dying. You're dead, remember? It's got to be better on the other side than in Limbo, surely. This endless passing in and out of worlds – look how tiring it has become.'

'It's just so final. So over. So *dead*. And what if I can't ever come back through? We may never speak to each other again, and you know' – he actually looked directly at her – 'that makes me very sad, Lucy Diamond. I'm very glad that we met.'

She could never get bored of hearing her name spoken with his 007 tones and her eyes began to fill.

'Laura loved the ring, didn't she?' He was going over the same territory. 'Perhaps she can move on now. I just wish I could stop thinking about what might have been.'

'Jonathan. Don't. That way Limbo lies. You were here long enough to learn the lessons you had to learn. That's what they say.'

'Oh aye, that's what they say. But I loved life, Lucy. I loved the smell, the sight, the taste, the sound of living with all its ugliness and unpredictability. I loved the elements – sea salt on my face and rain in my hair – I had no choice, I'm Scottish – but where I'm going there's no wind, no sun, no storms—'

Lucy cut in. 'No disease, no poverty, no injustice either. And you had a charmed life, Jonathan, with every advantage. You had no right to not love life. Remember that. Be grateful for that. You were truly loved and you loved truly, I know that. And at the end of it all what more can we ask?'

Jonathan was thoughtful, not entirely at peace, but he nodded his head in agreement, his mouth set in a grim straight line.

'How did you get so wise, Lucy Diamond?'

'I think I read it on a birthday card once.'

'We were quite a team, weren't we?' He said it almost as if speaking to himself, and then, before Lucy could answer, 'God! I hate long goodbyes.'

Lucy nodded, not trusting her voice to speak without breaking first. 'Jonathan, I just want to say . . . thanks. I mean I don't think you chose me any more than I chose you, but I'm glad it happened. All of it. Even the Tony Russell business. You were so right about him.'

'And I'm right about Simon,' interrupted Jonathan. 'Call him, e-mail him at his stupid magazine. Just listen to what he has to say before you write him off.'

'No. No way.' Lucy shook her head. 'No, that's over,

Jonathan. Over. It hadn't really begun. Not all men are like you.'

'Take a chance, Lucy. Take a risk. Open yourself up to the possibility that he might have made a genuine mistake. You only get one shot at— Oh, shit, it's here.' There was a tremble to his voice.

A tiny pinprick had appeared in Lucy's peripheral vision. It expanded slowly, opening outwards like a flower until the whole of her left side was lit from its reflection. A shaft of bright white light, as bright as the sun but without the burning glare, stretched upwards almost infinitely, reaching through the ceiling, up and beyond. She turned her head and could see Jonathan silhouetted against it. A fully defined silhouette as though the light had filled him up, replenished what Limbo had taken out, so that she could clearly make out his outline from the epaulettes on the shoulders of his trench to the slight wave in his hair. The light was wide where Jonathan stood and narrowed to a point in the far distance.

There were figures inside the light, indistinct, though some looked broad-shouldered and masculine and others were curved and womanly. She was reminded of ET going into the spacecraft and wished she could think of a better, more worthy analogy. Tears were spilling down her cheeks but, childishly, all she wanted to say was 'Phone home' to the man who had swept into her life one dull Monday and changed everything. There was no need to utter the imperious-sounding commands taught to her by Keith and Mrs Gamble. He was moving to the light, absorbing it and in turn being absorbed by it until he seemed to blend with the edges of it and become a part of this vibrant, shimmering beam. Then, without warning, he turned. Turned away from the magical white light and came back towards her.

Suddenly, there was a banging. An insistent banging on the door, like someone being chased by the hounds of hell or the hounds themselves leaping and pounding at the door to break it down, to get through, to spill their dark, vile shadows into the light.

Lucy was filled with terror, remembering Hallowe'en, recalling Joe. She'd have to fight this battle herself. Jonathan was hesitating. That was enough, Keith said, to let in the darkness. Enough for Jonathan to be lost for ever in Limbo.

'No, Jonathan! The light, the light!'

Bang! Bang! Bang! The door was jumping at the force. The light was shrinking now, closing like a lens shutter, and Jonathan was moving towards her as vivid and colourful as he must have been alive, but before she could scream another warning, a very earthly-feeling kiss was planted on her cheek and Jonathan had turned and leapt like a schoolboy springing over a gym horse through the shrinking aperture, shouting, 'You're a Good Friend, Lucy Diamond!' and he was gone, and the light with him.

Her hand unconsciously rose to touch the warm spot where his kiss had landed. The banging had grown louder. Lucy took a deep breath to steady her resolve, splashed around a bit of the spring water from Barrockby church and flung open the door, ready to tackle whatever presence of the underworld was trying to burst across her threshold.

It was Simon. She punched him squarely on the jaw.

*

Luckily there were no bones broken although Lucy's knuckles smarted a little. Simon, not expecting that sort of greeting, had stepped backwards and aided by the force of her fist had toppled backwards down the twisting flight of stairs and landed in a heap on the first-floor landing.

She ran to him, but still adrenalised from Jonathan's crossing she was ricocheting wildly between wanting to punch him again and wanting to kiss him. She was still sobbing great gulps for Jonathan. The soup of emotions swirling within her meant that she was bouncing around Simon's prone, twisted form like a champion boxer. Miss Crump opened her door to see what the commotion was all about, saw it was Lucy and slammed it shut in irritation. Simon was rubbing his chin and trying to straighten out his limbs.

'Where did you learn to punch like that?' he groaned.

'You shit!' Lucy Diamond's vocabulary always had a tendency to suffer when she was angry. 'You nearly ruined his final crossing over. What was with that banging on the door? And you lied to me! Are you OK? Why did I ask you if you were OK? You don't deserve to be OK. You're a . . . you're a . . .'

'A shit, yes, you've already told me.' He was sitting up now. Lucy was still shouting and he tried placating gestures, hands held up, surrender-style. 'I get it. You have every right to be angry with me. I lied. I lied big time and it snowballed out of control but what I said about how I feel about you is true. Every word.'

Lucy was still now, but blowing through her nose like a winning racehorse.

'But you're not an agricultural worker—'

'No, I'm not. I'm a journalist.'

'And you have no special gifts.'

'No, I don't and yes, I thought that spoon-benders, Ufologists and psychics were all deluded, loony freaks. And, Lucy, I still don't know what to believe.' He was reaching for her hands and she was snatching them out of his reach. 'But I believe in you and I see what you do and I don't know how you do it. Whether it's body language, brain waves . . . I don't know.' Sensing Lucy's growing sense of outrage, he grovelled some more. 'But I've seen it and what you do and it's . . . it's amazing. There is no other word for it.'

He was kneeling in front of her now and she had relented and let him grasp her hands. He was earnest. He was pleading. She was staring at the floor but taking sly looks at him and noting that he looked more slick, more urban and even more shagable in obscure-label skatewear.

'What you do after this is up to you, Lucy, but just hear me out. Hear my side. I can't help what I was doing when I met you. I'm a journalist. It's what I do. I entered into it in the spirit of investigation – sorry, no pun intended – I just wanted the truth. I'm not digging dirt about footballers' sex lives. I'm trying to help people just like you are. I'm trying to stop innocent people being conned and throwing their money away. I can't help my job. And I can't help the way I feel about you. I've missed you, Lucy. And I think you feel the same.'

She still wouldn't look directly at him, but she had sunk down to sit on a step so that they were at eye level.

'But what I've learned, what I've seen, won't lend itself to objective reporting. I've learned that there are things that can't be explained. Things that science and the naked eye cannot reasonably explain, and I've learned about you, Lucy, and everything I've learned I like—'

Footsteps were clattering up the stairs and a cynical voice said, 'Am I interrupting something? Hi, Lucy. Hi, Simon.'

It was Nigel, looking dapper and Mod in a tank top and Levis, trim and toned. Still off work but minus a tumour and ready for a bit of gentle exercise and being waited on by Lucy. He stepped over Simon's legs and squeezed past Lucy, starting up the stairs to Walthamstow Heights as if it was the most natural thing in the world to find them in that position on the first-floor landing. He looked better than he had in months and the odd thing was, Lucy didn't even notice. She could sense his jolly mood but her eyes were now on Simon.

'Door was wedged open,' Nigel said by way of explanation and whistled his way to the top of the flight. 'Cup of tea, anyone?' he sang out.

'Um . . . yeah,' said Lucy distractedly in Pavlovian response. Simon was still kneeling in front of her, the flow of his pre-prepared speech interrupted, and he was beginning to lose the feeling in his legs below the knee. A strained silence descended between them. As Simon was mentally searching for the remainder of his script, Lucy didn't know what to say, but she was thawing, weakening, secretly marvelling at the movie-style way he had come to find her.

They could hear Nigel whistling, his mood in stark contrast to the conflicting emotions between them, and the kettle was bubbling.

'Tea, Simon?' Nigel's tone was chipper and warm.

Impossible to believe that the last time he had seen Simon, he had exposed him as a fraud and been chief witness and prosecution at his public dumping.

'White, no sugar.' But Simon was glad of Nigel – it had bought him time and now he knew what else he wanted to say. Had to say. He launched back into his spiel.

'Lucy – give me another chance. Let's start again. Totally honest with each other. Simon the journalist and Lucy the medium. No more lies.'

Chiding herself for weakening, Lucy suddenly remembered why she was mad with him.

'You expect me to forget that article? You wrote about me as if I was a stranger, as if there was nothing between us, as if I was some sort of . . . failed *Britain's Got Talent* audition act.'

'I told the truth in that article and if you'd read it properly you would see clearly that I said—'

There was no way Lucy was going to let him speak.

'Your exact words were "no trickery that I could see". Which implies that there might have been, that there could be, and just because you couldn't see it doesn't mean that there wasn't any. Do you see what I'm saying?'

Simon nodded mutely. He thought he had the gist of it, but there were too many sees for him to keep track of.

She ranted on. 'I don't know how this happens. I didn't want it landed on me and I can't explain it and for a long time I thought I was going nuts. Crazy. Jojo and Nigel nearly had me sectioned but it's for real. It's happening. You can't see microwaves but they heat up your TV dinners.'

'Lucy—'

She still would not let him speak. 'Simon, if you can't accept it and believe me—'

It was his turn to interrupt. 'Lucy—'

'No, wait, Simon. I want to finish.' She could understand why Nigel loved the power of speech so much. 'You've had your turn. Now it's mine. This is part of me. No, it *is* me, and you know what? I like it and my friends like it and I don't care if the people I'm helping are alive or dead. It's—'

'Lucy – I can't feel my legs.'

'What?' She was irritated now.

'I've got pins and needles. You're gonna have to help me up.' Simon was trying to struggle to his feet and she seized his elbow as she'd seen people do who help the elderly. They looked about as easy and graceful as a pair of waltzing farm animals.

'Tea's up,' Nigel trilled breezily from above.

'Lucy, I do believe in you. In what you are. The spirits – I saw it . . . I know.' Before he could say any more his legs gave way and he toppled down another flight to the tiled floor of the hall below, straight to the feet of a well-dressed, designer-stubbled man who looked from Simon to Lucy, who had the wild-eyed look of the first Mrs Rochester, and without missing a beat said in a voice about as heterosexual as a night of song with John Barrowman, 'Excuse me, I'm looking for a medium. A Lucy Diamond? She left a note at my home in Manchester. Something about a rug.'

23

Lucy Diamond may look, to an unbiased outsider, fairly ordinary. There is nothing about her that is out of this world. No over-siliconed HH boobs, weird tattoos or observable quirks that would have Channel Five chasing her to make a caring/freakshow documentary. Lucy is averagely pretty . . . well, more than average these days. She has that inner sparkle, that sun in her eyes, that goes along with being happy, confident, secure in who you are. All the magazines, self-help books and life coach gurus tell you that beauty comes from within. And it does.

Ever seen a stick-thin model weep at a wedding buffet because she can't bring herself to eat trifle? That's not a pretty sight and all the photogenic cheekbones in the world don't make it so. But Lucy turns more than a few heads these days, particularly the innocent and the wise. Little boys clinging to their mothers on the bus say, 'Isn't that lady nice, Mummy?' and old men smile with eyes that say, quite wholesomely, 'Oh, if I were forty years younger!'

Even her friends look quite usual. Jojo Gray, best friend since the first year of senior school and arch nemesis of all the nuns in all her time at Our Lady and St Margaret of Cortona's, even she is quite run of the mill like so many single working mums juggling a career with eco-washable nappies. So nothing to get Lucy on the Jeremy Kyle show there.

There is Nigel, and although he might be gay (he definitely is – there is no might be about it), as he says, 'Isn't everyone these days?' Since the camp opening of the Sydney Olympics, and what with the armed forces parading at Pride, it seems like the whole of Western civilisation is in touch with their inner gay man. What is unusual is that a chance meeting over a pot of tea and the quivering legs of Simon in Walthamstow Heights has led to the longest (and happiest) relationship in Nigel's sexual history. There are rumours of a civil ceremony. They already share a cat. He still meets Lucy for lunch – salads of super foods and echinacea-enhanced organic smoothies. The surgeons took one testicle but gave him a second chance. Post-chemo, he works out; and these days he doesn't do depressed. There's no point looking on the dark side, he says. He's been there and it's nothing to write home about.

When Lucy Diamond sits on the tube in the mornings, dressed in her chic trench (she likes the look, it reminds her of a good friend), you would think that she's off to work; a place that involves filing, meetings and long hours spent tapping away in front of a screen whilst looking at horoscopes on Google but pretending she's not.

You'd never think she was on her way to crawl about on her knees, clean up poo and kiss the softest of feet. No, she hasn't become some sort of specialist call-girl in order to publish her memoirs, she is caring for her unofficial god-daughter whilst Jojo goes to work and Lucy can't think of a better way to idle away an afternoon than cuddling little Martha.

Probably like yours, Lucy's mother drives her crazy. It's what mothers do. It's their job and Jasmine is always on the communal phone – the hippies got a landline at last – to ask if Lucy has cleansed her chakras properly and has she considered a moon-cup? But Lucy kind of likes having a mother who worries, who nags. Maybe the novelty will wear off one day.

Stepdad Ert has found his niche doing home-grown. Vegetables, that is. It seems that the advice he and Jasmine gleaned from the old boys of Ploxbury at Nan Peters's 'do' means his marrows might win prizes in the next village show.

Lucy's grandmother pops in from time to time, more than she should but then, as Keith Richards says, the wraiths aren't going to chance her staying on in Limbo. Her old house is sold. Once she was gone it was no longer home, just bricks and a few sticks of outdated furniture. There was no point keeping it. It was snapped up by a young couple who viewed it as they were followed around by a television crew for daytime television's jewel in the crown – *First-time Buyers*. You could just see Nan Peters's orb to the left of the screen as the newlyweds moaned about the swirly carpets.

Though the house is sold it doesn't stop Lucy visiting her old friends in the north at the Barrockby and District Society for the Academic Study of Anomalous Phenomena meetings. Its membership has doubled. The village hall has been rebuilt. She takes Raven with her when she goes. He passed his A levels and escaped the sturdy-vests-and-packed-lunch suffocation of his mother to get to university. Studying parapsychology by day, he is DJ of a goth club called the Bat Box by night and has made his way through a series of interchangeable girlfriends who all have an air (or the hair) of Morticia.

Like so many in the rat race, Lucy hasn't time to see all her friends who live far away as often as she would like, but somebody rearranges the magnets of the fridge into rude comments about her hair and she suspects that it's Jonathan because her truthful, open-book, one hundred per cent honest boyfriend adamantly denies that it's him.

Boyfriend? That's kind of usual for a young woman, isn't it? Almost textbook, you might say. Nothing unusual there. They do boy/girl-friendly stuff. They go to the cinema, walk around art galleries and window-shop together. They buy each other presents like rare cheese (for him) and girls' comics from the seventies (for her).

He's two years older, a journalist who writes a column about obscure clubs and societies like the BBC Test Card Club and people who only eat food authentic to 1928. He was under quite some pressure to give up his old job, a sceptical editorial on the paranormal. Luckily, his editors agreed that it had run its course.

He ticks the boxes of sexy (he does quite a trick with silk scarves in the bedroom) and romantic (vintage-style carving of initials on a tree – is that eco-friendly?). He works from home and his home is London these days in a little flat at the top of an old doctor's house in E17, though in the future he'd like to go back to New Zealand. Especially if he ever gets married. Or has kids. With Lucy. Perhaps. Who knows? He hasn't talked to her about it yet. But he thinks about it. And so does she.

So if you were to see Lucy Diamond on a bus or a

tube or hold a door open for her as she entered a shop, you'd probably think she was quite ordinary. Just your average city girl getting by with overdrafts and concerns about humidity-sensitive hair. If she smiled you might think *We could be friends*.

But if you were to see her look past you, through you, to another place beyond, if she talked and you couldn't see to whom, if she looked at you, her eyes in a kaleidoscope trance, as though she might tow your heart right away, then you might doubt her sanity. You might say she's different. But she's more than that. She's extraordinary.

Lucy helps all the lonely people stuck between this world and the next. Where would they be without her? She can connect to lost souls who wander the earthly plain, unseen and unheard. She can start to make it better for those left on this side and those on the other. She can take their messages of love, the words that she knows only the recipients will understand, to those they left behind, because where machines and technology cannot go, the strongest, most enduring of all human emotion can. Love is all you need. But then the Beatles knew that, didn't they?

Lucy Diamond. Lucy Michelle Eleanor Jude Rita Diamond to be exact – yes, that really is her name, and you know what? It suits her, fits her well. It's taken her a while but she got there. She likes it.

little black dress

brings you fantastic new books like these
every month - find out more at
www.littleblackdressbooks.com

Why not link up with other devoted Little Black
Dress fans on our Facebook group? Simply type
Little Black Dress Books into Facebook to join up.

And if you want to be the first
to hear the latest news on all things
Little Black Dress, just send the details below to
littleblackdressmarketing@headline.co.uk
and we'll sign you up to our lovely email
newsletter (and we promise that we won't share
your information with anybody else!).*

Name: ————————————————————

Email Address: ————————————————

Date of Birth: —————————————————

Region/Country: ————————————————

What's your favourite Little Black Dress book?

————————————————————————

How many Little Black Dress books have you read?———

*You can be removed from the mailing list at any time

...ick up a *little black dress* – it's a girl thing.

TRASHED
Alison Gaylin
PBO £5.99

Take two suspicious, Tinseltown deaths and add them to the blood-stained stiletto of a beautiful actress who's just committed suicide... Journalist Simone Glass is finally on to the story of her life – but is she about to meet a terrifying deadline?

Hollywood meets homicide in Alison Gaylin's fabulous killer-thriller.

978 0 7553 4801 5

SUGAR AND SPICE
Jules Stanbridge
PBO £5.99

After the initial panic of losing her high-flying job, Maddy Brown launches Sugar and Spice, making delicious, mouth-wateringly irresistible cakes. Can she find the secret ingredient for the perfect chocolate cake – and the perfect man?

A rich, indulgent treat of a novel – love, life . . . and chocolate cake.

978 0 7553 4712 4

You can buy any of these other
Little Black Dress titles from your
bookshop or *direct from the publisher*

FREE P&P AND UK DELIVERY
(Overseas and Ireland £3.50 per book)

TO ORDER SIMPLY CALL THIS NUMBER

01235 400 414

or visit our website: www.headline.co.uk

Prices and availability subject to change without notice.